D1363662

LEAP OF FAITH

LEAP OF FAITH

RACHEL BUKEY

Rat City Publishing
www.ratcitypublishing.com

LEAP OF FAITH. Copyright © 2014 by Rachel Bukey.

This is a work of fiction. Names, characters, places and incidents either are the product of the author's imagination or are used fictitiously. Any resemblance to actual persons, living or dead, events, locales, or the operations of the *Seattle Times* is entirely coincidental.

RAT CITY PUBLISHING
1463 E Republican, #187
Seattle WA 98112
www.ratcitypublishing.com

ISBN 978-09-83571452 (paperback)

For Dave—always.

Prologue

The sun glowed faintly pink over Lake Union, washing Capitol Hill and downtown Seattle in a rosy haze that early August morning. Driving in to work, Dwight Heffron sang along with the radio and looked forward to his usual stop for a latte. As the front wheels of his old Volvo rolled onto the Aurora Avenue bridge span, Dwight spotted her up ahead—a young woman, teetering on the wrong side of the guardrail. He squinted, slowed down and looked again, not quite comprehending the image that would later haunt him for months, the way her hair tossed in the breeze, her body leaning out from the rail, fingers lightly grasping it. Then, "Oh my God, no!" He slammed on his brakes, the SUV on his tail swerving into the left lane and speeding past as Dwight screeched to a stop against the high cement curb. The woman glanced his way and smiled. Her lips moved as if to say something to him right before she let go and dropped two hundred feet to the cold water below. Dwight fumbled with his cell phone trying to control his shaking hands as he punched in 911. Later, he remembered the time on his dashboard: 7:08.

1

It was one of those late October mornings in Seattle that I always think of as the beginning of the end. No more baseball, no more sun. Dragging myself out of my down cocoon by sheer will, I raised the blinds and watched the room imperceptibly lighten. At seven a.m. the huge cedars behind the house were reduced to dark shapes looming outside my window. The wind picked up, whistling in the trees and rolling the mist through the ravine toward Puget Sound like a ghost moving down a long dark corridor. I shook the remnants of a disjointed dream out of my head—Nancy calling for help, manic laughter, orange robes—and felt an involuntary shudder as my own ghosts scratched at the edges of my consciousness.

Another image, more recent, had gotten under my skin. The image of a young woman taking a dive off the Aurora Avenue Bridge back in August. Her sister didn't think it was suicide, wanted me to investigate the circumstances surrounding Julia Comstock's death. I had to admit I found the facts compelling, and grim. Distraught over her husband's untimely death—a heart attack at age forty-three—Julia got herself involved with some kind of New Age bullshit church and its resident psychic medium. She gave them a large chunk of money. Now she was dead. It reminded me too much of my sister Nancy's involvement with a notorious religious cult several years ago and the painful way that ended. I did not want to dredge up my past right now, neither the cult nor my own husband Ben's impossible death. There was only so far I would go for a story.

I forced the disturbing memories from my mind and made my way to the front door to let my dog out. Waiting for her to take care of business and retrieve the paper from the lawn, I noticed four toxic-looking mushrooms had popped up in the crack of the driveway overnight. Relentless. The slime, fungus, moss, and pervasive damp seeped into my psyche even before my first cup of coffee. Cursing the weather, I promised myself that today I'd go out and get one of those full spectrum lights before the full weight of my seasonal affective disorder set in.

After a quick shower and some coffee, my brain began ticking off all the tasks left unfinished from the day before and my schedule for the day. Today my big scoop involved the new arts high school in Seattle Center; I had an interview with the principal at ten. While landing a job as a reporter with the *Seattle Times* five years ago seemed perfect—I'd escaped the horrendous Midwest winters and left the small regional paper behind—my heady visions of investigative reporting, Woodward and Bernstein and all that, hadn't exactly materialized. Because of my background as a teacher, a brief stint teaching high school English, my editor liked me to cover education.

Only after I'd pulled on my boots and checked myself in the mirror did I chuckle at my unconscious choice: kicky tweed skirt, navy sweater—good for my blue eyes—and hair pulled back. Not bad for pushing forty, but just because I was visiting a high school didn't mean I should try to look like a teenager. Who was I kidding? I decided against the ponytail and let my curly brown hair fall loosely around my shoulders instead, then changed the tight sweater for a tasteful collared shirt, reminding myself how distracting ample breasts can be to high school boys, even on older women.

I drove south on I-5 toward downtown with the windshield wipers on high and arrived at the *Seattle Times* building in less than twenty-five minutes—pretty good for a rainy weekday morning. Michael Ray sat in his usual spot manning the front desk along with a guy I hadn't seen before.

I smiled and waved at them.

"Hey, Ann, this is James. He'll be working the late shift when he learns the ropes. James, Ann Dexter, reporter extraordinaire. Anything you want to know about education, you just ask Ann here."

I stopped at the desk to shake hands with James before making my way to the far end of the lobby and the door to the stairs. There's an elevator but I've convinced myself that trotting up the two flights to the newsroom keeps the unwanted flab off my slight five foot four frame. The din of morning conversation, ringing phones and clicking of computer keys cheered me as I moved through the familiar pods of cubicles on the way to my own.

I spotted Poppy tapping away at her computer in the tech pod.

"Hey Poppy, you see I registered?"

"Sure did. Good job!"

"Hope I did it right."

"No worries. I've got a whole stack of them to check. I'll let you know if I need anything else."

I'd just registered for Twitter and needed Poppy to check, make sure I hadn't screwed it up. She's the best—a whiz at all those techie things that drive me crazy. Her purple hair and eyebrow ring had thrown me off at first. But then, I never could trust my first impression of people.

I listened to Caroline Schuster's voicemail and dialed the number while thoughts of her sister's suicide darkened my mind. An old-timey answering machine picked up: "You have reached 365-4760. Please leave a message for Caroline after the beep and she'll get back to you as soon as possible."

"Caroline, Ann Dexter returning your call. I wanted to—" In mid-sentence the phone picked up.

"Hello! Caroline Schuster here. Sorry, screening calls. I'm so glad you decided to help me. I don't know who else to talk to in Seattle."

"Wait. Wait a minute," I said. "I haven't decided that at all. I'm calling to tell you that I think you should talk to the police. I can't imagine what I could do for you."

"I have spoken with the police. Their case is closed. Suicide! That's it as far as they're concerned."

"I'm sorry." I paused, wondering what else I could say.

"I came across your article in the *Seattle Times* about the Ramtha cult during my own online research. And I recognized your name. You're Nancy's sister right?"

Apparently Caroline had seen my feature article, a rare departure from my usual education column, about the Northwest's resident New Age guru: J. Z. Knight from Yelm, Washington. Knight claimed to channel Ramtha, a 35,000-year-old warrior philosopher from the vanished ancient city of Atlantis. But it was the other part of her comment that got my attention. She knows my sister?

"I am. But I'm sorry, I don't recognize your name. Do you know Nancy?"

"It was a long time ago. Nancy and I were friends at Macalaster, but I was Caroline—Carrie—Bradford back then, before I got married. You and I actually met right after Nancy dropped out and you came to campus looking for her."

"Carrie Bradford. Sure, I remember your name now." I said, trying to match her name with the faces of the young women I'd met on my trip to St. Paul that September. Nancy had called to tell me she was going to leave school for a while, travel around, find herself. It was right after our parents died—we were both pretty screwed up. She'd met some guy while camping at the end of the summer and I'd had a hard time talking her into going back to school. After her call, I'd flown to Macalaster hoping to change her mind, but she had already left. So I spent a couple of days on campus talking to her roommates and friends—Carrie Bradford was one of them.

"You were one of her roommates?" I asked, still trying to picture her.

"No. We were in the same dorm but I lived across the hall. Anyway, I was sorry how that ended up." When I didn't respond, she continued. "What's Nancy up to these days? I haven't heard from her in years."

"I wish I knew. I haven't heard from her either."

"Not after the cult went down?"

"No. Not then. Not since."

"I always wondered what happened to her after all those indictments, and the guru getting sent back to India. I mean, I half expected to read Nancy's name in the paper then; she was practically the voice of the cult at one time."

"She got out before the shit hit the fan. Then she just disappeared."

"And never contacted you? But you two were so close. That's intense."

"Yeah, we were." I said, and had a flash of the two of us together singing karaoke to "I Feel Good" and how we once improvised a tap dance to our own rendition of "Me and My Shadow" using beer bottle caps as taps on our feet. She was the wild one who could always pull me in, lighten me up.

"Do you think she *had* to disappear? That she was in danger? You know some of those people were totally wacko, tried to poison the water supply or something, didn't they?"

"I thought about that. I talked to some of Nancy's friends at the time, those who were still around. I even hired a private investigator. He didn't come up with anything. Then my money ran out."

"I'm really sorry, Ann. I had no idea. When I came across your name I thought you would be sympathetic to my situation. But I didn't realize that you had lost your sister too."

"Nancy's not . . ."

"Of course not. She's always been a free spirit. One day she'll probably show up on your doorstep. I didn't mean to imply . . ."

Caroline stopped mid-sentence and I listened as the silence on the other end stretched on.

"So, do you think you'd like to help me bring down Victor Lloyd and the Nirmala Church of Self-Actualization?"

"I'm sure there's no comparison between Nancy's experience and Seattle's current version of New Age. It's quirky, yes, but fairly harmless."

"It's not harmless!" Caroline replied, her voice becoming shrill. "I'm sure this so-called church and especially this guy who calls himself a psychic medium are quite treacherous. I've discovered some disturbing connections between him and my sister."

"I'm so sorry about Julia. But I really don't see how I can help you. I'm a newspaper reporter who writes about education."

"This could be a much bigger story for you—you could expose these frauds for what they are. I'm sure Julia would never jump off a bridge on her own, no matter how desperate she felt after Warren's death." Her words brought back the feeling of desperation I had after Ben's death, a hellish momentary déjà vu. I remembered the darkness that swallowed me then, how hard it was to back away from the abyss.

"Desperate people do desperate things."

"I know that. But I'm telling you something's off here, something dreadful. Please meet with me," she pleaded. "I know I can't bring my sister back, but I need to know what happened to her. Surely you understand that."

I did understand. And I knew I'd regret the words before they even came out of my mouth, but I couldn't stop them. "Okay, I'll meet with you," I said.

Caroline's grief had touched a resonant chord in me, though it would be a long time before I admitted that outwardly. Instead, I told myself, it was all about the story.

2

I spent most of the workday dealing with the usual minutiae, and trying not to think about Julia Comstock or Nancy. The highlight of my day—a visit to the Center School—reminded me just how much I'd enjoyed working with teenagers. These kids were enthusiastic, curious, funny, and in your face. Their teachers had ambitious plans for them—rigorous academics coupled with real arts experiences, working side by side with local artists, actors and musicians. It sounded fabulous and I wondered whether the school district would ever figure out that these kinds of innovative programs should be cloned. Doubtful.

Caroline and I had agreed to meet at five thirty at Diva Espresso on Greenwood at 145th. It was on my way home and close to Julia Comstock's house in The Highlands, where Caroline was staying. As I pulled into Diva's parking lot at 5:25, my thoughts turned again to Julia's suicide. I had talked to David Bolton, the reporter who covered the story of Julia's death, and learned that the only witness, Dwight Heffron, swore there wasn't anyone else on the bridge that morning except some guy in an SUV who almost rear-ended him when he slammed on his brakes after spotting Julia on the wrong side of the guardrail. She looked happy, he'd said in his statement, and she waved at him and said something right before she jumped.

I got out of the car, leaned into the driving rain, hopped over a few puddles, and opened the door to Diva. Inhaling the warm pungent air thick with freshly roasted coffee beans, I felt the muscles in my neck and shoulders relax.

"Hi, Ann. How's it going? I liked your article about the school board candidates in yesterday's paper. Very informative." My favorite afternoon barista smiled as she packed the coffee into the basket, tapped it down, and flipped the switch to push the hot water through.

"Thanks, Kristie. I'm sure the Seattle School Board election is a burning issue for you college students."

"It keeps my mind off of terrorists. Your usual skinny mocha?" she asked.

"Perfect."

A quick glance around the room and I knew Caroline Schuster hadn't arrived yet. The familiar late afternoon crowd included a young guy clicking away on his laptop, a couple having an intense discussion, complete with long pauses and deep looks, and two young moms talking about reliable babysitters while their preschoolers munched away on biscotti. I took my favorite seat on the plush crimson Queen Anne sofa in the corner, which I'd always thought of as an odd choice for a coffee shop but the perfect piece for a bordello. The door pushed open and a woman wearing a light gray double-breasted raincoat over a soft gray turtleneck sweater and black wool slacks paused to scan the room. Caroline. I raised a hand and she hurried toward me in sensible but not quite stylish boots. She tucked a wisp of dull brown hair back into the large clip at the back of her neck and extended her well-manicured hand for me to shake.

"I'm so glad you agreed to see me," she said, shrugging out of her raincoat and smiling at me. "You've hardly changed at all."

Surprised at the rush of emotion that her polite comment aroused in me, I swallowed hard and mumbled something about how great she looked too, thinking instead how much we'd both changed and recognizing my own pain and loss mirrored in her eyes. While she ordered a chai tea, I studied her face. She had meticulously applied her makeup, making the most of her regular features and softening the lines around her sad brown eyes. We made a brief run at small talk: the weather and how long she had been in Seattle. Then I figured we should get to the point.

"Let's talk about your sister. Tell me what you think happened. How she ended up on that bridge."

"Right." She took a deep breath and squared her shoulders, readying for the task. "It's so unlike Julia," she began. "If she were going to kill herself, she might take an overdose of pills or something, but a dramatic leap off a bridge?" She shook her head. "No way! I know the police say there was no one else there that morning. But I know someone pushed Julia off that bridge. Maybe not physically, but someone, possibly this guy Victor Lloyd, pushed her psychologically. You know she left most of her money to Lloyd's New Age church?"

So that's it, I thought, it's all about the money. "What about you? Do you inherit anything?" I asked.

Caroline's eyes flashed and her hands tightened around her cup. "It's *not* about the money." Caroline's angry voice startled one of the preschoolers who'd been wandering around the room tapping her biscotti on the empty tables. She ran to her mother's arms and the mom glared at us over her daughter's head, patting her back reassuringly.

Caroline lowered her voice. "Julia and I haven't been close for years. We haven't spoken to each other since she married Warren. I'm sorry about that now. Maybe I could have prevented her death if I had forgiven her."

"Forgiven her for what?" I asked.

Caroline looked down at her boots for a long while before she replied. "It's messy. I'd rather not talk about it."

"Look, Caroline, you need to tell me everything you know about your sister's life at the time she died, especially if it pertains to her mental state."

She settled back in her chair, closed her eyes briefly, and nodded.

"Okay. So, I met Warren ten years ago while working on an audit at Comvitek for Findlay & Preston."

"Comvitek. That's the dot com company Warren Comstock and Nick Villardi founded after leaving Microsoft several years ago, right?"

"That's right. I'm a CPA. Our firm conducted an independent audit. Anyway, Warren was an incredible man, good-looking, brilliant, and so much fun. I fell head over heels." Caroline's brief smile faded as she paused, shook her head, and lowered her voice for emphasis.

"It was the first time I'd felt anything for another man since my divorce," she said.

I nodded, knowing only too well how hard it is to open up after losing someone you love.

"We had a brief torrid affair in Seattle those few weeks. After I went back to San Francisco, we continued to see each other when we could. Whenever Warren came to town for business, he'd call and I'd drop everything to see him. It was worth it." She smiled and looked out the window, lost for a moment in her private reverie. "Warren appreciated the convenient sex, I suppose. I discovered later how little I meant to him."

I winced at her comment thinking about the convenient sex I'd been having with Jack. Assuring myself he meant something more to me, I asked, "How long did your relationship last?"

"By the calendar, just over a year. But we only saw each other about once a month."

I nodded, waiting for her to continue.

"During one of his trips, Warren met my sister. She'd stopped by my apartment one Saturday afternoon when he was over and I introduced them; they seemed to like each other and that made me happy. Ha! Little did I know." She shook her head. "Anyway, later that year, Julia enrolled in the Art Institute and moved to Seattle. She didn't know anyone else here so she looked up Warren. It seemed a natural thing to do—I probably even suggested it." Caroline pressed her lips together, massaged the back of her neck and continued.

"You can fill in the rest of the story. He continued to see me whenever he visited San Francisco. We'd tear each other's clothes off the minute he walked through my door, spend hours in bed, and then he'd go back to Seattle and presumably do the same thing with my sister." Caroline shook her head and snorted, "What an idiot! I only found out about it when Julia called to tell me they were getting married. I was completely blindsided, and furious. I swore I'd never to talk to either one of them again."

As if for punctuation, Kristie turned on the steam and began frothing a stainless steel pitcher of milk. The loud noise buzzed in my head as I thought about Caroline's story. When Kristie switched off the steamer, I turned to Caroline and asked, "You didn't try to patch it up with your sister, once the shock wore off?"

"Julia kept writing to me. She wanted to salvage our relationship, even came to San Francisco to see me. We had a huge fight and she left. I never saw her again."

"What about when Warren died? Did you come to Seattle for the funeral?"

Caroline shook her head. "No, when Warren died, I was on vacation in Europe. I should have flown back, been there for her. I know that now. Instead, I sent her a note. I wanted to see her suffer a little, I think." Her eyes welled up. "I meant to come to Seattle to see her. But I waited too long."

Caroline pulled out a tissue, dabbed her eyes, and blew her nose. The young moms shot disapproving looks in our direction, hurriedly wrapping their darlings in raingear and shuttling them out the door. Kristie caught my eye and winked over Caroline's head. She seemed oblivious, lost in her own grief.

"I came here because I needed to figure out what happened to Julia. How she could have committed suicide, whether I could have prevented it."

I didn't need a degree in psychology to recognize Caroline's desperate need to assign blame for Julia's death to someone other than herself. Victor Lloyd appeared to be a convenient stand-in.

"Now I understand why you're here. I know that you believe Lloyd pushed your sister into suicide. But even if he did push her psychologically, I don't think you'll ever get satisfaction from the legal system. I mean, the police aren't going to arrest him for messing with her mind."

"I know. I've talked to them. They're sympathetic, but they say just what you do. That's why I need your help, Ann. Will you at least read Julia's journals? Then decide if you can help?"

"Why don't you tell me what's in them?"

"Right. Well, they show her getting more and more sucked into Lloyd's weird ideas." Caroline shook her head. "She thought she had a friend talking to her from the grave, for Christ's sake! But the really scary part is that the journal ends several weeks before she jumped."

I mulled that over. "Maybe she felt so depressed that she gave up on writing for a while. That doesn't seem too strange to me."

Caroline grabbed my arm, leaned forward until she was inches from my face, and raised her voice slightly. "That's impossible. Julia wrote every day, ever since she was a teenager. She couldn't sleep if she didn't write her daily entry. Maybe she started another journal and someone took it because he was afraid it would implicate him— probably that Lloyd character." She sat back, smoothed her slacks, and said in a low tone, "It's too late for Julia, but if you can expose Victor Lloyd and his scam in the press, then maybe you can stop him from hurting anyone else. Please consider it."

I considered it. She sounded like me in my college days, when I thought the press had that kind of power. And Lloyd sounded like a charismatic ass who thought he had a direct line to God. Oh, I'd seen it before, and I would definitely enjoy dragging any exploitative cult through the dirt.

"Tell you what. I'll take a look at Victor Lloyd and his church. I'll ask around and talk to him personally, read through your sister's journals and anything else you think is relevant. Then it's up to my editor at the *Seattle Times*. We'll see what he thinks and go from there."

This one's for you, Nancy.

3

A gust of wind blew my raincoat open and whistled through the trees bordering the Seattle Golf Club across the street as we hurried back to our cars and out of the rain. Caroline turned west toward the exclusive gated community of The Highlands while I wheeled my aging Toyota north onto Greenwood for a half mile, turned off the main road winding downhill past the community college and on to my little street tucked into the wooded landscape.

The garage door opened and the front lights flashed on as I touched the remote clipped to my sun visor and pulled into my garage. I'd bitched about the cost of installing this system last summer when Jack suggested it, but every wet blustery night I say a quiet thanks—worth every penny. Gathering up my bag and fumbling with the keys, I heard whimpering and two clipped "hurry up" barks as I opened the door from the garage to the laundry room. Her tail high, alternately slapping the doorjamb and my legs, Pooch strained to keep herself from jumping up to lick my face, a retriever characteristic we were working on harnessing. Her front paws lifted slightly from the floor and her back end wriggled from side to side. She pushed her golden furry face into my legs. "What a good girl. Yes, I missed you too."

Okay, I talk to my dog—usually when no one else is around. Pooch and I have an understanding. We were meant for each other. I plopped onto the couch, scratched her ears, and thought about how we met. The year after Ben died, the shrink I'd been seeing suggested

I get a pet or do some volunteer work to lift me out of my depression. But I wasn't ready for any new relationships yet, not even with an animal. Then I saw a program on TV about this volunteer organization that trained dogs to work with disabled people. I thought maybe I should try it. It was meant to be temporary so I couldn't get too attached and maybe I'd get some satisfaction knowing I'd helped someone worse off than me, even in this indirect way. It sounded perfect—I had no idea.

After much research and several weeks of instruction, I picked up my first puppy in training from Marilee Goodhue, a local golden retriever breeder and head of the volunteer program. The puppy was eight weeks old when I got her and when she reached her first birthday, I'd give her up for another six months of intensive training with the professionals. Those eight months of training were challenging and more therapeutic than I could have imagined. As her birthday approached, I realized with a gnawing dread how hard it was going to be hand her over, even though I recognized her as the greatest gift I could give someone—a once-in-a-lifetime dog who would make such a difference in the life of her new owner. I kept reminding myself that she wasn't going to die, just go off to live the life she was meant for.

On the Saturday morning when I had to give her up, I tuned into the Metropolitan Opera's weekly broadcast, as always. Butterfly's aria floated from the speakers in my living room while I gathered the dog's things, and I felt a twinge of emotional recognition. Ridiculous, I told myself, giving up a dog is nothing compared to Butterfly's sacrifice. But as the last note died, the dog nudged her wet black nose under my hand for a scratch and my eyes overflowed. I told her she would be the best helper dog they ever had; she would make me proud. And then we left.

The actual hand-off was brief and businesslike. Marilee met us in the lobby with a handler who thanked me and talked in a high-pitched voice to Pooch who immediately wagged her entire rear end, tail slapping the doorjamb as she moved happily through it.

"Goodbye, Pooch," I croaked. That's what I'd called her, "Pooch." I didn't want to give her a real name, imagining I'd get less attached. "Pooch" was generic, like saying "dog." It did nothing to lessen my attachment.

The trainer explained how the next phase of Pooch's life would go and I nodded, but the details kept evaporating like fog in the early morning sun. I was supposed to pick up another puppy that same day and start the process all over, but I couldn't do it, couldn't imagine going through the gut-wrenching goodbye again. How could I have been so stupid? Or maybe it was masochism—at least I'd felt something, the pain of losing Pooch, instead of the numbness I'd felt most of that year.

In the following months, I moved through the various stages of grief, an expert by now. I spent more time at work, writing about charter schools and other innovative educational programs. One evening, as I sat in my office polishing one of these articles, Marilee Goodhue called. Apologetic for calling me at work, she reminded me that I hadn't returned her calls to my home. About every two months she would call and ask if I wanted a new puppy, so I avoided her. I had spent several months neatly tucking away those emotions about Pooch just as I had tucked away those dealing with Ben, and I didn't want to tear the scab off another slowly healing wound. This call changed all that. Marilee told me that Pooch had done well in her training, but not in her placements. Too curious to work well with the sightless person she'd moved in with, Pooch moved on to a second placement, a paraplegic woman looking for a dog to cheer her up. Instead, the woman said Pooch saddened her deeply, that she was listless and had a "look of sorrow" in her eyes. Marilee had the vet check her out; physically she was fine. I'll always remember her next words:

"I think Pooch is depressed because she misses you, Ann. Are you willing to take her back?" I was and both of us recovered from our depression immediately. Instead of talking to a shrink, I talk to Pooch, usually about Ben. I like to focus on the good times, those are what I want to keep in mind anyway, instead of how much I miss him. I've had Pooch back for almost a year now. I gave her a "real" name right away, remembering that Saturday I let her go. "Puccini" seems to fit her brilliantly, "Pooch" for short.

I tucked the memory away and picked up the leash while Pooch ran for a tennis ball. We headed out the door, moving toward the beach path at the end of the street. Once there, Pooch sat waiting patiently for me to release her to run free toward the shoreline. Strewn with large maple and alder leaves and cushioned with cedar and pine needles, the soggy path squished under my feet. Overhead, the towering trees swayed sixty feet up and I recalled the article I'd read this morning about a young couple killed on their honeymoon driving into Mount Rainier National Park when a tree split and crashed onto their car. It reminded me of the randomness of life, how Julia Comstock might still be alive if she'd decided to stay home that weekend rather than visit her sister. She never would have met Warren, would not have become estranged from her sister, would not have been affected by his death, would not have become so lonely, would not have fallen in with Victor Lloyd, and, would not, presumably, be dead.

That night I logged onto the Internet to do a little more in-depth research on Victor Lloyd and the Nirmala Church of Self-Actualization. I discovered that the church had its beginnings in Northern California and that a young female church member had sued its head guru, someone called Jazrindi Bhopa, aka Joshua Booker, for sexual misconduct. Despite Bhopa's vow of chastity, he entertained young women in his private rooms where lofty discussions of spiritual matters quickly degenerated into more earthy pursuits. According to court testimony, those meditation sessions sometimes included massage. The guru liked young women to straddle his back while massaging him, then he would roll over and rub up against the women until he reached climax. He explained climax as just another way of transferring energy from one spiritual being to another and nothing to avoid or be ashamed of. When one young woman, confused and concerned about this behavior, went to talk to other church officials they reassured her, suggesting that she should feel pleased and privileged that the guru singled her out in this way. Disgusting.

My research into the California branch of the Nirmala church confirmed my belief that these places are breeding grounds for weirdos of all types. But I couldn't find much about Victor Lloyd. He taught classes on "realizing your full potential" at the local Nirmala Church and had published a book called *One Final Encounter*. The reviews were all over the map. Maybe I should pick it up, I thought. And I wanted to visit the church personally to see what I could find out there. But it would have to be something pretty juicy before my editor would let me go ahead with this investigation on the *Seattle Times'* clock. I still had the K-12 education beat to cover.

4

I couldn't remember how I got here, so close to the edge of the bluff. Leaning forward, I lost my balance and dropped fast, hit the water and sank like a boulder. Kicking my legs, churning and flailing and trying to grab hold of something, anything, to get to the surface to breathe, I opened my mouth to scream, swallowing water instead. Thrashing around the dark, murky lake, I grabbed hold of something at last. My eyes snapped open and I bolted upright in bed, gripping my pillow. Shaking off the familiar nightmare, I squinted at the bedside clock glowing in the pitch black room: 6:15.

I heard Puccini stir from her bed in the corner, a few thumps of her tail and a stretching "yawp" while she found her feet. I turned on the light, reached for a robe and wrapped it around me on my way to the front door. The wind had picked up enough overnight to add some color to my nightmare and cover me with a wet spray as I stood in the open doorway waiting for Pooch to retrieve the morning paper. I waved to my neighbor as she let in her cat Mocha, and gave Pooch a warning "stay" command to keep her from chasing after the cat, a favorite pursuit. I pulled on my sweats, poured coffee into my thermos cup, and took off for a quick romp in the park with Pooch and her tennis ball. When we got back, the phone flashed a message and I picked it up.

"Hey, it's me, just calling to check in. I'm back on Thursday. Can I take you out for dinner on Friday? Or maybe we could stay in for dinner and frivolity? Frivolity first? Mmm, looking forward to that. I'll check back when I can. Bye."

Ah, Jack, I smiled. I missed him too. But even though I missed him during his frequent business trips, when he stayed in town too long, I got restless, missed having time to myself. And he'd been raising questions about the future of our relationship lately that made me uncomfortable. I didn't like thinking about the future; experience taught me it was always uncertain, you could never plan for it. Just when you thought you had it figured out, life, or death, would slam you. Of course, of anybody I knew, Jack understood all that. After Ben died, Jack was the only one of our friends who stuck around. The couples we knew included me sometimes, but there was always that empty chair, that uneven number. Eventually, I stopped accepting their invitations and they stopped offering them. And Jack and I moved from being friends to friends with benefits. It always felt comfortable and safe. But he could never replace Ben. And he'd always remind me of him.

Knowing I should plan a conversation with Jack about our future, or lack of it, I pushed those thoughts aside, preferring to jot a quick note to Nicole while thinking of a Friday filled with frivolity. Nicole Burke is my twenty-year-old neighbor, buddy, and all-important dog walker. The arrangement worked well for all of us— Nicole got away from her suffocating mother, I could work late without worrying about the dog, and Pooch got some first-rate attention. A clear calendar this morning meant I could meet Caroline at Julia Comstock's house and go through her papers first thing.

As I drove west on 145th, past the Seattle Golf Club and up to The Highlands gatehouse, I wondered whether I took on this job just so I could get a look at this wealthy enclave up close. I had never been inside. The gate guy checked my name off his clipboard and gave me directions to the house.

"Follow this road, Huckleberry, down about a quarter mile. Turn right onto Dogwood. You'll see their name on the gatepost. Turn left into the drive. It winds around and up to the front door. White house with green shutters, you can't miss it." I nodded and he lifted the gate for me to pass.

Driving along the tree-lined roads felt more like traveling through a parkway than a residential community. Around each curve, a glimpse through the lush foliage of Puget Sound or a slice of the Olympic Mountains surprised me. The Olmstead Brothers created this neighborhood back in the early twentieth century, a time when they'd built some of the most prestigious formal gardens in the country. The roads were named for native trees and plants, and occasional gateposts marked intersections and listed the names of residents, a "Who's Who" of Seattle's established families.

At the Comstock gatepost, I turned down the road trying to figure out the geography. It occurred to me that I might be looking at the same stand of cedars up the hill from the beach path at the end of my street. I drove around for some time without seeing any sign of a house, so I looked for an opportunity to turn around in a driveway. Then I spotted it up ahead. Or was it? No, I'd somehow ended up at the golf clubhouse, a huge white colonial clapboard building with green shutters, and a massive double door flanked by four sets of windows on each side. Pulling into the drive to turn around, I noticed, hanging off a gas lantern, a brass sign welcoming me to the Comstocks'. Whoa, just two people lived in this place.

A line from *Doctor Zhivago* popped into my head: "The party has determined that six families could easily be accommodated in this house, Doctor. Do you not agree?"

"Yes, yes, I'm sure you are right. It's better this way," Zhivago says, surrounded by dozens of his new communist comrades.

I climbed out of my car and headed up the steps as the front door opened and Caroline emerged, along with a well-coiffed, impeccably dressed woman in her late fifties, wearing a broad smile. Caroline introduced the woman as Leigh Snodgrass from Windermere Realty. We shook hands briefly before Leigh went down the steps and got into her little green BMW.

"Ann, I'm so glad you're here. Come in." Caroline waved as the real estate agent pulled out of the drive, then turned to me. "I'm listing the house as soon as possible."

"I expect it will take a while to sell." I said. "I mean, it's not exactly in your average Joe's price range, is it?" Caroline led me through the front door and I looked around, trying to control my Midwest bumpkin impulse to say something like, *Holy shit!*

"Wow!" I said instead.

"It is pretty amazing, isn't it? The house alone is fabulous but the grounds still take my breath away, almost two acres including gardens, a greenhouse, gazebo, pond, and tennis court. And wait till you see the view of the Olympics. Too bad the Nirmala church will get the proceeds of the sale," she said, with a frown. "Leigh suggested offering it at $5,950,000."

"No wonder she had such a big smile on her face." I said, calculating her commission. We stood there awkwardly for a moment while I looked up at the vaulted ceiling and crystal chandelier and felt my feet warming from the heated stone floor.

"So, where shall we begin?" Caroline asked.

"Why don't you show me Julia's journals and anything else you think is pertinent and I'll get started."

Caroline led the way through the central hallway and I tried to keep my mouth from dropping open while taking in the living, dining, and sitting rooms and kitchen in passing. I jumped as we passed a staircase under which a man crouched in the shadows.

Caroline chuckled. "Yeah, that guy still catches me off guard sometimes." I bent down to look at the life-size bronze sculpture of a casually dressed middle-aged man and felt a shiver run through me. The peculiar look of concentration on his face and his posture made him appear frightening, waiting to pounce.

"Warren had a wonderful art collection. Just recently, he'd become interested in sculpture. You'll see more of these folks out in the garden. I can't help thinking this must have been some bizarre extension of the way he liked to collect people."

We entered the cherry-paneled library and billiard room where Caroline had set out Julia's journals on a desk in the corner. A wall of windows faced west, looking out over the landscaped grounds to Puget Sound with the snow-covered Olympic Mountains in the distance. The two other walls were floor-to-ceiling bookshelves. Running my hand over the smooth finish of the antique pool table dominating the room, I wondered what it was doing in the library. Then I moved to the bookshelves and found them filled with the kind of leather bound classic books more likely purchased by an interior designer than a reader—all for show. Interspersed among the books were a few art objects and some framed photos. I picked one up.

"This is Warren and Julia?" I asked. The photo, shot aboard a boat, portrayed the two of them wearing swimsuits and happy smiles. Warren had country-club good looks and exuded an air of self-confidence—the kind that, in my experience, is solely owned by the very rich. I studied Julia's image, comparing it to the more formal photo I'd seen with her obituary in the *Seattle Times*. Here she appeared so full of life, happy. She wore her unruly light brown hair to her shoulders and her mischievous blue eyes smiled at the camera from a perfect heart-shaped face, pink with the sun or simply good health. In the later photo Julia seemed not only older but tired, her hair cut into a more matronly style, with a haunting sadness in her eyes.

"Yes, it's them." Caroline said. "I think this must have been taken on Nick Villardi's boat just before they were married that August."

"Nick Villardi. That's Warren's business partner." I made a note to interview him sometime soon.

"That's right," she said, picking up another framed photo, apparently taken on the same boat, of a good-looking man, darker and about the same age as Warren Comstock, pictured with a magazine-gorgeous blonde. "Nick and Liz Villardi," she offered by way of explanation. "Nick has been great through all of this—very kind and helpful. Warren's death upset him quite a bit. His wife Liz told me that Nick hasn't really been the same since. They were very close, had known each other since college."

"What about Julia and Liz? Were they friends too?"

"No, at least not recently."

"They had a falling out?"

"Not exactly, more like they never had much in common to begin with. Julia has always been shy, while Liz is the opposite. She's the consummate high-powered executive wife—entertaining all the time, involved in the community. In fact, she runs Comvitek's charitable foundation. Julia just wanted to paint." Caroline sighed. "I guess she never really fit into this lifestyle."

I thought about how easily I could fit into this lifestyle, but kept it to myself.

"Did that cause problems in their marriage? Did Warren expect Julia to be more supportive, more of an executive wife?"

"I don't know about that. But I do know that Julia wished he'd taken her painting more seriously. In her journals, she says Warren thought of it as her cute little hobby."

She shook her head sadly.

"Look, why don't I leave you alone with them? They're a pretty clear window into Julia's psyche. It's disconcerting, really, reading them now." Caroline met my eyes briefly, then turned to the staircase. "I'll be upstairs in the office if you need anything. Or you can let Maria know."

"Maria?" I asked.

"Maria is the housekeeper. Sorry I didn't introduce you. You'll probably find her in the kitchen. She's been helping me pack up Julia's things and organize the estate sale. She's a godsend." Caroline walked to the doorway and stopped, looking back at me. "Ann, thank you so much for being here. I can't tell you how much I appreciate what you're doing."

"I haven't done anything yet," I said, but Caroline was already gone.

I picked up the journal on top—less than a hundred spiral-bound pages lined on one side. Someone, presumably Julia, had made a collage on the navy blue cardboard cover featuring the *Mona Lisa*, a piece of a Seattle map juxtaposed next to an old photo of the Space Needle, a wooded landscape, flowers, and the corner of an air mail envelope. A shiny red valentine heart held it all together. It looked like something I might give Nicole as a gift. Flipping through the entries from six years ago, I noticed their simplicity right off. Few of the entries included Julia's inner thoughts, most were mundane recaps of her activities:

> *June 17. Continued with yellow painting. Warren worked late. Dinner at nine. Still light so close to solstice. Garden looking good.*

> *August 12. Lunch w/ Warren. Hot out today. Wondering about new series—circles and spirals, no straight lines. Muted tones earth green/blue. More energy.*

Picking up another journal, this one from the first year of their marriage, four years prior to the last entry, I read:

> *October 12. Saw a deer run through the grounds followed by her fawn this morning. Beautiful! Warren is so wonderful! Today he went in to the office late so we could stay in bed and play. Yum. Maria served us breakfast in our room and we talked about everything, Warren's plans for the company, my work, the possibility of a gallery in Pioneer Square putting up a show. I know it will happen! Painted all afternoon to the steady rain in the greenhouse. Red, red hot and hungry red jumps into everything I touch. Fabulous!*

Wondering if Julia ever got that gallery show, and whether any of the art hanging around the house belonged to her, I made a mental note to ask Caroline. I would also ask her if I could take the journals home with me for a closer look. Then I went looking for the housekeeper.

Maria sat at the kitchen table, talking on the phone and writing on a yellow legal pad. She glanced up as I entered the room but continued her conversation. "Yes, Ms. Schuster needs an appraisal for the furniture. Yes, I will check with her about tomorrow. Thank you, yes. Good-bye."

Maria turned to look at me as she hung up the phone. She appeared to be in her middle fifties, tall and solidly built. She wore her hair, brown flecked with gray, pulled back and away from her open face. No makeup. Greeting me with a relaxed, confident expression and inquisitive brown eyes, Maria crossed the room and extended her hand. "You must be Ann Dexter. Ms. Schuster told me you'd be here. How can I help you?"

"I'd like to talk to you briefly about Mrs. Comstock's connections with some people from the Nirmala church. Did you ever meet any of them?"

Maria nodded, suggested we sit. "Mrs. Comstock went to classes and church regularly. I never met the man, Victor Lloyd, but a couple of women from the church came by at least twice that I know of."

"When was that?"

"One time, early on, when Mrs. Comstock first started going there, a woman came to welcome her to the church community. She told me they liked to personally call on new visitors." Maria's eyes moved from me to a spot outside the window.

"Did the woman give her name?"

"I can't recall. Several months have passed since then and I suppose I didn't think much of it at the time. You might check with Roger; he may have records of visitors. I don't know how long he keeps them."

"Roger?"

"Oh, yes. Roger is the head gatekeeper. You probably saw him when you came in."

"Right. I'll check with him. Do you remember what she looked like?"

"She looked like kind of a hippie, if they call them that any more, long hair, wore a gauzy dress and smelled like incense. I don't remember her face very clearly."

"And the second time—when did she come again?"

"Someone came by the day Julia died, that afternoon. But I'm pretty sure it was a different woman. At least, she dressed differently, a more tailored look, had a nice haircut, wore makeup. And I do remember her name—Sylvia Carter. She said she worked as Victor Lloyd's assistant, that she had an appointment to see Julia. Roger had noted the appointment in his book, so he let her by. It struck me as odd, because she appeared to know about Julia's death, said she heard it on the radio, but yet she came by anyway."

"Did she explain why?" I asked.

"Said she just couldn't believe it and had to talk with someone about it. She asked me whether Caroline, Mrs. Schuster, had arrived, and I found that very strange. Mrs. Comstock hadn't talked to her sister in years. Very few people even knew she had one."

"Did you tell Mrs. Schuster about this visit when she arrived?"

"Yes, I did. She asked me whether I had ever met Victor Lloyd. I told her just what I'm telling you now. I also know that, according to the police, Victor Lloyd doesn't have an assistant. They never found anyone named Sylvia Carter associated with the church, or anywhere else for that matter."

"Can you describe her, Maria?"

"Sure. She was a little shorter than me, about five-six, I'd say, thin, very fair complexion, light brown hair with pale blue eyes and regular features. Pretty in a cookie-cutter kind of way. At first I thought she was just a girl. She reminded me of the actress who played Peter Pan in the old movie. You know, the one who had this childish way, even when she became an old lady?"

I smiled, thinking of Mary Martin. "And what did she say, can you remember?"

"Yes. She seemed nervous, upset, said she'd heard someone jumped off the Aurora Avenue Bridge. Then she asked me straight out: 'Did Julia jump off the bridge this morning?' I was stunned by her impertinence." Maria shook her head before continuing.

"She also said she'd been unable to get a hold of Victor Lloyd and how upset he was going to be. Then, in the middle of our conversation, one of the neighbors rang the bell. She'd heard about it too and came to—quote, unquote—express her sympathy. It made me so angry! I'm sure she just wanted some gory details to share with her friends on the golf course. These people!" She sniffed and shook her head.

"Which neighbor was it, do you know her name?"

"Sure, Whitney Hatcher."

"Did the two of them meet? Mrs. Hatcher and Sylvia Carter?"

"No, they didn't. Sylvia Carter and I were in the kitchen talking when Mrs. Hatcher rang the bell."

"When Mrs. Hatcher left, was Sylvia Carter still in the kitchen? Could she have gone anywhere else in the house?" I wondered whether Sylvia Carter had enough time to snoop around, maybe steal Julia's missing journal.

"I don't think she would have gone anywhere else. Of course, there are stairs from the kitchen to the second floor. But I only spent a few minutes talking to Mrs. Hatcher. I thanked her for her concern, didn't invite her in."

I looked for the stairs, spotted them next to the SubZero fridge. "One other thing, Maria. What can you tell me about Mrs. Comstock's behavior in the months before she died?"

"I've told the police this, and Mrs. Schuster too, but the fact is, I think she was getting better. I mean, she had been terribly upset after

Mr. Comstock's death, very withdrawn, quiet. I thought going to that church might be a good thing, really. She had more energy and even started to paint again. She seemed a little distracted, I guess. But she smiled more often."

Maria shook her head and looked out the window again before she continued. "That's what doesn't make sense to me. Why would she go off smiling and all dressed up that morning if she planned to jump off the bridge? No. It never made sense to me, Ms. Dexter."

It sounded nonsensical to me too, but then, life, or death, never played by any rules I could make out. Maybe Julia's behavior was normal for someone who had decided to take her own life. Once she made the decision to let go, she could be happy knowing she would finally be free of pain and despair. I thanked Maria for her time and asked if I could look at Mrs. Comstock's studio.

Maria grabbed a key from a hook near the side door and led me out into the yard to an old greenhouse built near the back of the property where the grass ended and a wooded ravine sloped down to the Sound. As we made our way across the lawn, I watched the Olympic Mountains, visible half an hour ago, disappear behind a curtain of clouds. The drizzle started up again and the wet grass felt spongy under my feet. While Maria unlocked the door, I asked her to tell Caroline I planned to leave in ten minutes or so, as soon as I had a brief look at Julia's studio.

The greenhouse, crowded with taped boxes and crates packed with canvases, looked more like a storage shed than an art studio. A few unpacked paintings sat propped against the two far walls. As I moved to get a closer look, I began to understand why Warren Comstock considered his wife's art a cute hobby. Julia's paintings featured random splotches of color, similar, I thought, to what Puccini might be capable of, given a few containers of paint and a tennis ball. Then I noticed a canvas in the corner that was much different from the rest. It featured a hazy but discernible human face, slightly off center, amidst what I now recognized as Julia's characteristic swirls of color. As I bent to get a closer look, I heard a voice behind me.

5

"What do you think?" Caroline asked. "I'm kind of at a loss here. Julia wanted so much to have her own showing in a gallery and now, after her death, the Giordano Gallery is offering one."

"Really?" I asked, biting my lip, trying not to show my astonishment.

The trace of a smile crossed Caroline's lips. "Ah, not a modern art enthusiast, either? Have you been to the Museum of Modern Art in San Francisco? Astounding! My personal favorites are the canvases painted one solid primary color. That's art?"

I laughed, relieved that I wasn't offending the memory of her sister.

"Hey, Julia might be the next Frank Stella for all we know."

"Right." I noticed a touch of sadness in her voice. "Doesn't it seem a bit morbid though? No gallery would show Julia's paintings during her lifetime. I can't help thinking they're interested now only because of the circumstances of her death."

I had to agree that our society has a voyeuristic fascination for suicide. "Tough call," I said.

Caroline agreed to let me take the journals home, so Maria wrapped them carefully in plastic bags and tied them up with kitchen string. I tucked the bulky package into my trunk before heading over to the Nirmala church—time for me to get a feel for the place, see what I could find out about Victor Lloyd and Sylvia Carter. I drove south on I-5 through downtown, past Safeco Field and the huge neon green "T" lighting up the mist at Tully's Coffee headquarters. As I turned onto the West Seattle Bridge, I began thinking about how to best approach the church. I could pretend to be an interested soul looking for a place of comfort, introduce myself as a *Seattle Times* reporter writing an article on religion, or tell the truth. That last option was the least appealing. People like reporters when they think they're going to get some good press, especially if it will bring in money along with good will, but they clam up immediately if they get the slightest whiff of negativity. I decided to play it by ear, just an interested soul for now.

The church was on California Avenue, just off Fauntleroy Way, a street of small businesses tucked into a middle-class residential area. I spotted the "church," an old storefront really, next to the New Age Connection bookstore, found a parking space half a block down, and searched my bag for a credit card to pay the meter. Gold lettering on the door read "Nirmala Meditation Center and Church." I peered into the large front windows displaying books, small shrines, candles, and CDs, then turned back to the door to read the notice posted there: "Sunday Meditation at 9:00, Worship Service at 10:00." Tuesdays and Thursday evenings included meditation hours with chanting beginning at seven. When I read, "Welcome all," I turned the knob and went in.

A subdued tinkle of bell chimes announced my entry. The intense odor of incense assaulted my nostrils and made my eyes water, while soft New Age "music" drifted from speakers hidden somewhere in the ceiling. Immediately craving fresh air and hoping olfactory fatigue would set in before the inevitable headache, I decided to make this visit as brief as possible.

The small foyer, clearly set up to make visitors feel relaxed and welcome, made me antsy and need to pee. A fountain burbled on a table to the right of the door, an upholstered bench covered with jewel-toned velvet pillows rested against one wall, and a large wooden podium displayed a blank book opened to a page filled with scribbled names and addresses. The longest wall held books and more displays of statuary, CDs, DVDs, and candles. Behind the podium, an open, arched doorway led into a larger room filled with rows of folding chairs facing a small raised stage. Just as I began flipping through the sign-in book, a young thin blonde with freckles across her nose walked into the foyer. She gave me a shy smile and said, "Welcome to Nirmala." Dressed in layers of gauzy fabric, the young woman emitted the scent of incense so strong I thought I might sneeze. "My name is Rose," she said. "May I help you?"

Happy to be on a first-name basis so soon, I gave her mine. "I've always been curious about this place." I said. "Is it a church or a place for yoga classes and meditation?" Rose smiled again. "Yes," she said. "It's all of those things. We have yoga classes, meditation sessions, and Sunday worship services. Would you like a copy of our newsletter? It explains more about who we are and the services we offer." She moved to the podium and pulled out a newsletter. "Of course, it's on our website too."

"Thanks," I said, looking it over.

"We have a beginning meditation class starting later this week if you're interested. Let me get you the flyer for that."

"Great," I said, realizing that I had easily shifted into the role of nervous soul looking for comfort.

"And we'd love to have you come to services on Sunday at ten. That way you could meet the ministers and our members at the social hour afterwards."

"Thank you," I said. "I'll do that. What about you? Have you been a member long?"

"Oh, yes, about three years. It's such a welcoming community, the best family I could have." She beamed at me. "You'll see. There's something for everyone at Nirmala."

"Really?" I hesitated. "Personally I'm into in psychic stuff, communicating with people who've died, like that."

"Oh, you're definitely in the right place! You've heard of Victor Lloyd, the psychic medium?"

"I have."

"He teaches classes right here at the church." She moved to the podium, but came up empty-handed.

"Darn. I'm out of flyers for his workshop, but I'm sure you can get one next door at the bookstore."

"All right, I'm there," I said. "You've been really helpful, Rose."

"I hope we see you on Sunday," she said, giving me a little wave as I walked out the door. I took a few gulps of fresh air while looking into the window of the bookstore. It looked pretty innocuous, books on feng shui, Buddhism, simple living, and CDs of New Age music.

Again, small bell chimes jingled as I walked into the bookstore. My brief taste of fresh air would have to last me a while. The shelves overflowed with aromatherapy candles, soaps, bath crystals, perfume sprays, lotions, and massage oils—just about all things smelly. A display held flyers on upcoming events. I flipped through them and picked up a hot pink flyer announcing a workshop called "Opening to Channel," taught by Victor Lloyd. I stuffed it into my pocket as I moved through the shop, taking in all it had to offer: portable fountains, botanicals, clothing, and books on yoga, meditation, divination, astrology, tarot, Buddhism. It went on and on. They hadn't missed a thing. I was jotting down some notes on my observations, a journalistic habit, when a salesperson startled me. I hadn't heard her approach.

"Are you finding everything you're looking for?"

"Pretty much," I said, pulling out the pink flyer. "I'm curious about this workshop with Victor Lloyd. Can you tell me anything about it?"

"I'm told they're fabulous, though I've never taken one myself. We do have his book, if you're interested." She gestured to a table covered with books on New Age religion, meditation, and holistic health—a fine hodgepodge of twenty-first-century topics. She handed me Lloyd's book, *One Final Encounter*, and walked back to her post at the cash register. The cover graphic showed a stormy sea with a blazing sun rising on the distant horizon. I turned the book over and examined Lloyd's face, idly wondering how many shots were taken before the photographer caught just the right effect. Lloyd's head seemed to float in the black square, a slight backlight creating a glow around him. His eyes, dark, deep-set, and intense, were offset by his expression which was open and sincere, engaging. He looked like someone you could trust. A lock of his brown hair had escaped its part and fallen over his left eye. This, along with the hint of stubble on his strong chin, created a slightly tousled and sexy look.

"I hear he's even hotter in person."

I looked up and the salesclerk smiled at me as if reading my mind. I feigned indifference. "He kind of reminds me of someone. I was trying to place him." Flipping to the dust cover, I scanned the quotes praising him as an "internationally acclaimed psychic medium" who had appeared on television shows. I didn't recognize any of the names attributed to the flattering quotes and presumed these were famous folks in the New Age realm. Feeling slightly peeved at the $23.95 price tag, I handed the book to the salesclerk anyway.

"Is there anything else I can help you with?" she asked.

"Yes, actually. I wonder if there are any other psychic mediums who teach classes here. Any women? I think I might relate better to a woman and I heard a woman sometimes works with Victor Lloyd?"

"I'm pretty new here. Let me check." The clerk walked back to the checkout counter and spent some time clicking through a computer database, including a list of classes and speakers, but came up with only one female psychic from California scheduled to speak at Nirmala in the next several months, no one working with Victor Lloyd regularly. She suggested I talk with Lloyd personally, assuring me, "He's very accessible."

On my way back to the office, I stopped at The Sunfish on Alki Beach, scarfed down some fish and chips and checked messages left on my home phone—nothing but a hang-up call. What the hell? It really annoys me when someone listens through the whole message, waits for the beep, and then hangs up.

6

Back at the *Times*, I called the number listed on the flyer for the "Open to Channel" workshop.

"Victor Lloyd here." The deep voice in my ear caught me off guard. I wasn't expecting Lloyd to answer the phone himself.

I expressed interest in registering for his upcoming workshop.

"Sure, sure, let me see here," he said, sounding pleasantly amused. "Yes, there are still a few spots open. Can I take your name and number and have Rose call you back? I'm just answering the phone while she's at lunch. She can get all the information from you then. The fee is $85.00 for the two-hour session and I think you'll need to give her a credit card number since it's too late to mail in a check at this point."

"Rose? Is she your assistant?"

"No, no. Rose is a volunteer from the church helping me out with paperwork."

When I explained that I would probably sign up for the course, but wanted to know a bit more about it first, Lloyd suggested I pick up a copy of his book, *One Final Encounter*.

"It has some background on my work and past workshops. I think it will give you a pretty good idea of what I'm about."

"Great. One other thing, can you refer me to someone who has taken one of your seminars?"

"Oh, satisfied customers, you mean?" He chuckled. "Sure, why don't you check with Rose? I'm sure she'll be able to answer most of your questions and come up with some names."

After hanging up, I sat at my desk and tried to reconcile Lloyd's easy-going demeanor with my preconceived notion of him as potentially dangerous—someone capable of driving an unstable young woman to suicide. I couldn't wait to meet him in person. In the meantime, I made a to-do list: finish reading Julia's journals and Lloyd's book; talk to some other members of the church; interview Nick Villardi, Warren Comstock's partner, and his wife Liz. That was it. According to Caroline, there were no other people close to Julia. She had lived in Seattle for nine years and appeared to have no friends at all. I added Dwight Heffron's name to my list. Maybe the only witness to Julia's leap would remember something worthwhile.

I spent the rest of the day polishing my article on the Center School and preparing for the news conference the next day at John Muir Elementary School announcing the opening of a fundraising campaign to complete a state-of-the-art "school in the woods" currently under construction on Bainbridge Island. The project struck me as a sign of the times in Seattle. A high tech couple developed the idea for the school, purchased the land, and began building on the site, while Boeing, longtime Seattle icon, donated a mere million to the mix. According to the advance press kit, the school would provide a two-week outdoor learning experience in science and the environment to every fourth-and fifth-grade student in the district. They needed fourteen million more to complete the project.

Later in the day, I did some preliminary Internet research for background on the company Nick Villardi and Warren Comstock founded back in the 1990s. According to their website, Comvitek was an e-business company which had grown tremendously over the past several years into one of the largest in the online industry.

I wondered how the death of CFO Warren Comstock had affected the company but found only one article on the company's "news" page, announcing the appointment of a new CFO and VP last spring. The biggest news seemed to be the company's "exciting new expansion" into European markets, beginning with Italy.

A call to the Comvitek number got me through to Villardi's

secretary and gatekeeper Cheri. Since Cheri didn't recognize my name, she asked about the nature of my call. Describing myself as a friend of Caroline Schuster, I explained that I wanted to speak with Villardi about Julia.

"I'm sure Mr. Villardi would be happy to talk with you," she said. "I'll have him call you as soon as he gets out of his meeting."

True to Cheri's word, Villardi called me back within half an hour. There was a long pause after I explained the reason for my call. Then Villardi said, "Sure, I'll talk to you. But I don't think I can explain why Julia decided to kill herself. I still don't understand it."

We scheduled a meeting at his office the following day at eleven, and he gave me his home phone number so I could call his wife to set up a separate appointment with her. She wasn't in, so I left a voicemail.

I was scanning my notes for the school news conference when my editor, Jeff Skinner, popped his head into my cubicle.

"Hey, Ann, what's up?"

"I'm getting ready for the press event at John Muir. Looks like Boeing really needs some good press."

He grinned as he plopped into the chair facing me. "It's going to take more than a token million-dollar donation. I can't believe how badly they screwed up the press with the Dreamliner problems."

"No kidding." I smiled, trying to figure out how to tell him about Nirmala. "I've been meaning to talk to you about something."

"Shoot."

"I've been contacted by Caroline Schuster, sister of Julia Comstock—remember her?" I watched the wheels spin in his encyclopedic brain.

"Wife of gazillionaire Warren Comstock, Comvitek dot com, right? She jumped off the Aurora Bridge last August and we had a hell of a time keeping the press to a minimum—suicide ethics and all that. What does her sister want with you?"

"Caroline thinks Julia was pushed off the bridge, if not

physically, then psychologically. After Warren's death, Julia got involved with Nirmala, a New Age church in West Seattle, and particularly with a 'psychic medium,' named Victor Lloyd."

"He talks to dead people?" Jeff asked, with a smirk.

"Or pretends to, apparently. Anyway, Caroline read those articles I did early in the year about Ramtha and the New Age business boom in Seattle, and she sent me some e-mails asking for help."

Jeff winced and shook his head. "As I recall, the police closed their investigation pretty quickly. One witness saw her jump. She was all alone." He had an amazing memory.

"I know, but Caroline says her sister's journal is missing, the one covering the weeks just before her death. She thinks this guy Lloyd stole it, probably destroyed it, to cover up his role in her murder." Jeff was paying attention, so I continued.

"I've done a little preliminary checking on the church. Nirmala is a big money-making concern founded in California with at least a couple of pending lawsuits—one of their gurus is a pervert. I can't stand to think about how many people have been ripped off by them."

"Yawn. People have been giving money to churches from the beginning of history. Plus, perverts are everywhere. We already have David working on the latest Catholic Church thing. Forget it, Ann. You need to concentrate on all those happy Seattle school kids absorbed in their study of environmental science thanks to the high-tech industry and Uncle Boeing," he said, getting up to leave.

"Jeff?"

"Yes?" He turned back to look at me.

"How about I spend a couple of days on it and report back to you early next week? If it's bogus, I'll let it drop. If it gets interesting, it might be a great Halloween feature. The guy talks to ghosts after all."

Jeff's head moved back and forth, saying no, but his eyes were smiling. Finally, he shrugged. "Okay Ann, spend a *little* time on it.

We'll talk about it next week."

Pleased with my persuasive skills, I considered his comment. I knew that I would spend more than a little time on it—I was hooked on the possibilities and wouldn't give up easily. Not this time. Not like I had given up on Nancy.

That night I curled up with Julia's journals in front of a roaring fire in my living room with Pooch at my feet. It felt a little creepy at first, reading the private thoughts of this dead woman I didn't even know. But by the time I'd been through a couple of them, I felt stupid about the whole thing. These journals appeared to be useless except possibly as a sleep aid. I found myself dozing off after only half an hour of reading. Most entries included comments on her paintings and occasional notes on interactions with Warren and others. But those were few. Mostly it was a kind of diary of her work and her thoughts on things she'd read—dull stuff. I decided to turn to the days just before and after Warren's death. Julia had scribbled a bleak note on the day Warren died, just two words:

Warren. Gone.

The next day's entry overflowed with fear and grief:

I can't believe Warren is dead. Leftovers from the meal he cooked on Sunday are still in the refrigerator. I keep expecting him to walk through the door. There are plans to make. Nick is trying to help. I'm thinking of calling Caroline. Maybe now that he's gone. What should I do? It will never be the same.

My stomach flipped and I squeezed my eyes shut to keep back the tears. "Stop it," I said out loud. "It never helps." Instead, I went into the kitchen and made myself a cup of tea, forcing the thoughts of Ben's death, the feelings of helplessness, back into that deep place at the back of my brain.

"Did I ever tell you about how I met Ben?" I asked Pooch, while waiting for the water to boil. She'd never met Ben but she's heard all about him since I discovered that telling stories to Pooch was easier and just as therapeutic as telling them to a shrink.

Pooch wagged her tail at the sound of my voice and followed me back into the living room where I sat on the floor, leaned against the couch, and launched into the story. The dog plopped down next to me and looked up expectantly while I scratched her ears.

"When I bought this house, it was a fixer. I hired Jack as the architect, and Jack suggested I hire his friend, Ben Gregor, as a general contractor." I remembered the night Jack brought Ben over to introduce us and talk about the proposed schedule. I think my mouth dropped open the moment I saw him.

"It was love at first sight, Pooch." Actually it was lust. Ben was so gorgeous, like a fantasy of a hard-body contractor you'd expect to see on one of those home makeover television shows. "He was very handsome, Pooch." I patted the dog's head as she stared at me with her doleful eyes.

"Yes, you have nice eyes," I said. "But Ben's eyes, they were something else." I remembered Ben's eyes, which were dark brown and expressive, how they sparkled with delight when he was amused, bore into you when he was serious or questioning, and melted into liquid chocolate when he was passionate.

I sighed audibly as Pooch put her head in my lap and I just let the memories roll. I'd been so embarrassed to have a crush on my contractor—so cliché d. Nevertheless, I found myself getting up early to have coffee and talk to Ben before work and coming home early hoping he would still be there. He put in a lot of late nights and I got to know him pretty well.

He talked about the year he spent at the University of Hawaii mostly surfing, how he'd dropped out of college for a while to work with a general contractor in Seattle, and how eventually he finished a degree at the University of Washington in business. He worked as a broker for a while—"the dead years," he'd called them—until he made enough money to buy a sailboat and went back to building houses. He loved the freedom it gave him and the satisfaction of creating something with his hands.

During the months of the remodel Ben never hit on me even though I sent clear signals that I found him attractive. Then one morning it occurred to me. He must be gay! I was devastated but it made him the perfect escort for the office Christmas party. I invited him "as a friend" and he accepted. That night, again so clichéd, I had too much to drink and tried to seduce him. I said it was too bad he didn't like girls because I'd sure had some amazing fantasies about how great he'd be in bed. He was amused at my comment but explained he had a personal rule about never getting involved with his employers, despite how much he might want to. Since the job was nearly complete, I suggested he make an exception. Instead he hired someone to help him finish sooner.

Those next weeks were quite amusing. Ben would show up extra-early each morning with a young guy to help him, he would call me "Boss" with a twinkle in his eye. There's something really wonderful about anticipation. The Friday afternoon he finished the job, I left the office early, bought a bottle of nice champagne on my way home, and paced around the new kitchen until the doorbell rang. It was the first time we were ever ill at ease with each other, trying to make conversation, when all we wanted was to head right for the new bedroom loft. After a few awkward moments, I asked him if he wanted to see how nice the new bed looked upstairs, now that it was all finished. He grinned. We took the bottle of champagne with us and didn't come down, except for food, for the next two days. Ben was definitely good with his hands, and his mouth, and, well, everything else that mattered. On Monday when I went into the office, Poppy gave me a wink and said, "Hey, girlfriend, you have a good weekend? Looks like you've been horseback riding for days."

We were married eight months later. I smiled as I tucked the memory away and noticed Pooch had fallen asleep beside me.

I picked up Julia's journal once again and began paging through it. Later entries described Julia's unsuccessful attempts to contact Caroline and Caroline's curt message from France saying she would call her when she got back. Julia's reaction to her sister's message was mostly confused:

> Caroline won't be coming back for a few weeks. It doesn't look like she'll be coming to Seattle. She still hates us.

The tone of the entries changed once Julia started going to classes at Nirmala. They began to reflect her excitement about the new concepts she was learning, her ideas about the "eternal nature of the soul," and her experiences with Lloyd's workshops. Her descriptions of the meditation hour at the church and the benefits of meditation made me crazy. I could hear my own sister's voice in my head. *Oh Ann, you can't imagine the feeling of peace I get after the dynamic meditation sessions. It's amazing. You should try it.*

The way Julia described Lloyd's workshop exercises reminded me of her paintings: they were encouraged to visualize colors swirling around, moving through every color in the spectrum. Julia had no trouble with the first part of the process but was frustrated by her inability to reach the final stage, imagining a dazzling gold light shining down within the other light. That's where Lloyd suggested she might see the face of a loved one or maybe a "spiritual guide."

"What crap!" I blurted out loud, startling Pooch from her nap on the floor. "I think the dazzling gold stuff is money the poor saps are pouring down on him." Pooch cocked her head, waiting for me to use a word she understood like "cookie" or "walk." I got up to move around for a while and decided to have some Ben and Jerry's straight from the carton, much more satisfying than mucking around in dead people's thoughts, though not a great substitute for what I really missed.

7

"Who's that bald guy?" The fourth-grader's indiscreet query bounced off the auditorium's cement walls as the room quieted. Muffled laughter followed as the school district superintendent approached the microphone to begin his PowerPoint presentation on the new "school in the woods." Noting the boy's location in the audience, I decided to interview him afterward—it might make up for the tongue-lashing he would get from his teacher.

Sitting up on stage with the Boeing CEO and the high-tech couple were two women and one other man who were unfamiliar to me. Reminding myself that all the pertinent information would be outlined in the press kit, I waved to Jeanine, the *Seattle Times* photographer, smiling at me from the front of the room, and found a seat among the folding chairs reserved for adults. She looked cheerful so I figured she must be getting some good shots. No doubt the fifth-grade student council president would be featured on the front page of the local section tomorrow grinning and holding an oversized check for one million dollars from the other "bald guy," the one from Boeing. Checking my watch and jiggling my leg in impatience, I turned to find a teacher frowning in my direction. Drawing on the endless store of guilt instilled in me as a child, I smiled back and pretended to make some notes in my book.

After the mercifully short presentation, the principal gave some final solicitous remarks and dismissed the children and teachers to "line up" and return to their classrooms "in an orderly fashion," another reminder of why I'd detested elementary school. Getting these kids out of the classroom and into the woods would be a great improvement. I leaped over to the line where my favorite inquisitive boy stood and asked for his opinion of the new school. Tongue-tied at the attention of a newspaper reporter, he stammered, "It's cool, especially if we don't get homework." I thanked him, sent him back to his classroom, and spotted Jeanine packing up her camera equipment.

"I'll have the photos on your desk by early afternoon, Ann. Gotta run." Jeanine bolted toward the door and I wondered if she had the same feelings I did about elementary school.

The round school clock above the auditorium door read 10:45. I'd be late for my meeting with Villardi, even under the best driving conditions. Bordered by Puget Sound on the west and Lake Washington on the east, Seattle had few north-south alternative routes to I-5, making it second only to Los Angeles in traffic congestion. I called Comvitek from my cell phone. Cheri would let Mr. Villardi know I was running late.

Exiting the freeway at Fairview, I spotted my destination immediately. The low-rise building, all green-tinted glass with "COMVITEK" in block letters on the roof, sparkled on the west side of Lake Union, in one of those rare "sun breaks" we Seattleites live for. I grabbed my sunglasses from the dash and turned onto Westlake Avenue. Little known fact: Seattleites own more pairs of sunglasses per capita than folks in any other US city. Like moles above ground, we're unused to such brightness.

According to the directory in the lobby, Villardi's office occupied the top floor. I stepped out of the elevator into a tastefully decorated reception area done up in muted tones. Soft leather chairs surrounded a coffee table strewn with technology magazines. I gave my name to the receptionist who spoke softly into her hands-free headset, then assured me that Mr. Villardi would be out soon. Drawn to the windows overlooking the lake, I watched a floatplane set its pontoons down gently on Lake Union. Thanks to Seattle's other gazillionaire, Paul Allen, this stretch around South Lake Union had been transformed with new buildings, lots of high-tech businesses, including, a little farther south, the real giant—Amazon.com. You couldn't go into a bar or restaurant around here without running into hordes of young up-and coming-techies, and sometimes, their dogs. Amazon's dog-friendly policy meant their employees could bring their dogs to work with them. Pooch would love that.

A man's voice behind me interrupted my musings.

"Hello, Ms. Dexter. Ann, isn't it?"

I turned to find Nick Villardi smiling at me. The Comstock's photo hadn't prepared me for his powerful good looks. Watching his dark eyes flick from my face to my breasts and back again, I felt myself blush, instantly aware of the snug fit of my green sweater and black leather skirt. Annoyed at my involuntary reaction, and pretending not to notice his attention, I returned the smile.

"Yes, it's Ann," I said, hoping my voice sounded all business. "So nice to meet you, Mr. Villardi." I couldn't help noticing how nicely his chocolate-brown cashmere sweater brought out the color of his eyes and how his chest hair showed over the top of the V-neck.

"Please, call me Nick. Mr. Villardi is my dad."

"Right."

He led the way to his corner office and I breathed in his aftershave, a lemony citrus scent, not too sweet, and shamelessly checked out his behind in snug jeans. I remembered that he'd played college football, figured him for a quarterback, not big enough for the line. I also figured he must put in regular hours at the gym—the guy looked fit. With difficulty, I turned my attention to the rest of the environment. We passed a few cubicles of folks clicking away at their keyboards and an open space just outside his office where four employees sat around a large table in an animated discussion. Nick suggested we sit at the small round table in a corner of his office to talk. I appreciated the gesture as leveling the playing field.

"So, Ann, what can I do for you?"

Poor question. I didn't want to think about what I really wanted him to do for me. Instead, I explained that Caroline had asked me to look into Julia's death.

"Why don't you start by telling me your impressions of Julia Comstock," I said.

Villardi sat very still, looked down at the table and then back at me. He ran his hands through his hair a couple of times, then leaned forward resting his forearms on the table. "Julia was a beautiful girl, quiet, sensitive, and intelligent, always a little introverted, even when Warren first met her. But she had a playful, mischievous side, too. She seemed naïve, younger than her years, childlike almost. I think that's part of what attracted Warren. He'd dated many powerful and demanding women over the years. Julia was different, happy to stay at home, in the background."

I raised my eyebrows.

"I don't mean it as a criticism. Julia certainly was not the ideal wife for Warren—she disliked all the trappings of the corporate wife role, never bought into that. But it worked okay for both of them for quite a while. Warren took refuge in their home, kept his life with Julia separate from his work life—a kind of sanctuary. Then Warren started to travel quite a bit—we began consulting with firms all over Europe—but Julia would never go along. I know that bothered him. When Comvitek became highly profitable, we wanted to give back to the community. We set up a foundation, began to donate large sums of money to education, the arts, that kind of thing. But Julia had no interest in working with the foundation either."

"You think they were having marital problems?"

"I think Warren was disappointed, but he didn't talk about it much. He spent less time at home, more time at the office or on the road, always pushing himself. That's what did him in: a heart attack at age forty-three. Pretty scary." Villardi leaned back in his chair and shook his head. "Sorry, you were asking about Julia and I got to talking about Warren's death. It's still so hard to believe."

"You were close, you and Warren." I said, recognizing his need to talk about it.

"We met at Boston College, first-year roommates, luck of the draw. I was on a full scholarship, a poor Catholic kid from an Italian neighborhood, unlike Warren, this rich kid from California, the Bay Area. I figured we had nothing in common. Turns out we both played football during the day and were closet computer geeks at night—an unlikely combination. We had some great times." He paused, glanced out the window, lost in his memories.

"After college you stayed in touch," I said.

He turned back to me, nodded. "After college, Warren's family expected him to go to medical school. Instead we hatched a plan to come to Seattle and get into the computer business. We worked together at Microsoft for a couple of years, long enough to make the money to start Comvitek. It sounds corny but we were living our dream. Until last spring, that is." Villardi looked down at the table for a moment and when he lifted his clear brown eyes to mine, they were swimming. "I miss him."

Wow. This amazingly attractive man was not only smart and successful, but sensitive. And clearly married, I reminded myself. I tried to get back to the subject.

"I'm sorry. I know it's hard to lose someone you're close to," I said, resisting my strong urge to touch him. "And then Julia's suicide so soon after Warren's death. Did you see it coming? What can you tell me about her behavior last summer?"

"Useless," he said, with a harder edge to his voice now. "I mean, she walked around in a daze for several weeks after Warren died. She wouldn't participate in any funeral planning and then, at the funeral, she was out of it—drugged, I suppose. For weeks after that, she wouldn't answer the phone. She refused to come and stay with us. And once she joined that church she went completely bonkers. Started talking about 'spirit guides' and how people talked to her from 'the other side.' Weird shit. I guess she jumped because she wanted to get back together with him. At least, that's how it seemed to me."

"Did she say that to you?" I asked. "Did she share her feelings with you at all?"

"To tell you the truth, I never asked her about her feelings. I figured she joined this church as a way of coping with Warren's death, that it was a harmless phase she would eventually grow out of and get on with her life."

"How often did you see her during that time?"

"About once a week right after Warren died, then less often. I was busy trying to keep the business together. I had Liz check in with her though, until she got fed up with it. Not surprisingly, it didn't take long for that to happen."

"Why 'not surprisingly'?"

"When Julia invited Liz to join her for one of those sessions, Liz gave up, couldn't put up with that."

"Liz is your wife," I said, hoping I didn't sound too interested in his marital status.

"Yes, Liz Villardi, my wife," Nick said, narrowing his eyes and rubbing his chin, as if puzzling over that concept, then changed the subject. "Have you talked to the people from Nirmala? You know Julia spent most of her time there toward the end."

"I've talked with Victor Lloyd over the phone. I expect to meet him in person later this week. Have you met him?" I asked.

"Oh yeah. After Julia's death I called him up, paid him a visit, actually." A bit of an edge crept into his voice.

"You know, he surprised me at first, seemed like a regular guy until he started talking about death, or life after death, I guess."

"What did he say?" I asked.

"Lots of things. Like, he understood my anger about Julia's death. He said anger was a normal part of the grieving process. It was natural that the loss of my friend disturbed me."

"That makes sense."

"Yeah, it made sense until he started talking about his beliefs, that when people die they go to 'another side' or something like that, where they find peace. Then he had the nerve to suggest I should try to contact Warren through him sometime. Can you believe that?" He shook his head. "Trying to get me to buy into his bullshit."

"Amazing," I agreed. "Did he say anything else specific about Julia?"

"He denied that he pushed her over the edge, said he would never interfere in the natural order of things. I don't know, Ann, maybe Julia just wanted to die."

"Her sister feels that Julia was incapable of killing herself," I said.

"Her sister. Well, she hadn't seen her sister in a long time. Do you know the story?" he asked.

"I know that Caroline and Julia were estranged but I don't know the circumstances," I lied, waiting to hear his version.

Nick related pretty much the same story I'd heard from Caroline. I pretended I hadn't heard it before and scribbled down a few notes. When I looked up, Nick was glancing at his watch. I guessed I had taken up enough of his time.

"Well, thanks for talking with me." I stood up to leave.

"It has been a pleasure." He gave me another penetrating look. "Please let me know if there is anything else I can do for you. Call me anytime."

"Please tell your wife she'll be hearing from me," I said, thinking that a reminder about Mrs. Villardi was a good idea for both of us.

"Will do," he said, holding the door open for me. "I'll see you out."

Photos from the morning's press conference were on my desk as promised after lunch. My eyes moved from the faces to the caption that Jeanine had provided, identifying the individuals pictured. On the far right stood Liz Villardi, next to a woman named Kelly Long, both representing Comvitek. I held the photo up to the light, trying to get a better look at Nick Villardi's wife. Even from this distance and long camera angle she looked stunning, in an ice queen sort of way. Maybe that's what made Nick such a flirt—maybe he simply needed a little warmth.

8

I walked through the Nirmala church doors just before the "Opening to Channel" workshop started at seven p.m. The large gathering room had been transformed into a more inviting space, with candles flickering on the altar and in recesses along the walls. The sound of small fountains burbling had the usual effect—good thing I had remembered to hit the bathroom beforehand. As my nose registered the pungent tang of incense and my eyes adjusted to the darkness, I looked around, guessed there were about twenty people in all. Each had staked out his or her territory on one of the multicolored cushions scattered randomly on the carpeted floor. Most were sitting silently, staring off into space, but a few talked quietly with those around them. I counted only three men in this group of mostly middle-aged women. It felt a bit like the beginning of an aerobics class, except for the low lighting, candles, and piped-in "music." How anyone equated canned sounds of waves crashing, synthesized wind, and an occasional lilting flute with real music astonished me. I would have preferred Pavarotti, or Dave Matthews, maybe. I grabbed a sky-blue cushion, found a spot towards the back of the room where I could watch all the action, and waited.

At exactly seven o'clock, the side door opened and a shaft of light burst into the room along with Victor Lloyd. Like moths, we turned toward him. All talking and music ceased. Dressed in light gray sweatpants and an oversized white cotton shirt, Lloyd strode purposefully to the front of the room and turned to face his audience. From my vantage point, his facial features were indistinct, but I could see he wore his brown hair rather long, covering the tops of his ears and just brushing his shirt collar in back. Stepping into the wash of soft light flooding the small platform area, he smiled broadly and looked around the room.

"Hi, I'm Victor Lloyd," he said, in a warm, resonant voice. "This is the 'Open to Channel' workshop. I'm here to teach you something about connecting with the spirit world. So, if you thought you signed up for a yoga class, or aerobics, you might be disappointed, or at least surprised, by what happens here tonight." We chuckled nervously, and on cue. As he continued to speak, a lock of his hair fell forward into his face and the way he flipped it out of his eyes seemed somehow like an invitation. I felt the heat wash over my body as he looked directly at me, sure the invitation was something personal, something intimate. Embarrassed, I looked around and saw that every woman there felt the same way. I reminded myself to be careful. This guy was good.

"Seriously, I'm so glad you're all here tonight," he said. "I'm looking forward to a great workshop. How many of you have been to a psychic reading before, or are familiar with my work?" he asked. About two-thirds of the group raised their hands.

"I recognize some of you from the church. That's great. Hopefully I'll get to know the rest of you over the course of the workshop. We'll have time to socialize during our breaks. Right now, I'd like to get started with some relaxation techniques. We'll get the basics of meditation practices going and then, when we're all feeling more receptive, we'll move into some specific exercises you can use on your own to connect with the spirit world." Lloyd sat down, positioned himself cross-legged on a yoga mat, and dropped his hands into his lap. I noticed that his large feet were bare.

Committed to keeping my guard up, I listened attentively as Lloyd described his views on posture. Rather than assuming a formal meditative posture, he advocated finding any comfortable position as long as we could stay alert. In other words, don't fall asleep. Then he got started:

"Close your eyes lightly. Begin by affirming your intention to be kind to yourself tonight, to be patient with yourself, to be present with yourself in a non-judgmental way, to be aware. Feel your body relax. Let go of your tensions. Allow yourself a quiet space from your hectic life.

"Concentrate on your breath as the air moves slowly in and out of your body. Feel the coolness of the air as it passes through your nostrils, sense the movement of the air in and out."

Lloyd went on quite a bit about listening to our breath and I felt myself relaxing despite my apprehension, until he asked, "Do you know your breath fully? Can you drop everything else and give full attention to your whole breath?"

Coughing to suppress a chortle and instantly recognizing my fate as meditation dropout, I couldn't help thinking that the times I knew my breath fully usually had something to do with the amount of garlic I had consumed.

After our initial meditation session and short bathroom break, we returned to our places on the floor for what I figured would be the real show: Lloyd teaching us techniques to increase our sensitivity to spiritual contact. These were the same exercises he used to prepare for a psychic reading, he said, a way to tune up the "psychic receptors." We began with more breathing exercises and then moved into some serious visualization. He had us imagine a bright light shining down from the sky, the brightest light we'd ever seen. Then we were to imagine the light taking the shape of a pair of hands, the hands beginning to massage our feet, slowly moving up our body.

As Lloyd continued, I opened my eyes to see if anyone else was having trouble with the concept of a light massage from the spirit world. Not a chance. My classmates were all totally engrossed. With lips pressed together tightly to keep myself from laughing or blurting out something inappropriate, I surveyed the room. All eyes closed, and everyone appeared thoroughly relaxed. A few wore blissful smiles on their faces. "Come on!" I wanted to shout. "This is straight out of

Saturday Night Live." Nevertheless, he went on and on and the absurdity of it all allowed me to loosen up—I wouldn't need to keep my guard up any more. Sure, Victor Lloyd was nice to look at, but as soon as he opened his mouth about this spirit world nonsense, it was all over for me.

Lloyd began describing a glass train moving through the countryside stopping at each station and taking on swirling light of different colors, and I recognized the imagery from Julia's journals. While his voice faded into background noise, I thought about Julia's paintings, large canvases filled with vivid swirls of color propped against the walls of her greenhouse studio. Lloyd's voice suddenly increased in volume, jarring me out of my personal musings.

"Extend this invitation: If there is someone on the other side who would like to pass on a message to me, please do it now. Within the sparkling golden light you might see a face. Closely scrutinize that face."

I remembered Julia's red painting, how a misty face was just visible in the swirling color. Who belonged to that face?

"Is it a loved one or someone you don't recognize—possibly a spiritual guide? Greet the presence. Be thankful for it."

I had to go back and look at those paintings again.

Lloyd went on to suggest that we talk to the spirit that might be visiting us, that we should ask it some questions without judging or adding any commentary. His next remark seemed directed at me. He said, "Pretend you are a reporter, your job is simply to gather information." Then, "We will now have ten minutes of silence."

I had a passing thought that if I believed in this bullshit at all, I'd be trying to get in touch with Ben. As much as I'd wished him back, I'd never wished he would send me messages. That was just ridiculous—and a tad scary in some way. After a few minutes Lloyd's now-agitated voice broke the silence.

"Is there someone here connected to a boat? I'm seeing a boat, a small boat, I think, an oar? The name of Cathy or Cassie is coming through. Does this have meaning for anyone? A very strong spirit is interrupting my meditation here, wants you to know that she is okay, that she loves you."

We all snapped to attention, looking around at each other, waiting for someone to acknowledge what Lloyd was saying.

"I'm being shown water, a storm maybe, huge waves. An accident, I'm getting a sharp pain in the left side of my head. Is it Shane or Jane?"

"Oh my God!" A shrill exclamation filled the room as we all jumped, turning to find the voice in the low light.

"My cousin Cassie had a boating accident last summer—she flipped out of a rowboat and slammed into the oarlock. They pulled her out of the water, unconscious. She was in a coma for several months." Very quietly the woman continued, "Cassie died two weeks ago. My name is Cheryl but she called me Jane because I've always loved Jane Austen novels. It was her nickname for me."

"Cheryl," Lloyd said, "Cassie is on the other side. She's telling me she is fine, that she is happy." Tears streamed down Cheryl's face as she smiled up at Lloyd.

"Thank you," she murmured, "thank you for bringing her back to me."

"Cassie is showing me another image, Cheryl, a bird. It's someone she is with, I think, on the other side."

Cheryl's face lit up with a smile of recognition as she flicked away the tears with the back of her hand. "Robin, Robin O'Grady, our grandma. We spent summers at her house growing up. She died several years ago." Cheryl looked to Lloyd for reassurance, "Cassie really is okay, isn't she? Will she come back, maybe talk to me?"

"Yes, Cassie really is okay. She's happy on the other side. If you want to contact her again, you can practice these exercises on your own. I'll have some CDs available after class. I think you'll find that staying open to the spirit world will help you find peace."

I watched Victor Lloyd at the front of the room, appreciating the quality he had of being totally comfortable in his own body, confident and relaxed. Then I noticed how tired he now looked. Not tired exactly, more like spent. My stomach did a flip and I looked away, relieved when Lloyd called for another ten minutes of silence, suggesting we continue to relax and meditate on our own.

I thought about Ben, wished I could imagine him somewhere just on the other side of this world—through the looking glass or down the rabbit hole—but it just didn't work for me. I tried to call up some happy memory of the two of us but couldn't seem to do that either. After witnessing Lloyd's very effective charade with Cheryl, I planned to catch up with her after class, see what she had to say. I didn't think she was in on it, just that Lloyd had been very thorough in researching his students.

After a while my mind wandered to more mundane matters: dinner plans with Jack this weekend, the deadline for my latest article. I'd moved on to thinking that I needed a haircut when the distinct sense of being stared at washed over me and pulled my eyes open. Victor Lloyd, gazing vacantly in my direction from his spot in the light, appeared a bit dazed. In the next instant, his eyes focused and narrowed, locking onto mine. As Lloyd craned forward, his eyes wider now and lips parted sensuously, an involuntary shiver moved across my shoulders. I squeezed my eyes shut again to break the connection while my heart pounded against my ribcage. My head buzzed in anticipation as I waited for him to say something, knew his next "visit" would have something to do with me. *Please*, I begged silently, *Don't say anything about Ben.*

"Nancy?" Lloyd's voice boomed as he moved through the room in my direction.

"I'm Nancy," a woman in front of me squeaked. "Do you mean me?"

Lloyd looked at the woman closely. "I'm getting the sense that this is a spirit *connected* to a Nancy," he said. "I'm being shown trees, a campground, I think, tents."

Butterflies swarmed in my stomach while my classmate Nancy's confusion changed to clarity.

"Nope," she said. "Not me, I wouldn't go camping to save my soul. It must be someone else." We all looked around as Lloyd scanned the room.

"Anyone else, connected to a Nancy?" he asked.

"I work with a woman named Nancy," a guy to my left blurted out. "But, I'm not 'connected' to her in any other way. And I don't think she's the outdoorsy type."

Lloyd frowned. "I'm sensing some resistance." he said. "This spirit is very persistent. It's showing me the numbers eight, and," he paused, closing his eyes for a moment, "and fifteen."

I gasped involuntarily, quickly covering it with a cough, as Lloyd spun around to look at me. He approached slowly, his piercing, somehow frightening eyes contrasting with the smile on his face.

That hot, muggy Midwestern day eight years ago came back to me in a flash, as vivid in my mind now as ever. I'd replayed it so many times: My sister Nancy, backpack slung over her shoulders, smiling as she explained, "I'm going camping in the Boundary Waters with some friends. Not sure when I'll be back. I need some space right now, you know?" But I didn't know, and that space she needed stretched on from Minnesota to California to the Northwest as she searched for something I never understood.

In my mind's eye I saw Nancy's sweet smile and her long blonde braids following behind her out the door. She left on August fifteenth of that year our parents died—8/15. Although I talked her into going back to Macalaster later that month for the beginning of her junior year, she never even made it through the first quarter. She dropped out to follow a guy she'd met on that fateful camping trip. *What is going on here? What does Victor Lloyd know about Nancy? What can he know? My sister is alive. I know she is.*

9

"Are *you* connected to a Nancy?" Lloyd's quiet voice brought me back to the present as I looked up at him. He was still smiling.

"Nope, not me," I croaked, the words catching in my throat as I looked around to see if anyone would bail me out here. I wasn't going to play this game.

"It must be a mistake," I challenged. "Do you ever make mistakes with these *feelings*?"

His eyes widened, then narrowed. He looked directly into my own eyes before he blinked and, with an exaggerated shrug of his broad shoulders, said, "This is not an exact science. I'm only telling you what I'm feeling from the spirit world. It's all I can do. Just reporting what they're asking me to." He emphasized the word "reporting."

I mirrored his shrug, feigning indifference, feeling a jumble of emotions—relief that he wasn't pretending to hear from Ben, fear about Nancy.

Lloyd went on, "I feel the spirit receding now, letting go. I think we should call it a night. It's just about nine."

Lloyd moved back to the front of the room where a few admiring fans approached, hoping for a chance to talk to him or simply hang out in his aura. Most of us were dutifully piling our cushions in the closet murmuring about the "amazing" experience we'd just witnessed. Pushing the thoughts of Ben and Nancy back into the recesses of my brain, I searched for Cheryl, eager to find out about her interaction with Lloyd, how he could have known those things about her cousin's death.

"Cheryl?" I touched her shoulder just as she placed her cushion on the growing pile. "Do you mind talking about what happened here tonight? I mean, it was pretty *amazing*," I said, hoping I sounded just like everyone else.

Cheryl smiled broadly as she replied, "Oh, I'm sure I'll be talking about it for a long time. Wasn't it something?" Sensing the impatience of our classmates to get their own cushions onto the pile, Cheryl and I began walking towards the door together as we continued our chat.

"Pretty incredible," I gushed. "How did you decide to take this class? I mean, had you met Lloyd before? Do you have any connection with the church, anything like that?"

"No, I've never met him, but I'd heard a lot about him from my friend Sara, who has taken some meditation classes at Nirmala and has heard him speak before. She recommended I take the workshop, in fact, knowing how devastated I'd been after Cassie's accident."

"Oh, so she's a friend of Lloyd's?"

"No, I wouldn't say that. She just has a great deal of respect for him, is all. Look, I'm pretty wrung out right now. I'd better go, see you." She ducked out the door and headed for the parking lot as I too got swept out with the other stragglers raising the hoods of their North Face rain parkas and making the mad dash through the rain to their cars.

Standing at my car and feeling around for my car keys in the black hole of my purse, I felt someone approach me from behind.

"Excuse me." At the sound of his voice, I turned and bumped right into Victor Lloyd. Startled, I jumped and nearly lost my balance in the slippery parking lot. He reached out to steady me and I felt my heart racing.

"Whoa, careful, don't want you to fall," he said, looking directly into my eyes. He smiled, then glanced down, breaking eye contact long enough for me to catch my breath.

"I had the feeling I offended you in some way during the workshop," he said, the smile gone from his lips now but not from his eyes. "And I wanted to apologize. We haven't really met?"

I shook his outstretched hand and flashed my best welcoming-committee smile. "Ann, Ann Johnson. No, we haven't met, but we talked briefly on the phone the other day when I registered for the workshop."

He nodded and waited for me to continue.

"And you didn't offend me at all. I just felt confused, I guess, and you were so persistent about the Nancy thing, my mind was spinning trying to think of all the Nancys I've known in my life and what they might want with me right now." I forced a laugh. "I couldn't come up with anything."

"No harm then?" he asked, smiling. "It's just that a spirit was showing me 'Nancy' and I was getting a strong feeling about you and I linked the two. I guess I missed the real connection. Maybe I'll get it another time. So, you decided to sign up for the workshop anyway. Good. I think I remember you had a lot of questions over the phone."

"Yeah, well, curiosity, I guess. I've always been intrigued by the notion of ESP, my mom was a little psychic maybe." Surprised at what just pops out of my mouth sometimes, I continued, "Anyway, that's it, just curious."

"Has your mom crossed over?" he asked, suddenly alert and cocking his head in a way that reminded me of Pooch when she heard the word cookie. Registering my confusion, he amended his question. "Has she died?"

"Oh, well, yeah, but it was a long time ago and I'm not really looking to get in touch with her or anything."

Lloyd stared at me for an uncomfortably long time before responding. "You're very skeptical, aren't you, Ann?" Now he really was showing his psychic powers.

"Well, I guess I am. But I'm curious too. Like, how did you know all that stuff about Cheryl's cousin?" I asked, pulling my eyes from his to follow the progress of a candy wrapper as it blew across the parking lot and slapped to a halt against the car next to mine. I flipped up my coat collar and pulled it shut against the rain falling in earnest now.

"The answer to that question is too complicated for an outdoor discussion at nine- fifteen on a rainy Wednesday night," he said, leaning closer, pushing the hair out of his eyes to get a better look at me. "Why don't we get together and talk about it another time?"

I felt the heat rise in my cheeks again as I realized he was hitting on me and I liked it.

It took me too long to respond, so he tried a different question. "Have you had a chance to read my book? I think I mentioned it to you over the phone."

I must have winced at the abrupt change in topics, but he kept talking. "No, I didn't think so. Why don't I drop a copy off at your office tomorrow and then we'll get together early next week, after you've read it? You'll probably have more questions then."

I finally found my voice. "Actually, I picked up a copy the other day. I just haven't had a chance to read it," I lied, thinking how clever he was. "But I would love to talk to you about it. Do you have an office in the church? Why don't I call you early next week and we'll see if we can get together before the next workshop?"

"Sure. If you'd rather do it that way, it's fine with me. I'll look forward to hearing from you."

He turned abruptly, jumped over a puddle, plucked the candy wrapper off the door of his dark blue Saab, got into the car, and drove fast out of the lot.

I got into my car, took off my sopping wet jacket and threw it into the backseat, then turned the heat and windshield wipers on full blast. Shivering, I wheeled my car onto Fauntleroy Way and headed for home, trying to process what had just happened and pretending I wasn't excited by the prospect of seeing Victor Lloyd again.

Nicole was in my living room in front of the fire, tossing a ball for Puccini, when I got there.

"How was it?" she asked, while I sat on the rug so Pooch could shove her head into my lap before flopping over for a belly rub.

"Very weird," I said. "And the guy, Victor Lloyd, followed me out to the parking lot and was hitting on me."

"Oooh, is he hot? Maybe you could make that work for you. You know, get all cozy with him and get him to spill his guts to you." I had told her a little bit about my investigation when she came over to watch Pooch.

"You've been watching too much TV. That's not the way it works in real life. He is attractive, though, or maybe 'charismatic' is a better way to describe him—sexy in a potentially dangerous kind of way. No, the last thing I want to do is get cozy with this guy."

"Oh yeah, I guess he could be a murderer, huh?"

"Maybe. He seemed pretty harmless tonight. Except, of course, he did pretend to talk to dead people."

"Tell me about it."

"Well, he had this whole show going where he said he was getting messages from some poor woman's dead cousin. The group ate it up. I talked to the woman afterward. Turns out she has a good friend who knows Lloyd. I suppose Lloyd gets information about people in the class and then uses that to put on the show. I don't think the woman was in on it herself. She seemed genuinely happy to hear from her dead cousin."

"Weird."

"Yeah, and then he really creeped me out by pretending to have a message for someone connected to Nancy."

"Whoa, how does he know your sister?"

"Well, I'm sure he doesn't, but he's really good at sensing people's reactions to what he says. He could see the mention of Nancy bothered me. I must have had some kind of involuntary tic that he spotted before I got myself together. With all the relaxation exercises we did, I could have fallen asleep in a minute. You know, my guard was down—he got lucky. It won't happen again."

"On second thought, you should stay away from him."

Nicole and I spent a few more minutes talking about Lloyd, her mother, the classes she was taking, and a guy she had a crush on who apparently didn't know she existed. She left before ten thirty and I sat down with my spiral-bound notebook and went through my notes on Julia Comstock and the people I had interviewed. I made a note to call Liz Villardi in the morning and to check in with Rose again at the church. Maybe she knew Julia; maybe I could get the names of the people who had taken workshops with her.

Reading through my notes, I latched onto the phrase "estranged from her sister." I began to think about Nancy, how much Lloyd's comments disturbed me. How could I connect Julia Comstock's death with a religious cult when I couldn't even keep my own sister from going down with one? I preferred to think we weren't "estranged," but who was I kidding? We hadn't spoken to each other in five years. Now Lloyd had planted the seed in my mind that Nancy might be dead. I couldn't believe that. I'd had enough death. When Nancy first disappeared, I was pissed off, hurt that she never contacted me. Then I just went on with my life, closed that door, and put up a pretty solid wall around my feelings. That wall began to crack when I heard Caroline's story about Julia; with Lloyd's "visit" tonight, the mortar was crumbling rapidly.

The fire made me drowsy and I must have dozed off for quite a while since I awakened with a start to a noise, which must have been the slap of the *New York Times* against the door. I could hear the low idle of a car driving slowly past the house and Puccini growling as I picked myself up from the sofa and wandered into my bedroom, pulling off clothes along the way. I willed myself not to look at the clock as I got into my bed and under the comforter. I didn't want to know how close to morning it was. Sometimes ignorance really is bliss.

10

Thursday dawned cooler than the day before and blustery. I hoped the early morning sun break would last at least as long as it took to drive to the *Seattle Times*, since my windshield wipers were iffy—my second pair this year. While stopped at a long light on Aurora Avenue, I punched in the number for the Nirmala church and left a message for Rose to call me on my cell phone when she got in. As soon as I got to my desk, and before I got inundated with the crisis *du jour*, I called Liz Villardi and left a voicemail, then shifted into work mode.

Rose called back shortly after ten, just as Nirmala Books opened for the day. She wanted to know how I'd liked Lloyd's workshop and she had already heard about the incident with Cheryl.

"Sounded wonderful," she said.

I agreed that it seemed wonderful to Cheryl, then changed the subject. "Say, Rose, could you get me in touch with some folks who've taken Victor Lloyd's workshops in the past? He suggested you might give me some names from his class lists. Or, if he has an assistant, someone he usually works with, that would be great, too."

"No, Victor doesn't have an assistant, although sometimes I help him out with paperwork and stuff, and, yes we do have lists, but our records are confidential. Reverend Waters is very strict about that. You could talk to my friend Patty, she's taken a couple of workshops with Victor. She's also very sensitive. I'm sure she'd love to talk to you."

I scribbled Patty Mitchell's number into my notebook and promised, after Rose's relentless urging, to show up for their Sunday service. Rose never missed an opportunity to proselytize.

Liz Villardi called back in the early afternoon. Yes, she recognized my name; Nick had told her about our meeting yesterday. Yes, she would find time to see me, although she made it clear that her schedule was quite busy. I suggested early the same evening. She hesitated briefly, then said she would be at home from seven o'clock to eight, if that worked for me. It did.

I arrived in the upscale neighborhood of Denny Blaine just before seven p.m. The houses here were nestled into the hillside, up off the street. I checked the address painted on the curb, then climbed the thirty or so slightly slippery concrete steps to the front porch clinging to the wrought iron handrail, thankful for the rare clear October night and the full moon lighting my way. I rang the doorbell of the Villardi's large brick Tudor home, and turned to take in the view. Lake Washington was an inky expanse, beyond which thousands of lights blinked from homes on the eastern shore—Bellevue. My musings about the geography, which neighborhood was directly across from the Villardi's, were cut short by the abrupt opening of one of the double doors. Liz Villardi looked down at me while the corners of her mouth widened into more of a straight line than a smile—she was no stranger to Botox. Her blonde hair was pulled back away from her face into a bun at the nape of her neck like a ballet dancer, and her expertly applied makeup showed off high cheekbones and unnaturally green eyes, probably colored contact lenses. She looked vaguely bored.

"Ann Dexter. Come in." Liz opened the door wider, allowing me to pass as her perfume slapped me in the face. She took my raincoat with a sniff and hung it in the entry hall closet while her eyes swept swiftly over me, from head to toe, possibly doing some mental math on the paltry price of my outfit. Quite a contrast to her boutique ensemble: slacks and a casual jacket over a fitted shirt in neutral tones, complementing her pale complexion and showcasing her stick-thin frame. Large diamond studs sparkled at her earlobes, more adorned her fingers, and two tennis bracelets jangled at her wrists. It occurred to me that the watch she wore probably cost more than my car.

She gestured me in and I moved through the hall into the tastefully decorated living room. A red-orange Chihuly glass sculpture shimmered on the table behind one of three plush sofas arranged around the marble fireplace. The color of the glass echoed in the pillows piled on the neutral sofas.

"Have a seat," Liz said, gesturing to the nearest couch as she slid onto the opposing one, tucking her long legs beneath her. She got right to the subject at hand.

"Nick told me you're looking into Julia's death for her sister Caroline, correct?"

"That's right. Caroline is convinced that Julia would not have committed suicide unless someone pushed her into it." Liz's green eyes narrowed as she took this in and her brightly polished crimson fingernails began tapping against the arm of the sofa.

"Figuratively, you mean. There was no one on the bridge when she jumped. I do remember that from the police investigation. What can I tell you that you don't already know?"

"Tell me about Julia's behavior after Warren died and she joined the Nirmala church? Any change you observed?"

"Right." Liz paused briefly, apparently processing and arranging her words carefully before she spoke.

"I suppose her behavior did change. Julia getting involved with that church was a change in itself."

"Tell me about that."

"Julia was always quiet, introverted. Warren saw that as her sensitive, creative nature. I saw her as spoiled and lazy. She did whatever she wanted, never got involved with anyone: no friends, no family, no community. It was surprising to me that she got involved with that church at all. I suppose it's some kind of community, even if it is . . ." She paused before continuing, "Odd. Perhaps she simply got involved with that medium, Victor Lloyd, and switched her dependence from Warren to Lloyd." She waited for me to respond.

"I understand you met him, Victor Lloyd. You went to one of his workshops with Julia?"

"Yes, I did. Nick kept after me to try to help her, suggested I go to the church with Julia, see how she was doing." As an afterthought, she added, "Nick loved Warren and felt responsible for Julia after he died."

"What was that experience like—Lloyd's workshop?"

"Utterly bizarre and totally spurious—Lloyd delivering messages from dead people to their family and friends in the audience. Really!"

"Did Julia get any messages? Did Warren appear to talk to her?"

"She hoped to communicate with Warren, of course, but that hadn't happened. She said she had connected with a particular spirit, Charlotte, she called her, a 'spirit guide.' I believe she thought this was the spirit of her sister from another life, or some such thing. Oh yes, it was completely ridiculous, and Julia was entirely taken in."

"Did she talk to this spirit, Charlotte, at the session you went to?" I asked.

"Lloyd did the talking. It was fairly vague until he said Charlotte was worried about Julia. That she should be careful whom she trusted, something like that."

"Did you talk with Julia about this comment afterwards?"

"Later, when I told her what I thought of Lloyd in no uncertain terms, she was outraged, said Charlotte must have meant me. I was the one she couldn't trust. I had never understood anything about her. She was doing very well, she didn't need any of my false concern and she suggested I leave her alone."

"Did you? Leave her alone after that?"

Liz shifted her weight on the sofa. "Oh, I persisted for a while. Nick insisted. I called and suggested we do lunch, tried to get her involved in some community service projects Comvitek was working on. No, she was finished with me and everyone else in this world. I never saw her again."

"Do you think Lloyd had something to do with Julia's death?"

"Maybe. He did put ideas into her head about how terrific the 'other side' is. But then, in the end, Julia killed herself. She was a misfit in this world looking desperately to fit in somewhere else, a spirit world that she wanted to believe existed."

Liz stood up, glanced at her Rolex and moved toward the front door. I followed behind.

"That's my input. Perhaps you can persuade Caroline to give it up. I'm sure she's furious about the money. She didn't inherit a thing, did she?" Liz asked with lips pressed tightly together suppressing a grin as she opened the closet door and removed my coat.

"I believe the money went to the Nirmala church. But Caroline's not contesting it. That's not what she's after."

Liz threw her head back and laughed full out. "That's really funny: 'not what she's after.' In my experience that's what everyone's after."

Back in Shoreline, I read the note Nicole left on my kitchen table. She and Pooch had a long romp on the beach after school; her crush, Andrew, had asked her to hang out on Saturday night. She was a happy camper. Glad that I didn't need to go out with the dog at this hour, I made myself some pesto linguini, poured a glass of cold pinot grigio, and settled in to read Victor Lloyd's book. Something about the crisp air and full moon made the prospect of reading about ghosts seem just right, as long as my own ghosts didn't intrude.

The book included a description of how Lloyd had discovered his psychic abilities as a teenager, but had tried hard to ignore them. What he wanted was to be normal, go to school, meet girls, play baseball. Only later, after the loss of a close friend, did he find it increasingly difficult to ignore his gift. The book was full of vignettes about messages Lloyd had received and delivered to people over much of his adult life.

Many of the stories made me laugh out loud, at least at the beginning. Not that the situations were funny—grieving individuals looking to contact dead loved ones—but more that the clues Lloyd professed to be picking up seemed so mundane, and vague. He was likely to be "shown" a letter in the alphabet and the person might fill in the name that would go with it. "I'm getting a name that starts with L, Laura or Larry?" "Oh, that must be my great aunt Lulu. She died last summer." Or, sometimes the person would have no apparent recollection of a name, but after Lloyd persisted, he would say, "Oh, I forgot, that was my uncle's name. He died last month. We were very close."

Lloyd's clients so obviously helped him along, searching for any connection with his "feelings," to the point of absurdity. I knew how hard it was to accept that someone you love is completely gone—that you will never hear his voice, never see his face, never touch him. I just couldn't understand how intelligent human beings could pretend Lloyd's charade had any basis in reality.

Several of Lloyd's clients had dreams in which they were "visited" by their dead loved ones. I didn't see how he could take credit for that either. I dream about my dead parents sometimes too and there is some comfort in seeing and hearing them in my mind's eye. Ben has never appeared in my dreams, though, as much as I have longed for that.

A hair-raising screech from the yard jolted me from my memories and sent Pooch running, growling and barking at the back door. I jumped up, flipped on the rear light, and screamed as the pair of eyes on the other side of the French door locked onto mine.

11

It was the biggest raccoon I'd ever seen, at least forty pounds. A large cat lay motionless at its feet. I pounded on the glass but the raccoon just stared at me, picked up the cat, and began moving slowly across the deck. I dragged a yelping and growling Pooch into the laundry room, slammed the door, and grabbed the first heavy object I could find to throw. The pot grazed the raccoon's back but it simply paused to examine it, glanced over at me, and ambled down the stairs into the ravine, taking the lifeless cat with him. Shaken, I let Pooch back into the kitchen, left her to whine at the back door, and grabbed the phone to call King County Animal Control—nothing but a series of recorded messages. I looked at my watch, twelve ten, too late to call my neighbor and tell her the bad news about Mocha.

A fitful night's sleep filled with bizarre and disconnected dreams left me feeling ragged when the radio alarm roused me at six thirty. I turned off the alarm, rolled over, and decided to get to work late. Nothing earth-shaking demanded my attention. Two hours later, the sun glaring through the slats of my mini blinds jolted me awake. It took me a minute to shake off the dream in which Nancy was dragged off by a huge cougar, and to remember what day it was and

I walked into *The Seattle Times* building at 9:55. Poppy waved at me as I approached her desk. Her smile and wink suggested she thought I'd had too much fun last night.

"It's not what you think," I said, shaking my head. Poppy arched an eyebrow in reply as she continued her end of the phone conversation, then raised her index finger, indicating that she wanted to talk with me. She clicked off the call.

"Jeff has called a meeting for ten on the newspapers in education project for next spring. He wants to go over your preliminary plan with the rest of the team working on it." She looked at her computer screen. "You have five minutes, girl, better hurry."

Thanks to my teaching days, I knew how to wing it. I grabbed my notes on the project and a cup of coffee and positioned myself at the head of the table in the small conference room exactly two minutes before anyone else arrived. *You are who you pretend to be*, I thought, and smiled, remembering my favorite aunt's advice.

The meeting went smoothly and I had just enough time to put in a call to Caroline before my lunch hour—time for a progress report and some more information. There were things about Caroline's relationship with Julia that nagged at me. And I couldn't get Liz Villardi's parting shot out of my head. Maybe Caroline was just interested in discrediting Nirmala so she could inherit Julia's money. Maybe she felt she deserved it—payment for her personal pain and suffering. Caroline suggested we get together Saturday afternoon at the Comstocks' place and expressed a keen interest in my meeting with Lloyd. I suggested we save the details for Saturday as I jotted down a list of ingredients for dinner, looking forward to my lunchtime trip to the Pike Place Market.

I checked my reflection in the full-length mirror one last time, before moving to the kitchen and the final details of dinner. Not bad. I'd settled on my new designer jeans and navy V-neck cashmere sweater, hoping a classic look would do the trick. Jack had been gone for nearly two weeks and I definitely needed some serious male attention.

Smiling in anticipation, I stirred the mushroom risotto, refreshed the baby salad greens, and glanced at the clock on the oven. Ten minutes before Jack's arrival and everything was under control. The salmon marinating in bourbon and brown sugar would take only a few minutes per side once the coals were hot. I'd wait and let Jack light them, a manly thing to do that we would joke about. One thing about Seattle: even in the late fall a barbeque could work as long as you weren't planning on spending too much time outside tending the grill.

I heard Jack's car in the drive just after Puccini did. She jumped to the door with her head lifted and tail thumping in anticipation. Giving Pooch the sit and stay hand signals, I opened the door just as Jack lifted his hand to knock. I pretended to duck the blow he was about to throw and we burst into laughter simultaneously and into each other's arms. Releasing me from the hug to take a long look, he said, "God, you look great," and, "Something smells fabulous in here."

Pooch's soft whining got louder as Jack leaned down to pat the barely contained retriever who was wagging her entire backside from side to side in joy. "Hey there, Pooch, looks like you missed me, too." Released from her stay command, Pooch bounded around the entry hall, ran into the laundry room, picked up a squeaky toy, and proudly dropped it at Jack's feet. As I watched Jack play a little tug of war with Pooch, I remembered how my friend Mary had been the first to suggest that my friendship with Jack might move into the friend with benefits realm. "He's just your body type," she'd said. I had to admit he looked pretty great: six foot tall, with curly blond hair and a runner's build. I loved his dreamy blue eyes and sexy mouth.

"Yeah, but he was Ben's friend," I'd replied.

"There you have it. Ben would approve. He liked the guy after all. He wouldn't want you to be lonely, Ann."

I'd definitely spent some lonely years. And I liked Jack. He was smart, well read and funny, a little too nice, maybe. Once Mary had planted that seed in my head, it didn't take long before Jack and I ended up in bed together. He has been attentive and warm, a fine lover. And he looked very appealing right now wrestling with the dog. I couldn't wait for my turn.

"I need to stir the risotto, and you can open up a bottle of wine. Follow me into the kitchen and tell me everything about your trip."

"The best part of the trip was getting back home," he said, eyes smiling.

I returned the smile and handed Jack the corkscrew as he pulled the cold bottle of French Chablis from the door of the fridge and set it on the counter. I reached up to get the wine glasses from the top shelf; Jack quickly came up behind me to help. Pressing against me as he took the glasses out of my hands, his fingertips tickled my wrists, and he covered the back of my neck with soft wet kisses, knowing exactly how I would respond. He placed the glasses softly on the counter as I turned into his arms and met his kiss.

Pushing him playfully away, I teased, "Hmm, Jack, a little lonely in Houston, were you? I'm flattered. But I need to stir this risotto, otherwise it will get all sticky."

"Hey, I like it that way," he said, following me to the cook top and kissing me again. I turned off the burner, pulled him into the living room, and kicked the door shut before Pooch could follow us in. Undressing each other as fast as possible and giggling at our urgency, we did our own kind of wrestling in front of the fire without the dog.

Satisfied and still smiling, we got back into our clothes and fixed dinner together, quietly exchanging our stories of the past week. Jack's trip had been a success. His new client, ecstatic over the plans Jack presented, was ready to move forward on the project: a huge storage facility outside of Houston promising to rake in profits from the packrats and organizationally challenged of the world. Three hundred temperature-controlled units would bring in large monthly fees and mounds of useless things, which the owners couldn't bear to discard, would pile up like so many hermetically sealed garbage dumps—a curious twenty-first-century trend.

When I told him what I'd been working on, Jack expressed concern about my investigation into Nirmala and more than a little skepticism about my motives.

"I know you hate these religious wackos, but try to keep some perspective here. Your sister chose an alternative lifestyle and got deeply involved with one of the most charismatic cult leaders of the century. But it doesn't sound like Victor Lloyd is in that league. So this guy thinks he's a psychic medium. He's not taking his followers off somewhere and asking them to give up all their worldly possessions to fund his lavish lifestyle, is he? Isn't it more likely that Julia Comstock was a lonely unhappy woman who decided to end her life? It's sad, but it happens."

"Gee, thanks for the encouragement, Jack."

"Come on. I'm just thinking about you. I'd hate to see you to dredge up the pain of Nancy's disappearance over this. You can't change the past. But you can choose to leave this alone," he said, taking my hand.

"No, I can't," I said, pulling away. "I just wanted to bounce some ideas off you. Never mind. Forget I mentioned it." I got up and began clearing the table and filling the dishwasher.

"I'm sorry. You're right. I was wrong. I do want to hear what you're thinking. Bounce away."

"Okay," I said, instantly swayed by the power of the three most important words a lover can offer: *I was wrong.*

"Why don't you pour us another glass of wine and I'll tell you what's happened so far."

I gave Jack the abbreviated version of my investigation, told him about my conversations with Caroline, Maria, Rose, Nick and Liz Villardi, about Julia's missing journal, her paintings, and my experience in Victor Lloyd's class.

"Does Lloyd benefit directly from Julia's money? I mean, does he get it, or does it go to the church?" he asked.

"That's exactly what I've been wondering. The church is a huge organization with branches in California as well as in Europe. I need to find out the structure, who owns what. I assume the church itself is a nonprofit, but I don't know about the rest of it. Are there shareholders? Is Lloyd the major shareholder? Something Liz Villardi said got me wondering about Caroline's real motives here. Maybe it really is about money after all and not about sisterly love."

"Well, money can't buy you love, but it can make you feel all right."

I wasn't sure what to make of the grin on Jack's face, but I was ready to change the subject. Time for an encore.

Jack left mid-morning on Saturday to catch up on household matters and I felt the usual lift as he walked out the door. I knew it wasn't fair. It wasn't Jack's fault; there was simply something missing between us. I loved his friendship and the sex was great. Maybe a little automatic, but he definitely knew how to push the right buttons. I tried not to think about how it felt to be with someone who could take my breath away every time, someone I loved completely, someone who touched my soul. I knew I'd never have that again. No, I was lucky to have Jack, and my work. It was enough.

After tending to the usual weekend housekeeping and errands, I still had plenty of time to meet with Caroline. This time, as I rolled past the gate and into The Highlands, I had no trouble finding my way to the Comstock compound.

I wound my way through the old-growth trees, catching the occasional ray of sunshine slicing through gaps in the thick fir and cedar canopy, with questions for Caroline running through my head. I pulled my car under the porte cochere, just as Caroline stepped out onto the front porch in a pair of tailored dark wool slacks and a soft ivory sweater, a long multicolored silk scarf tied loosely around her neck. She smiled and waved. She looked better than the last time we met, relaxed and energetic, more like she had spent the last week at a spa than attending to the details of her beloved sister's death.

"Come on into the sunroom Ann, Maria is just taking some scones out of the oven. Have you eaten?"

"Yes, but those smell wonderful. Just a small one for me, Maria," I said, sinking into the downy chintz sofa and looking out the window across the garden to Puget Sound. This morning the sound appeared flat and steely gray with a light fog hanging above the water—hard to discern where the water left off and the sky began. All hints of Bainbridge Island and the Olympic Mountains beyond were hidden under a heavy gray blanket. The wind picked up again and the tops of the firs swayed at the edges of the property while the alders dropped their yellow leaves in waves.

"I can't wait to hear about your meeting with Lloyd. What did you think of him?"

"I think he's pretty good at what he does. I can see how people, especially grieving people, are taken in by him. He seems very sincere."

Caroline shook her head. "Oh yes, I'm sure he does, the bastard. Did you find out anything about the kind of money he's making from grieving widows?"

"Not really. His classes aren't over-the-top expensive. He's not making much money there. But I'll be checking into his private clientele this week, looking for some answers about how the money comes and goes. Which reminds me, do you know the particulars of Julia's bequest?"

"Of course. Besides a small amount to me and to the Seattle Art and Design School, everything else goes to the Nirmala Church of Self-Actualization, earmarked 'to further the work of Victor Lloyd.' My lawyer says the Church is, in fact, a nonprofit, tax-exempt religious organization but also just one part of a larger privately held corporation with assets all over the world, real estate in the U.S. as well as Europe, Italy mainly. Lloyd is part of a multimillion-dollar dynasty, it seems."

"I'm not surprised," I said, thinking how familiar that sounded. "You said *your* lawyer—is that the lawyer for Julia's estate? Could I get his name? I'd like to talk to him."

"Sure, his name is Richard Jarndyce, with Jarndyce and Maxwell. But Richard is my personal lawyer and not the lawyer for Julia's estate. Julia's will is being probated by Jenkins and Phipps. Tom Jenkins is handling the particulars."

"Meaning you hired a lawyer to contest the will? Why didn't you tell me this before? I thought this wasn't all about the money."

"Come on! Did you think I would let the man who killed my sister get her money without a fight? It's not about me getting the money. It's about keeping the money from the murderer." Caroline's head snapped up as Maria entered the room along with the warm scent of vanilla, cinnamon, and a hint of lavender.

"Lemon lavender scones," Maria said, setting the tray on the coffee table between us. A small basket heaped with scones sat nestled between two oversized mugs, one steaming with coffee and the other with chai tea. I understood now why Caroline looked like she'd been spending time at a spa; this kind of pampering would do it.

After Maria left the room, we munched on the melt-in-your-mouth scones and talked about my plans to further investigate Victor Lloyd and Sylvia Carter—the woman who came to the Comstock house on the day of Julia's death. Pleased that Caroline agreed with my take on things, I resisted the urge to eat yet another scone and finally forced myself to leave.

"Good luck, Ann, and be careful," Caroline said, as she walked me to the front door.

"Right. I'll keep in touch."

I drove home considering Caroline's explanation for contesting Julia's will. It made sense. Of course she didn't want the money to go to anyone who might be responsible for her sister's death. But I wasn't naïve enough to think she would be giving it away to anyone needier than herself either.

I spent the rest of my Saturday running Pooch and looking forward to the evening. I had an excellent seat for Seattle Opera's production of Tchaikovsky's *Eugene Onegin*, thanks to my friend and former neighbor Mike Porter, who sang in the chorus. Mike said this production was incredible, I'd love it. But then, Mike never met an opera he didn't like. Too bad I couldn't convince Jack to go along. He had never developed a passion for opera, or even an appreciation of it. I settled into my seat wondering whether Jack had a passion for anything. He was always so even-keeled. Yes, I reminded myself, it was a quality I admired in him. Really.

The production lived up to Mike's enthusiasm—lavish sets and costumes, big party scenes, and a plot I could relate to. A young, inexperienced woman (Tatyana) confuses infatuation with love and eagerly confesses her love to the handsome, confident, and self-impressed young man (Onegin) only to face rejection and then humiliation when he flirts with her best friend at a party the next night. Years later, when it's too late to reclaim either his youth or her love, Onegin meets Tatyana again and realizes that he missed his best chance of happiness with a fabulous woman. Of course, since this is opera, there is a duel, death and banishment, and many dramatic arias. Even so, I left McCaw Hall thinking of Peter Dobson, whom I loved but who didn't give me the time of day in college, and how he would regret his loss when we ran into each other in the future.

I met Mike backstage after the show to tell him how much I'd enjoyed the gorgeous music and seeing him front and center dressed as a Russian aristocrat, but declined his offer of drinks. He scoffed at the idea of my getting up early to go to church in the morning, knowing as he did my cynical view of organized religion.

"It's research for an article I'm working on," I told him. He raised an eyebrow but left it at that.

"Say 'hi' to Toni and the boys for me."

"Will do. Wait till I tell her you've got religion!"

12

With very little traffic on Sunday morning and the drive to West Seattle relatively painless, I reached Nirmala a full ten minutes before the service began. I parked my car on Fauntleroy Way behind a minivan from which a woman and two young children emerged heading in the same direction. The family appeared dressed for church but they looked so white-bread that I supposed they were going to the coffee shop two doors down from Nirmala, after worshipping at some Presbyterian church nearby. As they approached Nirmala, the older boy surprised me by opening the door for his mother and sister and, seeing me approach, he held it for me as well. Once inside, we joined a few people milling about in the storefront area, talking with each other. Two men flanked the entrance to the sanctuary as greeters, handing out the order of service so I took one and made my way inside. It looked much the same as it had during the meditation class except for the rows of folding chairs facing the altar.

Only a few people were seated and all appeared to be in some meditative state, hangers-on from the earlier session, I supposed. A couple of musicians sat off to one side, behind an acoustic guitar and a keyboard synthesizer, even though the now-familiar noise of waves crashing against a shore, punctuated by the call of seagulls, continued to flow from the speakers overhead. Taking my seat in the back row toward one side, my eyes were drawn to the altar, a table draped with white linen and a gauzy fabric woven with gold and silver threads. A simple floral arrangement and a few white candles were the only adornments on the altar itself. Behind it in a recessed archway, five backlit paintings hung in a semicircle. I recognized Jesus top and center but the other four figures were a mystery to me. Above Jesus, at the very top of the arch, a large, glowing blue eye stared at the congregation like a disembodied cyclops. On each side of the altar, icons of both Eastern and Western gods and holy symbols were displayed—the Virgin Mary looking like she was straight from a Catholic baptismal font, the Shakyamuni Buddha—cross-legged and eyes closed, some saint whom I felt I should have recognized (St. Christopher?), a small statue of a man in the lotus position, and some intricately carved wooden artifacts that must mean something to someone, African, I surmised. It looked like they were covering all the bases here. A Bible passage involuntarily popped into my head— unavoidable to a recovering Lutheran with several years of youthful indoctrination under my belt—"Thou shalt have no other Gods before me." No earthquakes or thunder seemed likely to follow my internal admonition so I scanned the crowd.

Like the family who'd preceded me into the church, the other congregants already seated or wandering in were unremarkable. There were slightly more women than men. Most were middle-aged with a few younger folks—no one too terribly ancient. They could just as easily have been a group of Seattle theatergoers.

At just past ten, the recorded music stopped, the guitarist began strumming a tune, the lights brightened, and the ministers entered the sanctuary, one man and two women following behind. They were all wearing white robes and smiling knowingly as they approached the altar. The middle-aged assistant minister greeted us and introduced herself with an Indian-sounding name, though she looked Scandinavian. The ministers were then joined by a small group of individuals, apparently the choir. The hymn was agonizingly off-key and not particularly melodic but thankfully short. Next, the congregation stood to chant, repeatedly singing, "Thy name" and "getting drunk with Thy name." To me, this felt more like a hangover than getting drunk. The words to the chant were printed in the order of service but everyone around me seemed to know it by heart. Some began swaying slightly; others tapped their palms in a hushed semblance of clapping. I mumbled along, suppressing the grin I felt playing around my lips. The names we repeated included Jesus and the four other gurus or masters. I tried to match their pictures with their names. One was Krishna, I think, and the others had Indian-sounding names I couldn't pronounce, including Swami something and Yogi something else, possibly Yoginirmala. I couldn't help thinking of Yogi Bear—he was smarter than your average bear. Om.

When we finished our chants, we sat down and were asked to meditate for a few minutes on our own. We were to focus on God, in that important place between our eyes, the center of concentration, and there was lots of talk of light, the light of God. It was extremely quiet for an uncomfortable length of time and I found myself focusing on bodily fluids. In the packed eerie silence, all I heard were stomachs rumbling and swallowing and sniffing. The minister's invitation, finally, to stand and sing was very welcome.

We settled in to hear the homily, taken from the Bible and embroidered with the guru's experiences. Beginning with the passage, "Ask and it shall be given unto you, seek and ye shall find, knock and it shall be opened unto you," we learned that through prayer and meditation we were likely to get what we wanted, as long as we were at a certain stage of enlightenment and it was God's will. The minister illustrated this concept with a story about one of the swamis teaching in India, how he took young boys from the village to a waterfall for lessons. It was a dangerous place to cross but he always asked them before the crossing, "Do you believe in God?" and they would answer loudly and in unison, "Yes!" and no one ever had any trouble getting across the stream. When the swami returned to the United States, another teacher took his place in this village, but he was not as enlightened as Swami Nirmala and so one day a boy fell into the stream and drowned. Nice. The lesson, apparently, was that we should all continue to strive for enlightenment. To me, it was yet another example of the bizarre sense of humor most "gods" seem to have.

During the offertory, a young red-haired man approached the altar and began strumming his acoustic guitar. Startled at his beautiful tenor voice, after the chanting and off-key choir, I opened my purse and added five dollars to the basket. Only later did I wonder whether this relief, so timely inserted, was intentional.

According to my order of service, it was now time for the "Festival of Lights," a communion ritual of sorts. It began with the male minister taking the largest white candle from the altar and using it to light smaller candles held by his two female assistants. While music played and the congregants sang, the two women held their candles up to each picture of the "masters," performing a kind of sensual dance with their hands until they had each snaked around each of the five paintings. They then invited those who wanted to receive the light of the masters to come up and get it. I wanted to go up to hear what the ministers said as they ran their fingers around the rims of their candle vessels, dipped their fingers into the melted wax, and touched the foreheads of each individual in the most important place between the eyes. But my legs became so rooted to the floor that I had difficulty moving back to allow the man next to me to pass when it came time for our row to approach the altar. His puzzled scowl unnerved me even more as he shook his head and brushed past. Hopefully, he would be lighter when he returned. Feeling exposed as an obvious outsider, I checked my watch while my head began to throb as the final song, "The Thunder of Om," repeated again and again until the final person received the light.

We filed out into the storefront where tea and snacks were promised, and I was relieved to see Rose pouring a fragrant jasmine tea into cups. Looking up from her task, she greeted me warmly and introduced me to several folks, including her friend Patty Mitchell. I asked Patty about Lloyd and she gushed on about how fabulous he was.

"Too bad he's not at church this morning. I think he might be teaching a seminar on Bainbridge this weekend."

"Does Lloyd have an assistant?" I asked, adding, "I talked with someone in the channeling workshop who said he'd had one for a while but couldn't remember her name."

"Not as long as I've known him. And I've been here for six years now. Oh, sometimes women get attached to him and may want to help him, but officially, no."

"Do you know a woman named Sylvia Carter? That's the name I heard mentioned as his assistant."

"Sylvia? No, I don't think so. Sorry."

"Patty, will you introduce me to your friend? I'm sure I've not had the pleasure." I turned to find the minister smiling with only his teeth. He fixed his eyes to mine as he took my hand in both of his.

"Ann Johnson, this is Reverend Bob Waters, or, as we call him by his given title here at Nirmala, Swami Kriymala."

"A pleasure, Ann," he said, continuing to hold my gaze as well as my hand.

I nodded, temporarily tongue-tied and unable to look away from his steely blue eyes. He'd leaned in close enough for me to see the blonde stubble on his ruddy round face and smell his sickeningly sweet aftershave.

"I noticed that you are curious about us but reluctant to receive the light. Perhaps when you have learned more about the masters, you will be ready. In fact, Yoginirmala, the head of our church, will be at our spiritual community in Issaquah later this month. May I invite you to come and hear him?" He was still holding my hand and, as it began to perspire, I pulled away, abruptly feigning an oncoming sneeze and reaching for a tissue in my pocket. My face felt hot as I met his gaze once again and replied as matter-of-factly as possible.

"Thank you. Let me know the dates and I'll put it on my calendar."

"Ann has been taking a class with Victor, asking about an

assistant she'd heard he had working with him, Sylvia Carter?" Patty looked from me to Swami Bob.

"Sylvia Carter," he said, articulating each syllable clearly and shaking his head. "No. I don't know her. Of course, Victor works alone. Quite a talented young man he is too, providing an invaluable service to those he touches. Have you lost someone, Ann? Is that why you're taking Victor's workshop?" He adopted the same concerned attitude he'd met me with earlier.

"Haven't we all?" I shrugged. "No, I'm not trying to contact anyone in particular. I'm just curious about the afterlife," I said, feeling brave enough now to look directly into his eyes.

"I understand. A basic human need to know that some form of life continues after we take our last breath here on earth. I think you'd find the masters' teachings on this topic to be very comforting. Beginning with Jesus' promise of heaven to Yoginirmala's example in India when—"

"Yes, gosh, it's much later than I thought." I checked my watch and began buttoning up my coat. "I hope we can continue this discussion another time but I have a lunch date and I'm already late." I thanked Patty for introducing me to Bob, then thought maybe I should have called him by his title as I noticed a smile lick the corners of his thin lips and he nodded me out the door.

13

My one connection in the Seattle Police Department is homicide detective Erin Becker, daughter of a cop and married to a local criminal defense lawyer. I met Erin and her husband Matt socially a few years back and liked both of them. According to Erin, having a spouse on the opposite side of the criminal justice system leads to surprisingly few direct professional conflicts since Matt has a federal practice, but it sure ratcheted up the intensity of their dinner conversations. Ironically, it wasn't the criminal justice system that brought these two together, but their passion for motorcycles. They met at a local Harley Davidson club five years ago, were married after an intense six-month courtship, and spent their honeymoon riding across the country on their Harleys. It was a far cry from my only comparable experience, which involved an underpowered motorcycle in the South of France. But that's a different story and it happened a long time ago.

I dialed up Erin's number, remembering she'd worked on the Comstock case. We exchanged pleasantries and Erin told me all about her latest trip into British Columbia with Matt in September. It sounded like torture to me, being exposed to the elements, getting saddle sore, and camping in rustic spots. But Erin assured me they'd had a blast. When the conversation turned to what I'd been up to, I told her about Caroline Schuster—her views about Victor Lloyd and the Nirmala church. Then I asked her about Sylvia Carter. The name drew a blank until I filled in the background for her.

"Oh, yeah, now I remember. I also remember that she didn't exist. Lloyd never heard of her, the church records supported that, and we found no trace of her in a routine computer check. Since Julia's death was clearly suicide, we dropped our search for Carter."

"But someone named Sylvia Carter showed up at the Comstocks' home the same day Julia jumped off the bridge," I reminded her.

"Or somebody using an alias. It's a needle in a haystack, Ann. Forget it."

I hung up the phone, discouraged but unwilling to leave it alone. I planned to work my way into Nirmala's files for a look. Maybe if I dropped by to pick up the writings of Yoginirmala that Swami Bob had recommended yesterday, I could find a way. Maybe Rose would help.

"Yoo-hoo, Ann!" I looked up to see Jeff Skinner waving his arms and making a show of getting between me and the spot on the wall to which I must have appeared riveted.

"Wake up! May I get you some coffee?" He smirked and dropped into the chair across from my desk for, I assumed, one of his sporadic check-ins.

Sure enough. He wanted to hear about the progress of the newspapers in education project and was much more interested in whether I could get the Mariners' ace pitcher to appear at our kickoff of the program than anything to do with Nirmala. I switched gears for the rest of the day. Spring training was only four months away and there were lots of details to get together before then.

On my way home, I took a detour to West Seattle. The door to Nirmala was open when I arrived, but no one was in the vestibule as I walked in and set the chimes above the door tinkling away. Grabbing one of the books off the shelf, I moved behind the front table and into the small office area where several file cabinets, neatly labeled, lined the back wall. Scanning the labels while I yelled, "Hello! Anybody here?" I spotted several drawers marked "Workshops." Searching as fast as possible I scanned the dates as footsteps approached from beyond the sanctuary. I yanked at the drawer marked "Jan.-June." Locked. I heard a man's voice, getting closer,

"Hello. I'm coming!" Turning on my way back into the foyer, I saw them: a bunch of keys, each with round white neatly labeled tags, dangled from a hook on the side of the file cabinet. Grabbing and slipping them into my raincoat pocket, I leaped around the desk and back through the door into the foyer where I slammed straight into Swami Bob.

"Whoa, there! Hey, I didn't mean to startle you." The overwhelming sweet smell of his aftershave enveloped me as I stood inches from his freshly starched white shirt. His eyes narrowed as he looked at me, searching his memory for my name. I backed away and smiled, trying to appear composed.

"Ann, isn't it? Yes. We met at services yesterday. What a pleasant surprise." He glanced down at the book I was waving in his face.

"Yes, it is. Hi!" I replied as enthusiastically as possible. "I was thinking about what you said yesterday and thought I'd pick up one of these books. Would this be a good place to start?"

Grabbing my wrist and taking the book out of my hand, he appeared to consider the matter deeply as he studied the title. "No, I don't think so. I think you're getting ahead of yourself here." Fixing me with that penetrating look he had perfected and moving toward the bookshelves, Waters replaced the book I had chosen and pulled out one titled *Yogi and Me* and placed it into my hand. Glancing at the title, I bit the inside of my lip to keep that chortle from escaping. Didn't a publisher see the humor in this, I wondered as I again conjured up images of the smarter than average bear and imagined him saying something like, "What's new with you, Boo-Boo?"

"Great!" Perky me. "Can I buy this or is it a lending library kind of thing?" I asked.

"These books are for sale." He paused. "But you can borrow that one for a while. Let me know later if you want to buy your own copy." I nodded as he continued, "Most folks find that they like to keep the masters' works with them for frequent reference. You'll decide that on your own. I can see you have a very intense curiosity about our church."

"Yes, I—"

Waters interrupted with, "Let me give you one piece of advice about your curiosity." He spoke slowly, emphasizing each word. "Don't rush into superficial judgments about us. Like relationships, spirituality is something that deepens over time. Take the time to really understand us and we will begin to understand you as well."

"Right! Gee, that's great advice. Well, thanks Rev—, er, Master, ah …"

"Bob. You can call me just plain Bob."

He pulled out his wallet and handed me a card that read, "Rev. J. Robert Waters" and at the bottom, "Swami Kriymala, Spiritual Director, Nirmala Church of Self-Actualization." Stepping out onto the street and exhaling loudly, I stuffed Waters' card into my pocket and bumped up against the pilfered keys. Smiling to myself and closing my fingers around them, I gleefully planned my next move.

14

I crawled into my bed that night around nine with a book and some warm milk, hoping to hasten sleep. My alarm was set for three thirty a.m. By then I figured the late-night partiers would be home in their beds and the early birds would not yet be up—the perfect time for a little borrowing at Nirmala.

It seemed only moments after my head hit the pillow when the twang of Bill Frisell's jazz guitar jolted me out of a bizarre dream—something involving giant pterodactyls. I switched on the light, swung my feet over the side of the bed, and stared at Pooch as she lifted her head from her pillow in the corner. The dog scratched lazily while I pulled on my black yoga pants, dark turtleneck shirt, running shoes, and Gore-Tex layer. I checked my jacket pockets: mini flashlight, driver's license, credit card, Swiss Army knife, latex gloves. Everything a good Girl Scout needs for an evening heist.

"C'mon, Pooch, let's go." She looked how I felt, bleary-eyed and unsure about the whole thing. With one more stretch and a quick shake, she was awake and whimpering at the door, ready for anything.

Sheets of rain challenged my windshield wipers as we headed down I-5 toward West Seattle. The weather and the ungodly hour of our trip meant few other cars on the road and put me into a parking space around the corner from the church in record time. I turned off the engine and lights and looked up and down the street—dark and quiet, just one streetlight fizzling half a block away, about to go out. Leaving the car unlocked, I motioned for Pooch to jump out on the driver's side with me and gave her the hand signal to heel. Her ears pricked up and she tilted her head, listening as her nostrils flared open and shut, taking in the unfamiliar air. We walked briskly around the corner, then slowed at the church's storefront window looking, I hoped, like any other insomniac walking her dog in the middle of the night. The blinds were up, light pouring out and exposing the entry room with its books, tapes, and desk.

We rounded the corner at the south end of the street and I heard the thump of bass before the car came into view, windows open, young men's voices, drunk and rowdy mixing with an angry rap, something about an evil seed doing evil deeds. The ominous lyrics sent a shiver through me.

I ducked behind a large rhododendron at the side of Panda Dry Cleaning, pulled Pooch in beside me, held my breath, and waited. I could hear the whir of machines inside and smell the damp earth mixed with the unmistakable odor of urine. A minute later, certain the car had gone, we moved through the alley past the back of the drycleaners, tae kwon do studio, and café to the rear of Nirmala. I signaled Pooch to sit and stay while I looked through the back window and around the other side of the church building. All quiet. I pulled on my latex gloves, slipped the set of keys out of my pocket and into the flashlight beam, searching for one labeled "back door." It was an old Schlage deadbolt that required jiggling and a slight pull toward me before the lock would slide back.

Once inside I stood still, waiting for my eyes to adjust to the darkness. Taking one step toward the dim light at the end of the hallway, I clanged into something hard with my shin and caught the stack of folding chairs with my body just before they all crashed to the floor. Pooch let out a yelp and I grabbed her snout and said in a low, firm tone,

"No barking, no noise." She dropped her tail and remained silent looking up at me for further instructions.

Taking care to dodge the rest of the metal racks of folding chairs lining the hallway, I made my way to the far end, moving quickly, wet shoes squeaking on the linoleum with Pooch at my heels. If memory served, this doorway should lead to the sanctuary. Yes. Stepping into the large gathering room, my footsteps muffled by the soft carpet, I felt the hair stand up on the back of my neck as the blue eye glowed down at me from its recess above the altar.

Silly, I thought, *it's just a light, not Big Brother up there.*

I crossed the length of the room and passed through the archway into the front hall. The file cabinets were to the right against the wall between the small office and the well-lit storefront room. I took one step toward them when first the corner, then the whole room, filled with light, then darkened again—a passing car. Peeking around the doorjamb, I saw that the large glass window had a blind, now pulled all the way up. I considered my options. If the police regularly patrolled this block, they might know that the church kept the blind up for security reasons and get suspicious if I pulled it down. On the other hand, any patrolling cop would see me moving around if I left the blind up. I decided to go for it.

Dashing to the window I pulled the cord left, then right, then forward while hopping back and forth with it, looking, no doubt, like some strange bird performing a mating dance. The damn cord was tangled near the top. Pooch kept her eyes on me, squirming in her spot but not daring to move. The blind finally let loose with a crash, knocking the CDs and candles onto the floor. I jumped back, dropping to my hands and knees to round up the skittering mess and hurried to display them as best I could behind the blind. Rose would undoubtedly notice the random nature of the end result in the morning.

Moving quickly to the file cabinet marked "Workshops," I squinted in the dim light to read the identifying key tags in the beam of my small flashlight. Finally locating the correct key, I unlocked the first drawer, pulled it open and flipped through the hanging files crammed with manila folders. They were neatly organized by workshop facilitators, then seminar names, then date. Thankful for Rose's organizational skills, I unlocked the second drawer and found

Lloyd's records, dozens of them. I pulled the files for June through August, then ducked into the small office and flipped the copy machine out of its sleep mode.

"Please wait!" flashed the display, then, "Warming up."

While the machine was waking, I scanned the rosters for Julia's name, spotted it, placed the page face down on the copier glass, and pushed "copy."

"Please enter your ID code" flashed on the display.

"Shit," I murmured under my breath. Shining the beam of my flashlight over the desktop, I rummaged through some papers, then randomly opened and closed the drawers. Nothing. I wracked my brain, trying to think like Rose and imagine the most logical place to keep the codes. I searched the shelf above her desk for a copier handbook and found it between the printer manual and *Microsoft Word for Dummies*. Taped inside the front cover was a list marked "User IDs." I smiled, thanking God or Krishna for Rose's efficiency. I punched in her code and decided to copy Lloyd's entire workshop file. The more names I could get, the better. I finished the job quickly, folded the copies to fit into my inner jacket pocket, and replaced the files in their cabinet.

Just as I returned the keys to their hook, Pooch startled me by growling deep in her throat, hair standing up all along the length of her spine, ears forward. All I needed to do was pull the blind back up and head out the door. I held my breath and squinted in the direction of her stare. Over the pounding of my heart, I heard a car idling in the alley just outside the back door, then a woman's voice: "I'll just wait out here. Hurry up, or we'll miss our flight."

As the key slid into the lock, I grabbed Pooch and scuttled underneath Rose's desk, pulling a chair in front of the kneehole. I clamped my hand over the dog's snout and hissed, "Shhhh," while someone (a male voice, familiar) cursed the sticky lock and jiggled the doorknob. The door opened, a light flashed on in the hallway, and I thought I might wet my pants. My pulse throbbed in my ears and I squeezed my eyes shut like I used to as a child, thinking if my eyes were closed, no one could see me either.

When I realized the footsteps were receding down the hall toward the other offices rather than coming my way, I exhaled slowly, straining to hear anything beyond the car motor still idling outside. The footsteps stopped, another light flipped on, then off fairly quickly. Soon the footsteps were coming my way again and the man starting to sing an old Chris Isaak tune, "Baby did a bad, bad thing," and I placed the voice as just plain Bob's. At the sound of singing, Pooch gave a little whimper, began wagging her tail and raised her snout to the ceiling preparing to howl—the dog loved music. I grabbed hold of her before she could let loose, praying that Reverend Bob was headed back out the door and hadn't heard Pooch's response to his call. As the hall light went out, I exhaled but waited to move out of my hiding place until I'd heard the door slam and the car begin moving down the alley. It was way past time to get out of here.

I patted my inner pocket, making sure the copies were still there, took a last look around, and slipped out the back door with Pooch at my heels. Looking left, then turning right down the alley, we were in the car and heading over the West Seattle Bridge before my pulse was back to normal. According to the digital display on my dashboard, this entire escapade had taken only twenty minutes. I reached over and patted Pooch. "Not bad, girl, but we'll have to work on your singing before we try this again." The dog looked at me briefly, then flopped down in the seat to catch up on her interrupted sleep.

I flipped on the local jazz station and just caught the end of a familiar Diana Krall tune which, the nighttime host reminded me, was off her CD *Live in Paris*. Those three words triggered a profound memory of my trip to France with Ben. My eyes welled up and I blinked back the tears. I forced myself to smile, to call up the memory with fondness.

"Hey, Pooch," I said. The dog sat up and looked at me. "I was in Paris once. Did I ever tell you about the time that Ben and I went to

France?" I told her the story.

"We'd planned this trip to Europe as a last hurrah before we had a family. Yeah, Ben always wanted kids but I wasn't so sure about it." I thought about how Ben had finally convinced me that life would be full and wonderful with children. He'd wanted a family so much.

"We started off in London and took the Chunnel to Paris. We had a fabulous time there." I remembered spending hours at the Louvre and the Musée d'Orsay, browsing at Shakespeare and Company and—our favorite thing—starting and ending our days in cafés.

"But it was Provence that really did it for us." Pooch whimpered and I chuckled. "Sorry, Pooch, I can't scratch your ears while I'm driving." I reached over and patted the top of her head. She hunkered in to resume her nap and I replayed our fabulous trip to Provence in my mind.

I remembered taking the fast train to Avignon, how we fell in love with that amazing walled city and former papal home, how we meant to stay there a couple days, then rent a car and check out all the usual tourist hot spots: Aix-en-Provence, Arles, possibly Marseille. But we met a young couple at a café one night who convinced us that there were lesser-known places to visit and the best way to see them was on a motorcycle. The next day we rented the only motorcycle we could find, the French equivalent of a Honda 50. I laughed out loud remembering how the rental agent described it as a "*petit moto*," and how humorous we must have looked heading down the highway through the Châteauneuf-du-Pape vineyards once the mistral began to howl.

We'd read about the infamous wind, which whips through the Alpilles and gives a "peculiar sparkling sharpness" to the countryside, but it was unusual to face it so early in the fall. Our stop at Vaison-la-Romaine was brief and comical, in retrospect. We stopped just long enough to take a photo of me amidst the Roman ruins. There's the *petit moto* in the background (it blew over just after Ben took the shot).

I'm holding my helmet under one arm and my hair appears as a blur sticking up and out and into my face so that only part of my smile shows. After that I hunkered down behind Ben as he drove as fast as the bike would take us—thirty miles per hour tops—down the highway and into Orange. I remember the sun setting behind the coliseum as we arrived and how the lights of a patisserie poured into the town square like a golden welcome mat.

The owner, Madame Crottet, was as friendly and warm as her shop. She served us fresh croissants and a full pot of *chocolat chaud* that tasted unlike any hot chocolate I've had before or since—ambrosia, as rich and thick as melted chocolate bars. She asked us about ourselves and our travels, and we fumbled amiably through the conversation with our college French. She sent us off to a bed and breakfast across the square with warmed bodies and revived spirits and also recommended a restaurant nearby, a short walk through the narrow cobbled streets.

When the proprietor showed us our room, all sunny yellow with a warm tiled floor, and we saw the cozy bed covered with a thick downy white featherbed, we knew we'd found the perfect place. Dinner had to wait. We made slow and purposeful love right then, sure that the pot of chocolate we'd shared was a kind of magic aphrodisiac nurturing the conception of our first child. Later that night in the restaurant we ate lamb stew and joked about how we would embarrass this child we'd conceived by telling the story of how and where his or her life began.

"Oh, Pooch." The dog raised her head at the sound of my voice. "We were so sure then. And so wrong."

Sensing my distress, the dog placed her big paw on my leg.

"I'm okay, girl." I said, thinking how, months after that fabulous drive through the windy French countryside, we discovered why we hadn't conceived a child and why we never would. It was something even Madam Crottet's *chocolat* couldn't cure.

15

After a vain attempt to sleep for a couple of hours, I got up, retrieved the workshop lists from my jacket pocket, and wandered into the kitchen for some breakfast. I scanned the lists over oatmeal and coffee, starting with June fifteenth—a date I knew Julia had attended a workshop. Maybe there would be a name that stood out in some way. At first glance, I could see that there were six names that came up on more than one list—a good place to start, the true believers. I jotted their names, addresses, and phone numbers on my legal pad, looking for a pattern. Out of the six repeat customers, three lived on Capitol Hill, one near Northgate, and two listed post office boxes. I puzzled over their names, wondering if these women chose pseudonyms as well as post office boxes to conceal their identities—Penny Lincoln and Corey Gladstone. I called directory assistance to see if they were listed in one of the outlying suburbs with no luck. Okay, so back to the other four.

I picked up the phone, punched in the number for Jennifer Dixon with an address on Fifteenth Avenue East, and got an answering machine—the kind with the tinny mechanized voice. I hung up, figuring I'd come back to Jennifer if I struck out with the other folks. Two more calls went straight to voicemail until I got a real person, Blair Nolan. I explained my interest in taking a Victor Lloyd class at Nirmala and that my friend Patty had given me her name, saying they had been in a Victor Lloyd workshop together last year. Would she recommend it?

"Yes, I think I would," she said. "I'm hoping to take another one as soon as I can afford it. Are you looking to get a hold of someone in particular?" she asked, as if I were simply trying to place a telephone call.

"Of course not. I mean, I'm not sure." I backpedaled, tried to think of the right response.

"I'm sorry, I know it's hard, but I think you'll have a good chance of getting through with Victor's help. He's an angel."

"Right. So, do you need to take lots of these workshops before anything happens or what?"

"I took three because I was hoping to contact my boyfriend who was killed in a car accident." Her voice cracked.

"I'm sorry," I said, recognizing her pain.

"Yeah. Who did you say you were trying to contact?"

"I didn't. But I guess I have a lot to choose from. First my parents died, then my husband and now—" I gasped and stopped myself. What was I doing, talking to a total stranger about these things? "Sorry. Um. I'm just trying to figure out how it works. If it works."

"Right. Well, I never got through to Paul. But I did see it work with a couple of others. It's pretty powerful."

She wished me luck and I hung up the phone, thinking about what she'd said, what I'd said, and wondering what I really expected to find out about the whole psychic medium phenomenon. I knew it was bullshit but I wanted to understand how rational people came to believe in it.

"Whatever," I said out loud, then picked up the phone to make another call. The next three workshop attendees I talked to recommended the workshops, although none of them had "gotten though." I decided to put in one last call to Jennifer Dixon. This time she answered. At first, she was reluctant to talk about her experiences at Nirmala and wanted to know how I'd gotten her name.

I scanned my notes, circling the name of someone in the class with her.

"Corey gave me your name. She was in the same workshop you

took on June twentieth. She suggested you would have an interesting perspective on it." I was fishing, hoping she would bite.

"I don't remember Corey, but I suppose I do have an interesting perspective since Victor and I became really close. Until he dumped me." Jennifer was quiet for a long time.

"I see. I appreciate your candor, but I don't want to keep you right now. Could we meet sometime? Talk about this in person?"

More silence on Jennifer's end.

"I'll be straight with you. I'm a reporter with the *Seattle Times*, writing a piece on the Nirmala Church and Victor Lloyd. I'd love to hear about your experience."

She was still hesitant, but more receptive. "Well, I guess so. I mean, I wouldn't want you to quote me or anything, but I wouldn't mind if Victor got some bad press."

"Great!" Checking out her address, I suggested we meet at the Tully's on Aloha. She might even be able to walk there. We agreed to meet later in the day, four thirty.

In the meantime, I decided to give Victor Lloyd a call. His book had left me with more questions than answers. Writing in a self-effacing style, Lloyd seemed almost apologetic about his abilities to communicate with dead folks. I'd noticed a difference between Lloyd the performer, the guy conducting the workshop, and Lloyd the person, the one who wrote the book and took registrations for his own workshops over the phone. Maybe that was the nature of a "channel"—being a vessel through which other people communicated left no room for his real personality. I found Lloyd's wholehearted belief in himself—his confidence—compelling, but I couldn't help wondering how he did it. How did he know so much about the dearly departed?

Lloyd again answered his own phone and sounded happy to hear from me. I told him I'd finished reading his book and found it pretty interesting, though it raised some questions in my mind.

"Well, Ann, you're a quick study, or at least a fast reader. How about we meet for dinner and discuss it?" Lloyd suggested. "Are you free tomorrow night?" This guy worked fast.

The prospect of a cozy dinner with Victor Lloyd repulsed and intrigued me at the same time. Since I didn't want to pay him for a private session, dinner might be the best way to get him to loosen up and talk about his work. He offered to pick me up, but I declined, suggesting we meet at Sonrisa, a well-lit and family friendly Mexican restaurant at University Village, near the University of Washington where I pretended to have a meeting just before seven. No quiet candlelit dinners for me and Victor.

I spent the bulk of my afternoon looking over the proposals for the newspapers in education project and couldn't wait to pack it in around four to get to my meeting with Jennifer Dixon by four thirty.

Tully's parking lot was fairly empty but the place itself was jammed. Tully's succeeded much better than Starbucks in placing their coffee shops in neighborhoods where people still walked around and weren't totally dependent on their vehicles. Jennifer had said she would try to find a spot by the fireplace and had given me a description of herself so I would recognize her: tall, longish dark hair, wears glasses. I ordered my single short nonfat decaf, a drink I'd heard described by baristas as a "Why bother?" and glanced at the seating area around the fireplace—two leather chairs and a table between. Jennifer sat engrossed in a paperback, biting at the skin around her thumbnail. As I approached and said her name, she jumped.

"Sorry to startle you. Looks gripping." I said, gesturing to the book in her hand.

"Oh, yeah, it is." She showed me the cover, a black-and-white photo of the back of a naked woman wrapped in sheer fabric, which she held clasped shut over her derrière. I didn't recognize the title.

"It's kind of a gothic ghost story. A real page-turner." She motioned for me to sit down. While Jennifer dropped her book into her bag and rearranged herself on the chair, I had a chance to look at her close-up. Her face was very pale and free of makeup except for a hideous shade of near-black lipstick. Her clothes were black as well, except for her boots, which were red and exceedingly scuffed and worn, the sole pulling away from the toe on both sides. I was sure her feet got soaked whenever it rained. As if reading my mind, she tucked one foot under her and the other behind the bag at her feet.

"So, you're writing a story about Victor Lloyd. What's he up to these days? Still giving workshops and seducing half the women in them?" she asked with an odd smirk.

"Actually, I hadn't heard about that. Why don't you tell me your experience with him?"

"Sure. I took a couple of workshops with Victor last year. I don't know. I'm kind of into psychic stuff. I love ghost stories and movies that deal with the idea of people coming back after they die, either for revenge—like *What Lies Beneath*, although Harrison Ford just can't be convincing as a bad guy—or because they love someone so much, like *Ghost*. Of course there's revenge in that, too. Then there's the one about the dragonflies, have you seen that?" Jennifer was talking a mile a minute now and I wondered just how much caffeine she had ingested.

"No, but I've seen the others. So, what brought you to Victor Lloyd's workshop?" I asked, hoping to bring her back to the topic at hand.

"Oh, well, I was in a bookstore in West Seattle and saw a flyer for it. I figured he was Seattle's answer to that guy on television, you know the one who is always getting messages from dead people? I can't remember his name." I nodded, even though I didn't know who she was talking about. She rambled on.

"And that animal psychic, have you seen her? What a kick! She's hired by people who have pets with behavior problems? And she always says things like, 'Cuddles is telling me that she feels sad when you leave her home all day while you're at work. That's why she's pooping on your pillow. She's lonesome.' What a riot! Anyway, back to Victor. I took his workshop on getting in touch with your own psychic abilities. He puts on a good show, and it works for him: he gets a captive audience and lots of women to choose from." Jennifer looked at the fire and began chomping on her thumbnail again.

"Did you see Victor Lloyd outside of the workshops?"

"Yeah, I hung around after one of the classes to ask him a question and we ended up going out for a drink that night. And then we had dinner another time. We saw each other for a while until he dumped me for someone else he met in one of his workshops. The guy's got a short attention span when it comes to women. I'm sure he's gone through several more since then."

"How long did you date Victor Lloyd?"

"Almost a month. Just when we were getting close, he told me he didn't think we should see each other anymore." A spark of anger flashed in her eyes as she leaned closer to me, with a frightening twist in her expression.

"It sounds like you weren't too happy about that," I said, sitting back in my chair and marveling at the bizarre change in her demeanor.

"He lied to me, made me think we had a future together, seduced me, and then threw me away when someone else came along."

I started to laugh, thinking Jennifer was laughing at herself, playing up the drama. Then I saw how agitated and angry she looked.

"But you hadn't known him very long. I mean . . ." I trailed off, not sure what I meant but highly aware that Jennifer's agitation was way over the top. She jumped out of her chair, stomped her foot, sat back down, and slammed her fist into the arm of her chair before grabbing my hand and leaning in close.

"Oh my God! Whose side are you on here? I just told you that Victor Lloyd took advantage of me, then as soon as he got what he wanted, he took off. He refused to see me. Wouldn't even answer my telephone calls. We were in love! We had this fabulous future to look forward to and he threw me over for some slut from one of his classes. He humiliated me. I've been thinking about it ever since you called. You've got to write about this! Expose him for what he is!"

The coffee shop got very quiet as most of the other customers stopped talking and turned in our direction. I decided to cool this off as quickly as possible and get out of there fast, but couldn't resist one last question.

"So, you had sex with Victor Lloyd. He seduced you, then broke off your relationship and started seeing someone else from the class?"

"You do understand. You are the best listener, Ann. Can you imagine how humiliated I felt?"

"I can. You poor thing," I said in my most comforting voice. "I'm so sorry for what you had to go through. Do you know the name of the woman he started seeing?"

"Yeah, her name was Julia. You know, the woman who killed herself? She probably jumped off that bridge after Victor dumped her. He's evil. I think he's in touch with the devil himself." Jennifer's eyes were wide and wild now as she grasped my arm by way of punctuation.

Shocked by the mention of Julia's name, but more than a bit skeptical of Jennifer's view of reality, I stood up and slipped into my coat. Jennifer stood up as well, opened her mouth to speak but I rushed on, "Thank you for confiding in me, Jennifer. I understand the situation now. It's getting late. I've taken up so much of your time already. I think we should call it a day. Thanks so much for all your help."

I reached out, shook her hand, and turned to go. Jennifer opened and closed her mouth, like a goldfish at the side of the bowl, sat down, and mumbled, "Oh, okay, bye." I saw her staring into the fire through the window as I drove out of the lot.

16

Driving to my dinner meeting with Victor Lloyd, I thought about Jennifer's behavior—bizarre. She reminded me of Glenn Close in *Fatal Attraction* and I started to feel a little sorry for Victor, but only a little. You'd think Jennifer would have taught him a lesson about dating women from his workshops and yet, he was pretty quick to ask me to dinner. And what about Julia? Was there a kernel of truth in what Jennifer had to say?

I walked into Sonrisa at 6:55. Scanning the room, I caught sight of Victor Lloyd already seated and engaged in conversation with the pretty Mexican waitress, Anita, whom I remembered from my last time at the restaurant. In this setting and dressed in an olive green Henley shirt and casual slacks, he looked normal, like any average Joe Seattleite out for dinner. As I approached the table, Victor stood up to shake my hand, fixing me with his smoky eyes. He held onto my hand a little too long and the warmth of this brief intimacy sent a flash of heat to my face and a tingle to my nerve endings. No doubt about his sex appeal, and no doubt he knew how to use it. We sat down and I studied his face. He had regular features, high cheekbones, a straight nose, and a rugged square jaw with permanent stubble. His eyes were mesmerizing. They were hazel, a kind of murky cross between gray, green, and brown, changeable and intense, slightly disturbing until he smiled—showing off his very white straight teeth—and his face changed, lightened up.

We got through the first few awkward moments by studying the menu, deciding on drinks—Pacifico for both of us —and filling in the silence with small talk. I told him I'd finished his book and found his psychic experiences interesting but wanted to know more about how he'd chosen this path, how he'd decided it was a calling he couldn't deny.

"You know, when I was a teenager," he said, "I wanted to be *normal* like everyone else. It just wasn't in the cards for me, even then."

"You first recognized your ability when you were a teenager?"

"I think I had hints before that but somehow, during my adolescence, maybe because of all those raging hormones, I couldn't ignore the signs any more. I learned to live with it, tried to keep it to myself as best I could."

"When did that change? You refer to it vaguely in your book—the death of a friend had something to do with it?"

"Well, yes, but it's highly personal. I chose not to include it in my book, though I might consider it now that some time has passed."

I gave him plenty of time to decide whether he wanted to share this personal story with me. He seemed to be mulling it over.

Our beers arrived and we ordered dinner, the chicken mole for me and steak fajitas for Victor. I handed the waitress my menu. While I sipped my beer, Victor started talking.

"I was really into sports when I was younger, played a little baseball," he said.

I nodded. "I'm a big fan."

He smiled. "So, I had a friend, a teammate in college—the guy was an amazing athlete, a great pitcher, and a great guy. When he made it to the majors, I followed his career; we stayed in touch. I went to his wedding. Saw him pitch whenever I could. Then one day he was in the clubhouse suiting up, getting ready to pitch, when he dropped over and never regained consciousness. The docs said he died of a heart attack, out of nowhere, though it sometimes happens to athletes they said. He was thirty-two."

"I remember this. He played for Chicago, right?"

"Yeah." Victor nodded, looking me squarely in the face,

apparently surprised I'd remembered his friend. "Like everyone else who knew him, I was shocked. I couldn't believe that a guy could be in prime of his life one minute and gone the next." He paused and shook his head before continuing.

"I had always struggled with the Catholic faith I grew up with but my friend's death ended it for me. I simply couldn't reconcile the idea that God would allow this to happen. He had a wife, two young children. It was senseless, tragic. Of course, there's a lot of suffering in the world that can't be reconciled with a traditional notion of a personal God."

"Right." I could see how terrible this experience must have been, but I wasn't making the connection between that and how Victor Lloyd decided to follow his calling of becoming a psychic medium.

"So, did your friend come through to you? Is that how you started on this path?"

"No. He never did. But his death left such a void in my life, and so many others', that I needed to find some explanation that made sense. I began to study religion, how other cultures deal with death. I was particularly interested in Buddhist beliefs at first. For them death is a natural part of life, something we are born to do, before we move off into our next incarnation."

Victor talked about reading various religious texts, eventually traveling to India. My eyes glazed over. It sounded an awful lot like my sister's quest. He sensed my impatience.

"I'm sorry. It's probably why I don't talk about this much. It doesn't lend itself to casual conversation. Suffice to say, my friend's death was a kind of catalyst into my own spiritual quest. I spent two years traveling around, working when I could, trying to learn all I could about life and death, myself and my unusual sensitivity."

"Okay, at some point you decided to come back to Seattle and hang out your shingle as a psychic medium?"

He laughed. "It was a little more gradual than that. I've worked as a coach, personal trainer, a few other things. I started giving workshops, developing a private clientele over the years."

"How do you do it now, and keep your sanity? I mean, most of the people you work with are dealing with grief and loss. A pretty depressing business you're in."

"I prefer to think of it like this: I provide a service. I help those who have passed on by relaying messages to their loved ones. And I help the living find some peace knowing that their loved ones may have crossed over, but are okay, that they still care about them."

"I imagine lots of people are willing to pay for your service."

"I'm not exactly getting rich, if that's what you're thinking. It's a job. I think it has value, so I charge for it. Would you do your job for free?"

"Of course not." I said, then quickly asked him another question so we wouldn't get into a discussion of my job.

After our food arrived, Victor opened up about his psychic experiences over the years with very little prodding from me. Halfway through dinner I realized that, quite surprisingly, I was having a great time. Victor continued to explain his work to me in his self-effacing way while embroidering his experiences with a healthy dose of humor. He finished one of his more bizarre stories by whistling the theme song from *The X-Files*, and I caught myself laughing out loud.

Over coffee and dessert, those delicious tortilla thingies covered in cinnamon and honey, Victor got serious again and asked me what I'd thought of his workshop.

"Honestly, I thought it was pretty weird. I mean, I still want to know what the trick is. How did you know all that stuff about Cheryl's cousin?"

He shook his head. "I've been trying to explain how the spirits show me things, Ann, but I guess I haven't done a very good job of it. I know it's hard to imagine if you've never experienced it." He looked at me intently. "I thought so. You're a zealous skeptic."

I smiled but said nothing.

"So, what I really want to know, Ann Johnson, is why did you sign up for my workshop and why are you having dinner with me now? What is your hidden agenda?" He leaned forward, closing the distance between us.

I hesitated just a moment, then decided to go for it, shake him up a little. "Well, maybe you really are psychic," I said. "I am skeptical. I'm also a reporter with the *Seattle Times*. Last week I was contacted by Julia Comstock's sister. She believes that Julia did not kill herself, that someone else had a hand in it. She thinks *you* are a likely suspect."

Victor's head snapped up and his eyes flashed with anger. Then he frowned, looked away from me, slowly shook his head.

Anita arrived with our check. I rummaged around in my purse and put down a twenty and a ten, enough for my own dinner and a healthy tip.

When Victor finally looked up, his eyes were brimming. He squeezed them shut, pressing the bridge of his nose between his forefinger and thumb and looked directly at me.

"This is the toughest part of my work. It isn't dealing with grieving individuals, it's wondering why, when I've been given this sensitivity, I can't stop people from dying, even when I get some kind of spiritual warning beforehand. I couldn't keep my father from a fatal car wreck and I couldn't keep Julia from jumping off that bridge."

I remembered the story about his father from his book, but I didn't want him to shift the conversation.

"You had a warning about Julia?" I asked.

"Julia came to me a couple weeks before her death. She said she'd been working on her own with some of the techniques I'd taught her—visualization, tapping into her own psychic abilities, that sort of thing."

"She was trying to get in touch with Warren?"

"Yeah. I'd explained to her that when we lose someone we are often so distraught that we unconsciously block everything out in order to cope. We become numb, kind of like our psyche is anesthetized. It can't stand any more pain, so it shuts down. I think that's what happened to Julia at first, why I couldn't get through. A few months later she began to have some success with her own abilities through one of her spiritual guides."

"Do you mean a real person or a *spirit person?*"

"A spirit guide is someone who has crossed over but is still connected to helping the living."

"A guardian angel?"

"Sort of." Victor nodded. "Julia thought her guide might have been a sister from a previous life. She said her name was Charlotte."

"Okay," I said, thinking how weird this conversation was getting.

"Julia asked me if I thought it was 'better' on the other side. According to her guide, it was a happy place, the place where Warren had gone."

"What did you say?"

"I think I made light of her comment, turned it into a bit of a joke. If I'm so sensitive, why didn't I understand her real question?" He looked anguished.

"You think she killed herself to join Warren?"

"I do," he said in a solemn voice. "I also think I might have stopped her."

I mulled over what he'd said.

"Was Julia working with someone else, trying to connect with Warren?"

"Someone else?"

"I'm trying to identify the woman going by the name of Sylvia Carter who showed up at the Comstock house just after Julia's death. Some people say she's your assistant. Other people say you never had an assistant."

"I don't know this person but, yes, I do remember the police asking me about her after Julia's death. I had Rose check the church's records in case it was someone I had in a class but couldn't remember. Her name never showed up anywhere. I think the police looked for her for a while but also came up with nothing."

We sat in silence for a while. He stared off into the distance, then changed the subject. "So, Ann, if that's your real name. Why didn't you just ask me about Julia in the first place? Why bother taking a class, reading my book, and going out to dinner with me?"

"My name is Ann, but my last name is Dexter, not Johnson. Sorry. I wanted to get to know you first. I didn't want any false barriers to get in the way."

"Except the ones you set up. As long as you control it, deception is a fine way to get at the truth. That's a little ironic, don't you think? And why are you telling me the truth now? Did I pass some sort of test? Convince you that I'm not some psycho murderer?"

"Sorry," I said. "I don't blame you for being annoyed with me. It's just that I'm trying to figure out how Julia died and I think you know more about her state of mind at the time than anyone else, except maybe Sylvia Carter, whoever she is."

I tried a direct question. "Can you tell me anything about her?"

He shrugged. "The description I got from the police fit over half the women who take my workshops. A woman in her late twenties or early thirties, light brown hair, blue eyes, fair complexion, medium to thin build, medium height, soft-spoken, a bit nervous in manner. There is absolutely nothing that stands out about this person, nothing remarkable." His comment startled me, so similar were Victor's words to what a police officer asked me when I filed the missing person report on Nancy. *Is there anything remarkable about your sister, anything at all that would stand out?*

I shook my head, hoping Victor hadn't noticed my distress.

He continued. "I was furious that some woman calling herself Sylvia Carter claimed she worked with me. I'd never heard of her. She never took a class from me and she hadn't spent any time at Nirmala. And yet she clearly had some kind of relationship with Julia. She must have known just how unstable she was and got scared, thinking someone might blame her for Julia's death. I figured that showing up at Julia's house and naming me was a desperate attempt to shift the blame. And it worked too, for a while anyway. The police were all over Nirmala and me until they convinced themselves that Julia had killed herself without any help."

Lloyd stopped talking and shook his head. "Sorry," he said. As I looked at him, waiting for him to continue, his face shifted. He reached for my hand and my heart rate spiked with his touch.

"Ann, I'm getting that same feeling I had at the workshop. I'm seeing the name Nancy, someone off to the side, a sister, I think, but I'm also getting the name Ben. Look, I'm sorry to jump in with this now but I've been feeling this spirit almost since you arrived. Now it's very persistent, restless, a warning of some kind, I think."

At the sound of Ben's name, I froze. My head started buzzing. "Stop it!" I pulled my hand away, jumped up and moved as quickly as I could in the direction of the door, panic surging through me.

Outside, the rain and wind raged in frantic gusts, blowing my jacket open and my hair into my face. I managed to get one button closed and shove the hair behind my ears as I rushed past the shops toward the parking lot. I stopped under an awning and rummaged around in the bottom of my purse for the car keys, trying to forget Victor Lloyd's words and focus on exactly where I had parked the Camry. Simultaneously spotting the car and closing my shaking fingers around the rubber cover of the key, I made a dash for it. I slid the key into the lock and felt a firm grasp on my shoulder. I turned to face Victor, pushed his hand off my shoulder.

"Ann, please wait. Tell me what's going on here. What are you so frightened of?"

"Listen, you bastard, don't you *dare* talk about Ben. And my sister is none of your business either. She is *not* dead, just off somewhere with someone a lot like you, some other charismatic asshole who thinks he has a direct line to God. She's not dead. I just can't find her. She's not dead!"

17

The crying started then, wracking sobs I could not control. Victor tried to put his arms around me but I backed up against the car and punched him in the gut as hard as I could. He recovered quickly, grabbed my wrists, and pulled them to my sides.

"Hey, what's going on?" We both turned to see three young guys running toward us. They looked like UW students, in their Husky sweatshirts and backward baseball caps. I swiped the back of my hand across my face and straightened up against the car as Victor took a step away and smiled at them.

"Thanks for your concern," he said. "My friend is a little upset. I'm trying to calm her down."

"Are you okay, lady?" the biggest one asked, looking from me to Victor. "Is this guy bothering you?"

"No, thanks, I'm fine. I'm just leaving." While the four of them stood there staring at me, I got into my car and exhaled, releasing the breath I didn't even know I'd been holding in.

I pulled out of the parking lot and tried to concentrate on the road, but Victor's words kept gnawing at me: *Ben, Nancy, persistent spirit, some kind of warning.* What the hell was going on? How could he know about Ben? Jack was right: this whole investigation was wrong for me from the start. I'd call Caroline and tell her I'd had it. Nancy was bad enough, but I wouldn't let this guy conjure up the pain I'd worked so hard to move beyond. I wouldn't let him remind me of Ben even if it won me the Pulitzer. I picked up my cell phone and scrolled through the contacts until I got to Caroline's name, tapped the phone, and waited. Maria picked up on the second ring. Caroline was out while the real estate agent was showing the house to some prospective buyers and would return my call later.

Back at home, Pooch greeted me as if I'd been gone for days. All the jumping, licking, and whining, which usually made me feel appreciated, only made me feel worse. I simply wanted to curl up with Pooch's head in my lap so I could feel the warmth of a living, breathing being next to me right now. But she wouldn't settle down. I picked up the note Nicole left on the kitchen table and knew why— the dog had been let out briefly but hadn't been walked.

I sighed, "Left alone too long again, huh, Pooch?" The dog ran into the laundry room, picked up a tennis ball from her toy basket, and followed me into the bedroom as I changed into my sweats. She dropped the ball in front of her, then nosed it in my direction, wagging her tail and looking up at me expectantly. I tried to ignore her, kicking the ball away, but after it hit my foot for the fourth time, I laughed in spite of myself. I could learn a lot from Pooch—always in the moment.

"Okay, okay, we'll go out for a quick one, but not right now, Pooch. I have some things to do first." She followed right at my heels as I headed for the phone in the kitchen and hit 99 for voicemail. I had three messages. The Seattle Public Library called to say the book I requested was available for pick up. Jack called to say he was thinking about me and asking for a call back. Good old Jack. At least he was in the right time zone now that I needed him. I'd call him later. The last message had been left just a few minutes before— Victor Lloyd's voice, subdued but insistent.

"Ann, it's Victor. Look, we need to talk. We can discuss your personal situation or not—your call. But I can't leave things like this. You can ask me all you want about Julia Comstock. More than anyone, I'd like to know if there was some kind of foul play in her death. Please call me."

I replayed the voicemail and listened to his message again, jotted the number down on the pad next to the phone, and shook my head.

"Let's go, Pooch. Some nice wet fresh air sounds great." Pooch let out a howl of joy as we headed out the door and up the hill toward the college. On one side, the few houses hidden behind huge laurel hedges were dark. On the other side, the black expanse of Shoreview Park morphed into the community college grounds farther up where one hazy light glowed yellow near the tennis courts, though the gate was locked at dusk. I could feel but not see the huge cedars looming on the ridge.

We climbed the hill at a brisk pace—my heart rate rising and my face wet with the misty fog rolling in off the Sound. I welcomed the opportunity to get my thoughts in order as we hiked along the perimeter of the college parking lot to the top of the hill, then crossed over to the west side of the street and headed back down. I pulled Pooch in close along the narrow path and noticed a silver Lexus SUV now idling in the drive in front of the locked park gates—teenagers no doubt looking for a secluded place for a little intimacy, teenagers using Daddy's high-priced ride.

I walked by with Pooch, my eyes charitably averted until a little farther along when Pooch stopped to pee. I glanced up just in time to see the SUV turn out of the drive and come screeching down the hill way too fast on the wet pavement. Yanking Pooch out of the road and into the blackberry thicket on the upside of the ditch, I lost my balance and fell on top of her, heart pounding, as the huge Lexus swerved towards us. Pooch yelped as I rolled off her and back onto my butt, watching the SUV skid away and roar on down the hill. Jesus! I sat there for a moment, catching my breath and holding onto Pooch while the dampness seeped into the seat of my sweatpants.

I stood up slowly, picked off the thorny twig stuck to the back of my pants, and patted Pooch for reassurance. "You're okay, girl." Standing there dumbfounded, I tried to piece together what had just happened. This was no teenage couple out for a ride, that's for sure. In the split second as the car swerved past, I'd seen only one dark shape crouched over the wheel—no passengers. And he meant to hit me. Almost as quickly as the thought popped into my head, I dismissed it as paranoid, the product of a disturbing evening. I tugged on Pooch's leash, picked up the pace, and jogged the rest of the way back home. Once inside, I toweled off the dog, made myself a cup of peppermint tea, and was just sitting down to drink it when the doorbell rang. With Pooch barking like crazy, I got up, looked through the front door window, and saw Caroline standing on my front step.

I introduced Pooch to Caroline who, in the midst of the usual canine greeting—lots of tail wagging and the inevitable nose in the crotch—explained her unannounced arrival at my door.

"I called Maria to see if it was safe to go home and she told me you called and that Leigh was still at the house with the prospective buyers. I guess they were late but it seems like they've been there half the night. I hope you don't mind."

"Not at all. I could use the company. I've had quite the night."

"You look a little ragged. What happened?"

"First I had a fairly intense dinner with Victor Lloyd, then I practically got run over walking with Pooch up to the college. Some asshole took the hill too fast, barely missed the ditch and us. But I'm better now. Can I get you some tea?"

Caroline expressed the appropriate amount of concern for my run-in with the SUV while I poured her a cup of tea. As we settled in the living room, I decided to get right to it.

"Look, Caroline, the reason I called you earlier was to let you know I'm dropping the investigation into Victor Lloyd and Nirmala."

"What? Why? You've barely started."

"I don't think Victor Lloyd had anything to do with Julia's death, at least not intentionally."

"Just like that? You have one dinner conversation with him and you get sucked in too?" Caroline slapped the arms of the chair with her open palms, stood up, and walked toward the kitchen, turned around, folded her arms across her chest, and faced me. "Don't you see? He's very good at what he does. Why can't you see it?" Pooch started whining, her usual response to anger, and stood up, moving her tucked tail back and forth between her legs.

"Please, Caroline, sit down. Let's talk this through." Both Pooch and Caroline resumed their seated positions.

"I spent quite a bit of time talking with Victor Lloyd tonight, getting a better sense of what he's about. He seemed genuinely distressed by Julia's suicide and upset that he hadn't been able to prevent it." Caroline shook her head, but said nothing as I continued.

"Look, I don't pretend to understand what he calls his 'life's work,' but *he* certainly believes in it. And the church—well, it's not mainstream, but there's nothing terrible going on there either. No one's brainwashing anyone, or taking all their money, or holding them against their will."

Caroline sat very still and shook her head.

"In the final analysis, there's nothing newsworthy here," I said.

Pooch, still tuned in to the emotionally charged atmosphere, walked over and rested her head on Caroline's knee. Caroline scratched the dog's ears absently, then looked up at me. "But what about Sylvia Carter? How do you explain her?"

"I can't. I agree she probably knows something about Julia's death, but I don't have the resources to look for her. My editor already thinks I'm on a wild goose chase."

"So, there's nothing I can do."

"You could hire a private investigator. There's someone I would recommend."

"I'll think about it."

"I hired an investigator a few years ago to look for Nancy. His name is Tom Hill. I'm planning to call him anyway. I could give him your number and bring him up to speed on what we know."

"Why are you calling him now?"

"To see if he can follow up on some of his old leads on Nancy, maybe track her down. I'm worried that she might be in trouble after what Lloyd said."

"What? What did Lloyd say?"

"At the workshop, Lloyd said he was hearing from a spirit connected to a Nancy. Then he asked me directly if this message could be for me. I said no. Tonight he mentioned her again, but that isn't the most disturbing thing."

"Okay, what is the most disturbing thing?"

"He mentioned Ben." When Caroline looked puzzled, I remembered that she knew I'd been married, but I hadn't told her any of the particulars. I usually didn't.

"Ben. My husband. We were married for three short years before he was diagnosed with non-Hodgkin's lymphoma. He died within six months. He was only thirty-five." Caroline's expression changed from disbelief to pity, a look I'd seen too often and why I didn't talk about it.

"I had no idea. I'm so sorry."

"Yeah, I've spent two and a half years trying to move on, to fashion some sort of life without him. I thought I was doing pretty well until this whole Victor Lloyd thing."

"How could he possibly know about your husband? I mean . . ." Caroline's voice trailed off and I picked up.

"I know, it's crazy. He didn't even know my real name before tonight. I don't know how he does it, but I don't want any part of it."

Neither one of us knew what to say after that.

"But don't you see what he's doing?"

"I see that I can't have any part of it. Not now."

"Okay." Caroline's voice was softer now. "But I'm surprised you don't recognize what a snake this guy is. You start asking about Julia and he does whatever he can to throw you off. Don't you see?"

She wasn't getting it. I shook my head. "I'm sorry, Caroline. Call me if you want Tom's number." I stood and walked to the front door. Caroline followed. I put my arms around her for a quick hug and felt her body stiffen.

"I'm sorry too, Ann," she said coldly as she turned to open the door. "Goodbye."

After Caroline left, I returned Jack's call, vowing that I wouldn't mention a thing about Ben. It would be too painful for both of us.

"Hey, sexy, what's up?" His warm tone was welcome.

"Let's just say I've had a rough night starting with an awkward dinner with a psychic medium and continuing downhill from there." I chuckled at my unintended witticism, trying to keep things light. "The good news is I've decided to drop the Julia Comstock/Nirmala Church investigation."

"Great. And the bad news?"

"It's not really bad news." He waited. "I've decided to call Tom Hill and ask him to follow up on some of those leads he had on Nancy." Silence. "You can say something supportive."

"Okay. I hope it works out."

"Look, Jack, if there's any truth behind Lloyd's 'warnings' about Nancy, if she's in some kind of danger and I don't do anything about it, I'll never be able to forgive myself. I miss her, Jack. She's my only living relative." The words echoed in my head as I willed them to be true.

"I understand. And I'm glad you've decided to drop the investigation and to stay away from this character."

"Thanks. How was your day?" Turns out Jack would be off to Houston on Sunday so we made tentative plans to get together Saturday night to see a new local trio at Jazz Alley.

Hanging up, I thought about Jack's comment, "Stay away from this character." Instead, I thought about Victor's eyes, how sincere he seemed and the twinge of electricity I'd felt when he'd put his arms around me. Right before I'd slugged him. In emotional self-defense, I told myself. I moved through the house collecting laundry, straightening things, getting ready for bed, trying to avoid thinking at all. Picking up Victor Lloyd's book from the nightstand, I climbed into bed and began flipping through it.

I knew it was ridiculous, but I searched the book all the same, looking for stories about husbands who came through him to tell their wives how much they still loved them, or stories about how Victor sometimes misunderstood "warnings" he received. Instead, when I found a vignette about a woman who survived a car wreck in which her husband had died, I told myself this had nothing to do with me and Ben. This woman had survived the car accident and felt responsible somehow for her husband's death. Her husband "came back" to reassure her that he was fine; he didn't blame her. I didn't have any guilt over Ben's death—just anger, so much anger.

But I had to read on, see if I could find out how Victor dealt with warnings and sketchy information. I found a pertinent chapter and read through some of the stories. In one, Victor had a warning that a friend was seriously ill. Initially the woman laughed off his concern since she'd had a recent physical and had been given a clean bill of health. At Victor's insistence, she sought a second opinion and discovered her cancer soon enough to be successfully treated with surgery and chemotherapy.

Another chapter outlined Victor's brief experience as a police psychic. He had only worked on one case, which he viewed as a total failure. In that instance, Victor could only come up with the first name of the murderer, no last name, no other identifying characteristics. As a result, an innocent man—an acquaintance of the victim—was implicated and investigated by the police, causing him and his family much grief. There wasn't much solace for him when the real murderer, with the same first name, was arrested and convicted months later. Victor realized then that his spirit warnings were just too sketchy and too easily misinterpreted to be used in this way. I reread this story, convinced that any warnings Victor had about someone named Nancy had been misinterpreted, that while there was nothing that could be done about Ben, there was still time for me to find my sister. She would be okay. I closed the book, turned out the light, and tried to sleep.

Instead, long-suppressed memories of Nancy and me as children filled my head. I remembered endless summer days we spent in our backyard pool, the pool my parents put in after I conquered my fear of water and learned to swim. They didn't know why I had to do it. It was a secret Nancy and I kept all those years. I still had nightmares about that day.

Our parents had rented a cabin on the shores of Silver Lake in northern Minnesota for a week in August—an annual vacation we shared with our friends, the Stolpers. The late afternoon was hot and steamy so we kids were still playing at the lake while the grown-ups were beginning the cocktail hour on the deck. I had promised to stay on the beach with my sand toys since I wasn't a swimmer, but it was so hot, I couldn't resist putting my feet in. Nancy had abandoned her air mattress and was treading water close by, so I grabbed the floating toy, straddled it cautiously, making sure my feet touched the bottom and waved at her.

"Nancy! Look at me! I'm in the water!" I shouted joyfully.

She laughed and made her way over. "Hey, Annie, lie down and I'll give you a ride."

Tentatively, I positioned myself on my stomach while Nancy grabbed onto the side and kicked us out into the deeper water and jumped on. I was terrified and excited as the center of the mattress sagged with our weight and we bobbed along giggling, water sloshing over the sides.

"Kick your feet, and we'll catch up to Tim and Debbie." Our friends were floating on their own mattress, on their way to the dock where kids were jumping off. Nancy splashed them and they squealed, slapping the water with their palms in retaliation. In the laughing and splashing that followed, I lost my balance, slipped off the mattress, and plunged into the lake. Terrified, I kicked and flailed trying to get to the surface, to breathe, to grab the mattress, anything. Finally latching onto Nancy, I pulled her down with me. We struggled underwater, going deeper and deeper until Nancy unclasped my fingers from her arm, pulled away and was gone. I tried to scream and swallowed water instead. Swirling around in the murky water with my eyes wide open, I saw legs and feet kicking in slow motion, and then far off, a light, a dim, familiar face. Time slowed. I felt very tired. It was very quiet. I closed my eyes to sleep. The next thing I knew I was face down on the dock coughing up water while someone pounded my back, helped me to sit up.

"Welcome back," said the strange woman, rubbing between my shoulders. "You can thank your sister here for getting you out before you drank the whole lake. I saw her dragging you out of the water and helped her get you onto the dock." I looked over at Nancy who was sobbing, tears streaming down her face.

"I'm so sorry, Annie, so sorry. Don't tell, okay? Mom and Dad will kill me for taking you out into the deep water. I didn't mean for you to fall in."

I thanked the woman who had revived me and promised that I would take swimming lessons starting the very next day. When we got back to the cabin, our parents and the Stolpers were on their second round of gin and tonics and hadn't noticed a thing. And I never did tell. I knew Nancy had saved my life even before I learned about near-death experiences in my freshman psychology class and remembered how I'd seen the light at the end of the tunnel and Nana Dexter smiling at me.

We didn't talk about it much, but Nancy trotted it out like a totem whenever she did something she knew our parents would flip out about and I threatened to tell them.

"I saved your life," she'd say.

"I saved your butt," was my usual reply. We'd laugh.

We were allies growing up in the trenches of our parents' troubled marriage—we needed each other then. Maybe I needed her now. I wanted a relationship with the only person still alive who'd known me as a child, who shared the experiences that shaped me.

And life was short. Reminders of that fact were all too frequent these days.

18

With the memories of Nancy still fresh in my mind, I called Tom Hill's office the next morning and left a message, including my number and the reason for my call, then headed to the office. My voicemail included a message from Victor Lloyd. His voice was pleasant, normal—none of the tension from last night even hinted at.

"Hey Ann, it's Victor, hoping to catch you at work. Give me a call when you can." I hesitated with my hand on the phone and jumped when it rang—the PR person from the Seattle Mariners getting back to me about newspapers in education. We checked dates and player availability. I hoped we could get some established players to make an appearance at the kickoff of our latest project in the schools. She suggested a few rookies, a few even I hadn't heard of. Well, maybe anyone in a Seattle Mariners uniform would be exciting for middle school kids.

By mid-morning, I'd shrugged off my nervousness from last night and called Victor Lloyd. As always, he answered on the first ring. "Victor Lloyd."

"Victor, it's Ann Dexter."

"Ann, I'm glad you called. I'm sorry about last night, I—"

I cut him off. "I don't want to talk about last night. I'm just calling let you know that I'm no longer investigating Julia's suicide."

"Okay. Good. Is that because you believe I had nothing to do with it?"

"Pretty much. There are some unanswered questions, sure, but my editor doesn't see the point in my chasing after them. Back to baseball in education for me."

"I see," he said. "So that's it, I guess. Unless . . ." He hesitated.

"Unless?"

"Unless you'd like to explore some of the other issues that came up last night."

"Uh, no. I don't want to—can't really—explore those issues right now. Sorry."

"Okay. I understand. Do let me know if you change your mind. I'd love to see you again, Ann."

"Goodbye, Victor." I hung up abruptly and noticed the goose flesh on my arm as I replaced the handset into its base.

On my way home I stopped by the Comstock's to return Julia's journals—I wouldn't need them anymore. Maria opened the door seconds after I rang the bell and apologized for Caroline's absence before I said a word.

"Caroline will be sorry to have missed you. She went to her lawyer's office to sign some papers."

"That's fine. I'm just dropping these off." I said, handing her the bundle of journals.

Maria took the package and nodded, the look on her face betraying her disappointment. I felt compelled to explain.

"You know I really can't continue investigating Julia's death."

"Of course, I wouldn't presume." She shook her head and, with a tight smile, changed the subject. "It looks like the couple from last night may make an offer on the house. Caroline will be leaving soon. We'll all move on."

I drove out of the Highland's gate thinking it would likely be a very long time before I'd return, if ever. The lifestyle of the rich and famous didn't do much for me anyway. The other half have the same kinds of problems we all do; they just spend more money on them. As I passed the golf course, a car turned out of the drive behind me and momentarily blinded me with a flash of high beams.

"Turn them off, buddy." I muttered, turning around to glare at the driver as I pulled up to stop for the light on Greenwood. The guy clicked down to his regular lights, my eyes readjusted to the dim glow of nighttime in the burbs and my mind wandered to thoughts of baseball. I was counting down the days until the pitchers and catchers showed up in Arizona and wondering if the Mariners' cheap owners would shell out for the power hitter they'd need to have any chance at a winning season next year.

I turned down Innis Arden Way and noticed the guy still behind me, following a little close. Something clicked in my head as I looked into the rear view mirror and watched the silver SUV take the corner behind me. What the hell. How was this the new car of choice in my lowly neighborhood? I slowed to turn down my street and tried in vain to make out the license plate number. I exhaled as the SUV continued on down the road, relieved that my paranoia was unfounded.

After the usual mad canine greeting, I walked into the kitchen to check my voicemail. The first message was a male voice I didn't recognize:

"Stay out of other people's business—or you'll end up in a much bigger ditch. Understand?" I hit the replay number and listened again, my initial alarm at the threat morphing into anger.

"Jerk!" I murmured aloud, then listened to the second message, this one from Caroline.

"Sorry I missed you, Ann. Uh, there's something strange going on. Can you call me right back?"

Caroline answered the phone on the first ring.

"What kind of a car ran you into the ditch last night?" she asked, skipping any preliminary niceties.

"A silver Lexus SUV. Why?"

"The same car followed me earlier today so I asked Roger to keep an eye out for it. When I drove in tonight, he told me he'd spotted a similar SUV idling in the golf course drive late this afternoon."

"Yup. And it followed me almost to my door just now. Did you or Roger get a license plate number?"

"Just part of it—Washington plate, the first letters were J-O-Y, then six-something, I couldn't get the last two numbers. Do you think it's a coincidence? Now that you've told Victor Lloyd about your investigation, we're being followed."

"Victor drives a Saab," I said.

Silence.

"And I already told him that I've stopped investigating Julia's death. But I do think it's connected somehow. I'll call a friend of mine at the Seattle PD to see if she can get any information at all from a partial plate. I'll be in touch."

Erin Becker was surprised to hear from me so soon and joked that maybe I was looking for a career change.

"No, no, nothing like that." I laughed. "You know that I've been trying to help Caroline Schuster with some of the unanswered questions surrounding her sister Julia Comstock's death."

"I remember. Still looking for the mystery woman? What's her name?"

"Sylvia Carter, yes. But there's one other thing. It's probably nothing, but there might be some connection between Julia's death and the driver of a silver Lexus SUV. I wonder if you could get a name from a partial license plate number?" I wasn't going to tell her about my run-in with the same guy or she'd insist I file some sort of police report.

"It depends. I can call someone in the DOL but can't promise it'll get high priority. And the mystery woman, you think she's driving this car?"

"No, but I have another idea about Sylvia Carter. The Comstock's housekeeper spent some time with her on the day of Julia's death and has a fairly clear recollection of what she looks like. I'm sure she'd be willing to work with a sketch artist to come up with a likeness. I hoped you could recommend one."

"Ah, sure, I know someone who'd be great. Her name's Emily

Nakamura. She did a lot of work for the Department until they replaced her job with a computer program. Big mistake."

Erin was not a fan of the new technology. She went into more detail than I needed to know about how the computer program just couldn't get the nuance that an artist could with a pencil, not to mention how poorly trained some detectives were in working with victims and computers.

"It's a last-ditch effort," I explained. "If we can come up with a drawing of Sylvia Carter, we'll have a much better shot of finding this woman."

"So you are still looking for her."

"I guess I am," I said.

I hung up telling myself I *had* to follow this one lead. I felt challenged and I wasn't going to be intimidated into leaving it alone.

I called Emily Nakamura and she agreed to meet me at the Comstock house the next day, after she finished her work in federal court on a high-profile criminal racketeering trial. I followed up with a phone call to Caroline. She was thrilled that I had changed my mind about the investigation and said she and Maria would expect us at around quarter to five.

Driving up to The Highlands gatehouse the next day, I realized that the gate guy and I were on a first-name basis.

"Hi, Ann!"

"Hey, Roger, what's up?"

"Well, I haven't seen that silver SUV you're looking for—not today. But I'll keep an eye out."

I thanked him as the gate lifted and he waved me on.

I arrived at the Comstocks' and Maria showed me into the sunroom where Caroline was waiting. The sketch artist had not yet arrived. Maria appeared nervous, not at all comfortable in this situation. She kept getting up to refill coffee and wipe invisible dust off gleaming surfaces. All three of us flinched when the doorbell rang, even though Roger had called to let us know that Emily Nakamura was on her way.

The woman was younger than I'd imagined—probably in her early thirties. I'd also assumed that she was Japanese but she looked more Hawaiian, with smooth dark skin and eyes, her silky black hair pulled back loosely into an ivory shell clip. Emily stood in the foyer overloaded with several large books and a portfolio which Maria quickly offered to help carry into the dining room where they would be working. After carefully arranging the books, her sketchpad, and colored pencils on the table in front of her, Emily sat down and invited Maria to sit beside her.

Watching Emily prepare for her task, and listening to her converse with Maria and Caroline, I could instantly see why Erin Becker preferred working with this young woman rather than a police officer and a computer program. Her very presence was calming. Emily's eyes were warm and smiling and her voice had a musical quality, soft and mellow, like an Ella Fitzgerald ballad; she moved as she spoke, unhurried and yet with assurance. She began by making small talk with Maria and Caroline, complimenting the beautiful house and gardens, mentioning that she missed her mother's garden in Oahu. I suggested that she probably missed the sun as well and she smiled. "Yes, but it is the rain which keeps everything in Seattle so beautifully green."

Caroline went into the kitchen and Emily turned to the task at hand: explaining her plan to create a sketch of Sylvia Carter with Maria's help. She would begin by asking Maria to tell her everything she could remember about the woman, being as specific as possible. She would then start sketching the face with the information Maria provided and fill in details by asking her questions. If particular facial features were vague, she would use the books she had brought with her which contained hundreds of examples of individual facial features. There were separate books of noses, eyes, and mouths.

When Caroline returned and set the tray with a pitcher of water and several glasses onto the table, Emily looked up at the two of us and I understood her silent request to leave them to their work.

"Caroline and I will be in the sunroom in case you need anything," I said, nodding at Caroline who jumped up and moved through the front hall and into the next room. I followed her and we sat facing each other, lost in our own thoughts. Caroline broke the silence by asking if I'd had any luck with the SUV license plate number.

I shook my head. "My friend at the Seattle PD says she might be able to get some names, but it will take a while."

Caroline nodded.

"In the meantime, we'll need to reopen the lines of communication with Victor Lloyd. He says he wants to find out what happened to Julia, who Sylvia Carter is, as much as we do, and he might be able to help us."

"Or he could be sending his goons out to follow us around and scare the hell out of us. One or the other."

"Oh, I think he's pretty harmless—definitely a true believer in his psychic abilities—but harmless."

"I suppose you know what you're doing."

"Look, I really wanted to drop this whole thing—the last thing I need is to get sucked into Lloyd's 'I talk to dead people' world. But my original plan—to prove that Lloyd and his church have some kind of scam going on, one that turned deadly for Julia—doesn't seem likely. Now, I'm not at all sure what's happening here. But no one bullies me into giving up. I don't even care about getting a splashy story any more. I care about getting some answers," I said.

"I appreciate that, Ann. I just don't want to see you risk your own safety and I want to pay you for your time. I don't expect you to do this for free, especially if there's no story."

Caroline's comment made me pause. "Oh, there's a story all right. It's just a little different from what we thought at first."

"So what will you do now?" she asked.

"If Maria and Emily come up with a sketch of Sylvia Carter, that's great but it doesn't mean we'll be able to find her. We don't have police resources; we can't post her face in the media or send out an APB. We could do something on Facebook, I suppose, but I think our best bet is to show the sketch to some folks at Nirmala. Julia doesn't have any other friends. I think we need Lloyd's help."

"Remember that he's very good at manipulating things for his own benefit. He could send you off on a wild goose chase."

When I didn't respond, Caroline talked about the details of Julia's estate that she'd been handling. She'd arranged for the furniture to be picked up later in the week and sold at auction. The Giordano Gallery had been through Julia's work and had taken ten of her paintings to show at the First Thursday Gallery Walk in Pioneer Square. Three had sold on opening night for fifteen to sixty-five hundred dollars each.

"Julia would have been thrilled," Caroline said as her eyes clouded. "If only she had realized some success in her lifetime. Life is so unfair."

"It is."

At the sound of footsteps, we both turned to see Maria standing in the doorway, flushed and smiling. "Ms. Nakamura would like to see you. She has finished her sketch."

The artist was stuffing her books into her bag as we entered the room. Two sketches were set out on the table: one straight on and one profile. Caroline and I grabbed for the headshot simultaneously, chuckled nervously, then leaned over to examine it together. Sylvia Carter appeared to be in her early thirties with light brown hair cut just below her ears, short and choppy. She had pouty lips, a round face, pale blue eyes, and freckles across her small nose, which appeared upturned in profile. I smiled, remembering Maria's earlier comment, likening her to Mary Martin in Peter Pan. The woman looked vaguely familiar though she really didn't have any outstanding features, nothing to make her particularly memorable. I thought of those shampoo ads I'd seen in magazines featuring three different women all with the same color and length of hair, the same eye color and the same skin tone. They all looked startlingly alike.

"She looks familiar to me." Caroline said as she glanced over at me. "What about you, Ann?"

"Exactly what I thought. And that's just what will make her hard to find. She looks so regular. So like a million other pretty, brown-haired young women."

"Oh, she definitely has her own distinctive face," Emily said, looking from Caroline to me. "Maria did an excellent job remembering details. I hope you find her soon."

"Of course she's unique. But why can't she have a huge nose or a big scar, funny teeth? Anything to make her stand out?"

"Because those things are more the exception than the rule." Emily smiled. "Good luck with your search. It has been a pleasure working with you."

Caroline walked Emily to her car, discussing the details of payment for her services and helping her carry her things, while Maria disappeared into the kitchen. I sat alone studying Sylvia Carter's image. I couldn't quite shake the notion that I'd seen her before. Still puzzling, I picked up the original sketches and followed Maria into the kitchen. When Caroline returned, she thanked Maria for her work with the sketch artist, and I realized that her days at the Comstock house were numbered.

"So, Maria, what will you do once the house is sold? Caroline tells me the furniture is going to be auctioned off this week and that the couple who looked at the house the other night made an offer."

"Oh, I've put the word out in the neighborhood that I will be available to work for someone else soon. And then it's possible the new owners might want to keep me on. The real estate agent said she would mention me to them."

Caroline walked over and put her arm around Maria. "I'll

certainly give Maria a great reference, and I'll sure miss her pampering when I go back to San Francisco next week."

"Next week?" I hadn't considered that Caroline would be going back so soon. But then, she did have a job and life to get back to. And I hadn't found any answers for her about Julia's death; I had only raised more questions.

As if reading my thoughts, Caroline answered, "I have to get back to work. I do hope you have some luck with this sketch, Ann, and with the SUV, though I hope I never see it again. Do you want Julia's journals back, or shall I pack them up?"

"I'll take the most recent one with me and go through it one more time in case I missed something."

"Will you call me as soon as you have anything?"

I assured her I would, trying to convince myself that I might find something, then said my goodbyes to both of them and headed for a FedEx copy shop. While I waited for the copies, I put in a call to Victor Lloyd. I told him Caroline had convinced me to continue investigating Julia's death and that I hoped he would help. I didn't tell him about the SUV. He seemed surprised but pleased to hear from me and agreed to meet me at the Starbucks near my office in an hour. My turf, this time, and my rules.

19

I walked into Starbucks at 7:35 and spotted Victor sitting in a leather armchair near the window engaged in conversation with two young women seated at a table a few feet away. The guy never quit—I wondered if he was capable of sitting quietly anywhere without commanding an audience. Then again, I was struck by how normal he looked in this setting wearing a charcoal-gray collared shirt and jeans. Normal, yes, but better looking. We made eye contact and he smiled, stood up to greet me as if nothing awkward had happened between us.

"These girls were just telling me about the Halloween costumes they're planning," he said.

I supposed it was a natural conversation for this time of year, especially since the display case overflowed with seasonal reminders: pencils in orange and black with pumpkin erasers, stuffed bats, CDs of "ghoulish" music and overly frosted and overly packaged black and orange cookies. Just the sight of all that sugar made my teeth hurt.

"Halloween is one of his favorite holidays," I said to the girls, with a nod to Victor. "He has a thing about ghosts." The girls looked puzzled, but Victor laughed easily.

The girls returned to their conversation and I made my way to the counter to order coffee and a piece of pumpkin loaf in honor of the season. When I returned to the table, Victor stopped messing around with his iPhone and dropped it into a briefcase next to his chair. He began to apologize for how our dinner together had ended.

"Victor, forget it. That is, I want to drop it and go on. Okay?"

He nodded. "Okay. Where do we go from here?"

I told him I wanted to continue where our conversation about Julia had left off—about the "success" Julia was having with her own psychic abilities and the "warning" he'd had before she died—and that I didn't want to hear from any spirits that might have messages for me.

"I understand," he said, leaning back in his chair and crossing his legs while collecting his thoughts. "Here's what happened. Sometime just before Julia died—maybe the day before, two days, I can't be sure—I was working with a client trying to get through to her father. I kept getting the name Charlotte and seeing the image of a bridge. I was getting the name Julia as well, but my client's mother-in-law, her dead husband's mother, was named Julia, and so I wasn't connecting this warning with Julia Comstock."

"Okay."

"The reading went badly: we couldn't figure out what the bridge symbol meant and she didn't have any connection with anyone named Charlotte. Only later when I looked at my notes did I think about Julia and remembered that the spirit guide who came through to her was called Charlotte. The bridge image was a mystery, though, and the feeling of dread that I had at the time."

I nodded to show I was listening.

"You see, Ann, the spirits send *symbols* for me to interpret. When mistakes are made, they're in my *interpretation*, not in what the spirits send to me. It can be very frustrating."

"How so?"

"Well, some symbols are obvious. Like most often when I'm shown a white rose it means a celebration of some kind, a wedding or a birth. But when I'm shown a car it can mean many things."

"Such as?" I asked. So far, he wasn't telling me anything I hadn't already read in his book.

"A car might mean the person passed in a car accident, but it could also mean that he worked at a car dealership or that his hobby was building model cars. This is why the person I'm working with is so important. My clients help me read the symbols I'm getting because the spirits know what the symbols will mean for them, even when they have multiple meanings for me." Victor was on a roll now; he'd uncrossed his legs, leaned forward in his chair, and spoke with authority, like he'd practiced this part of his speech many times.

"Got it. But how do you mean you are 'shown' things? How does that work?"

"Good question. It's like this. Say I tell you not to think of a large gray elephant. What is the image you get in your head?"

"A large gray elephant. Okay, so these images just pop into your head when you're talking to your clients?"

"Well, yes. But often there are many images there and I need to sort through them to find the one that has the strongest association for my client."

Again, I nodded, trying to understand the concept. Of course a little voice in my head (I didn't think it was a spirit guide) was showing me how Victor could use the smallest bit of information he might have about the dead person or the circumstances of the death to perpetrate some major fraud.

"You know, Victor, this is all really fascinating but here's what bothers me. It seems to me that you could simply pick up bits of information from your clients before the formal reading and parlay that into vague messages and symbols. Your clients grasp at anything to hear what they want to hear and you take it from there. You're very skilled at working with what they're telling you already."

"I know this stuff sounds really out there, and that there are phony psychics all over the place. But I believe that I have this gift for a reason. It's my life's work. When I send messages of love from people who have passed away to their families and friends still here on earth, I give them tremendous peace of mind and hope. I don't expect you to understand it after just a few days. It has taken me my whole life and I still don't pretend to understand it completely."

Victor's eyes were shining with such intensity that, when he lowered his voice and looked directly into mine, I felt the full power of his belief. I sat back, grabbed my coffee cup, and, with great difficulty, pulled my eyes from his.

We sat in silence for a long moment and I realized just how much I wanted to know how it worked, though my motives were unclear, mixed up with the investigation and my own past.

"Victor," I said, "I'll admit I find this whole process fascinating but I still have major doubts."

He shrugged. "Maybe if you give it some time, try to stay open."

As I sat there thinking about psychic phenomena, an obvious question crossed my mind. "Have you ever thought of trying to channel Julia? Like maybe she could explain what happened?"

He frowned. "It's not like a TV show. I can't just tune it in. It's highly personal." He looked thoughtful, then asked, "Do you think Julia's sister would want to try a reading?"

"Uh, no. Definitely not." I shook my head and changed the subject. "I have something I'd like you to look at." I pulled out the Sylvia Carter sketches and explained about Emily Nakamura's work with Maria. He picked up the headshot, leaned toward the window and tilted the sketch to get as much light on it as possible. He examined it for several minutes.

"She's familiar, but I can't be sure I've ever seen her before. I'm fairly certain she never took a workshop from me. I think I'd remember her. She's quite lovely." He locked eyes with me again and I felt that tug from him, as if he'd just told me *I* was lovely and the woman in the sketch reminded him of it. Then Jennifer Dixon and her take on Victor popped into my head.

"I suppose you meet lots of lovely women in your workshops."

"Mmm. I met you, didn't I?" he said, eyes sparking at me.

I tried not to smile and to ignore the comment. "Seriously, though, isn't there some professional code of conduct that prohibits you from dating women you meet through your work?"

He laughed. "You mean like ethical guidelines for 'The National Organization of Psychic Mediums?'"

"Well, okay, but maybe you've developed your own code of ethics about it?"

He narrowed his gaze. "I'd like to think you're interested in my dating habits from some personal motive, but I doubt that. So, why don't you just ask whatever it is straight out?"

"Okay. What about Julia? Was your relationship with her strictly professional?"

"Unbelievable. First you accuse me of murdering her. Now you accuse me of dating her. Maybe you think I seduced her, then killed her for her money? Is that it?" Victor shook his head in disbelief.

"I just thought . . . all these vulnerable women. It could be quite a temptation. You are single, aren't you?"

"Yes, I am single and yes, I have been tempted. But I had a bad experience a while back and I'll never date anyone from a workshop again."

"What happened?"

"You ever see *Fatal Attraction?*"

I nodded and swallowed hard, remembering how I'd made the same association after my meeting with Jennifer Dixon.

"Yeah, well, since I'm not married and don't have any pet rabbits, it wasn't quite that bad. But it was pretty scary. No, I'll never do that again."

"And yet . . ." I raised an eyebrow.

"What? You mean, you? Well, you're different. You went to my workshop for research. And you certainly don't seem *vulnerable* to me."

I winced. "But you didn't know that at the time. You were quick to suggest we get together again."

"I was curious about you. I had this strong sense that night— something connected to the spirit world. I don't like unfinished business and I didn't think you were going to come back for another session. I was just trying to figure it out." He paused, then asked innocently, "I haven't made any moves on you, have I?"

Now I was embarrassed. It's true that he'd been friendly but anything beyond that was probably just in my head. "Uh, no," I said looking down at the table, feeling the color rise in my face. When I looked up, his eyes met mine.

"Well, you let me know if I'm moving in a direction you're uncomfortable with, okay?" he said, and I felt my stomach do that flip again.

"Okay, right." I said. It was time to go if I wanted to preserve some of my dignity. I gathered up the sketches of Sylvia Carter. "Why don't you show these around at the church, maybe to some of the people who took workshops with you and Julia? Someone might remember this woman."

Victor nodded. "Sure," he said, taking the sketches from me. "But I'm not going to call up everyone who happened to be in a workshop with Julia and ask them to look at these; they don't need to be reminded how she died. I'll show them around Nirmala, maybe post them in a common area. That's the best I can do."

I doubted that, but I wasn't going to call him on anything else tonight. Better to drop it for now. I stood up to leave and Victor did the same.

"Can I call you?" he asked.

"You mean if you find out anything about Sylvia Carter?"

"That, yes," he said with a mischievous grin. "And if I want to find out a little more about you?"

I hesitated too long and he could tell I was not totally opposed to the idea, even though I should have been. I shook my head and opened my mouth to speak but he was quick.

"Hey, I'm just a regular guy when I'm not working. Don't say no yet. Just think about it."

Before I found my voice he had reached the door. I stood there, still tongue-tied, watching him go. What the hell was I thinking?

20

I drove home mulling over my conversation with Victor, tucking away the embarrassment of our encounter and wondering if I should call him and tell him not to call me. Okay, that was ridiculous. I could just wait until he called, then tell him I wasn't really up for a date.

I had a voicemail from Tom Hill: he could be reached after eight tonight, but he didn't sound enthusiastic. I decided to call him back anyway.

Tom listened to me explain why I wanted him to reopen his investigation into Nancy's disappearance, but remained quiet on the other end for a long time. I recognized the powerful tool of a good investigator—give the other person plenty of silence and they'll fill it with whatever is on their minds. I explained Lloyd's warning about Nancy, highly aware of how bizarre it sounded, and finished by saying I didn't totally believe in Lloyd's psychic powers. My words sounded hollow as soon as they left my lips.

"Tom? Are you still there?"

"Sure, Ann, but I'm wondering what I'm hearing exactly. You want me to start looking for Nancy again because some psychic guy you just met says he had a 'warning from the spirit world' that she's in danger? Did I get that right?"

"Okay, I admit that sounds weird, but it has been so long since I've heard anything from Nancy. I've been thinking a lot about the past and I really need to know if she's okay."

Tom sighed. "Okay, I'll try to find some of the cult members still living in Oregon. Maybe someone would be willing to talk about Nancy now. But, Ann . . ." He paused to make sure he had my

144 • Rachel Bukey

attention.

"I'm listening, Tom."

"Do you want to give me a time limit? I mean, how many hours do you want me to spend on this? It's your money, you know, and it doesn't grow on trees even with all that rain in Seattle."

We decided on a budget. I'd been saving for a trip to Hawaii, but I'd swap that for some peace of mind about Nancy.

Before I climbed into bed, I pulled out the sketches of Sylvia Carter one more time. "Who is she?" I asked out loud. Puccini, already settled in for the night, raised her head from where it rested on her front paws and looked intently at me, expecting further instructions, something in her doggie vocabulary.

"Oh, never mind, Pooch. Go back to sleep. Tomorrow is another day." The dog put her head back down and I set the sketches on the bedside table, snuggled into my down comforter, and fell asleep in my usual three minutes.

I woke up with the alarm at six thirty, out of a disturbing dream filled with swirling colors, Victor Lloyd, and Sylvia Carter. That was it! The face in Julia's painting. I went through my morning ritual quicker than usual and wondered how early was too early to call Caroline. At seven thirty I decided to go for it.

She answered the phone with a sleepy voice but I jumped right in with my revelation.

"Caroline, I think Sylvia Carter is the face in one of Julia's paintings. You know the one, with all the red swirls of color?" There was silence on the other end followed by an audible sigh.

"Well, I remember the painting with a face but I don't remember the face very clearly. I do know that it went to the Giordano Gallery for Julia's show. You could go over there and see it, I suppose."

I scribbled down the number, told Caroline I'd be in touch, and called the gallery. Their message mentioned the current artists on display, including Julia, and ended with their business hours. They wouldn't be open until eleven a.m. Fine, I'd spend my lunch hour in

Pioneer Square.

When I arrived in Seattle's oldest retail district at 11:35, I noticed there were fewer homeless men than usual sitting on the benches lining the cobblestone square. I supposed the rain and cold had moved some of them along, hopefully to a dryer and warmer spot. The Giordano Gallery was across the square from the first bank building ever constructed in Seattle. The Seattle First National Bank has, of course, long since been subsumed by one of the mega national banks, but the building still stands and the old name remains etched in the brass plate at the entrance. I crossed the square and pushed open the huge old wooden door to the gallery.

Inside, a large open area, filled mainly with sculptures atop partial columns, flowed into four separate galleries. In the very center of the space, a meticulously put-together woman sat at a round mahogany table working at a laptop. She stood and smiled widely as I approached. Her look was what I thought of as "California:" very stylish, colorful, and a bit too tight and too young for anyone over forty. I spotted Julia's show in the room at a right angle to the aging beauty's table. Noticing my eyes shift away from her and in that direction, the woman introduced herself as Pepper Giordano and launched right into her sales pitch.

"Are you familiar with Julia Comstock's work? She does amazing things with color, doesn't she?"

"Yes, I'm familiar with it," I said, walking past Pepper and into the well-lit white gallery filled with Julia's paintings, searching for the red painting and the face. I spotted a similar painting in a corner and moved toward it. Not the one.

Pepper followed right behind me. "That is a nice one, isn't it? The touch of yellow swirled in with the red really makes it pop, don't you think?"

"You know, I'm looking for a particular painting I've seen of hers. It's similar to this one, red, but features a face kind of hovering in one corner."

"Oh yes, that one is fabulous. It sold on opening night. Sorry. You know, we'd be happy to bring any of these paintings out to your house and hang them for you there for a few days, just to see how you like living with them." She again flashed her perfect teeth at me. "If the red suits your décor, I could show you some other canvases we have in back that we haven't hung yet." She walked quickly toward the back room and I wondered whether business was so bad that she put the hard sell on all their customers or if it was just a slow time of the day.

"No, wait. It's that particular painting I need to see. Is it on approval with the person who picked it up on opening night, or purchased outright?"

"Oh, it was purchased outright, about five minutes after the show opened. I sold it myself," she said proudly.

My wheels began spinning; I needed to find out who was so quick to buy that particular painting. She'd never tell me if I asked her straight out.

"Darn it. I bet my friend Bobbi McCafferty bought it. She and I talked about coming to the opening together but then I didn't get back into town until late last night and had to miss it. Short, dark-haired woman, kind of dumpy." Pepper raised an eyebrow, smirked at my catty comment, and walked over to her desk where she began clicking away on her keyboard.

"I remember her as young and all business, not very friendly. I think she did have dark hair, but she wore a beautiful Jil Sander suit. Not dumpy. Let's see what her name is." She scrolled through the database and stopped suddenly. "Here it is. Oh, she paid with a corporate card: Comvitek. Her name is Kelly Long."

21

Thanking Pepper for her help, I quickly made my way out the door and into the square. The sky opened up, greeting me with a horizontal blast of drenching wind, a phenomenon known in the Northwest as "the Pineapple Express"—warm, saturated air moving across the Pacific from Hawaii. Leaning into it, I made my way across the square as the rain seeped into my shoes, washed over the cobblestones, and swirled into the sewer grates. With my stomach grumbling, I ducked into The Frankfurter for a quick lunch to go. Inside the tiny overheated restaurant, the lunch crowd milled around complaining about the weather. I waited impatiently, taking in the smells of damp hair and spicy sausage, while the young guy behind the counter packed my order: an old-fashioned hot dog with mustard, fresh-squeezed lemonade, and a warm chocolate chip cookie. Grabbing the bag and tucking it carefully under my raincoat to keep it dry and semi-warm, I headed to my car, hopscotching around the parking lot's rain-filled potholes (larger than some backyard koi ponds) and struggled to keep my already soaked shoes from washing off my feet entirely. In the dry car at last, I cranked up the heat, took a bite of my hotdog, and punched in Comvitek's number.

"Good afternoon, Comvitek." That voice immediately transported me to the plush lobby, where I pictured the perfectly coiffed receptionist purring into her headset.

"Hi, this is Sue calling from Cutter & Loeb," I said in my most efficient administrative assistant tone. "I have a letter here that I need to send to Kelly Long and I want to make sure that I address it correctly. What is her title there at Comvitek?"

"Ms. Long is Assistant Director of Corporate Giving. Do you need the address as well?"

I listened as she recited the address and then asked if Kelly Long was in this afternoon. "Right now, yes, but she's scheduled for a meeting at one thirty." I decided to go for it, driving through the rain to the south end of Lake Union.

The Comvitek receptionist apparently remembered my visit to Nick Villardi's office the week before and welcomed me with a large toothy smile.

"I'm sorry, Ms. Dexter, Mr. Villardi is out to lunch right now. Is he expecting you?"

"No, he's not. Actually, I have a few minutes between appointments and wondered if I could talk with Kelly Long briefly. I'm writing a piece on the Seattle Public School's new project on Bainbridge and I just wanted to check some of my facts. I know Comvitek is a major donor and thought Kelly might be able to help me out." I glanced at the small placard on her desk. "Kim."

I walked around the reception area looking at the paintings, half expecting to find something of Julia's among them as Kim rang through to Kelly Long's office, spoke briefly, then turned back to me.

"Ms. Long will be right out."

I sat and flipped through *Seattle* magazine, mildly interested in an article naming the city's top doctors, searching for my own practitioner among the list, when I heard Kelly Long approach. She introduced herself and I smiled thinking of Pepper Giordano's accurate description, although Kelly had dropped the all-business face in favor of one very friendly to the press. Kelly was young, somewhere in her late twenties, tall, slender, with dark hair cut in the popular choppy, sexy style, described by my haircutter as "bed hair"—with this cut, you want to look messy, as if you'd just come from a fun romp in the sack. She wore a dark blue suit, more formal than the other employees I'd noticed during my first visit to Comvitek. I told her a little bit about my interest in corporate giving, especially as it relates to education, as I followed Kelly to her office on the opposite side of the building from Nick's and decidedly less opulent. Small and nondescript, the room featured a desk, side table with laptop, two uncomfortable-looking chairs, and a bookshelf under the window, with a view of the parking lot. Only one piece of art, a traditional landscape, adorned the wall.

Kelly gestured to one of the chairs and sat behind her desk.

"So, what would you like to know about Comvitek?" she asked.

I jumped right in, asking Kelly about Comvitek's involvement with the School in the Woods, their general corporate giving philosophy and other projects they were supporting this year, then closed my notebook and turned to the real reason for my visit.

"You know, I just remembered where I've seen you before. I've been wracking my brain since we met. At first I thought it must have been at the School in the Woods presentation at John Muir School, but now I'm sure I remember seeing you at the Giordano Gallery, for the opening of Julia Comstock's show. Didn't you buy one of the paintings, the red swirly one with the face in the corner?"

Her smile faded and her eyes shifted from my face to the window behind me. She appeared uncomfortable only for a moment before her mouth turned up and she met my eyes once again.

"Well, you really are observant. I wasn't at the gallery very long. I had a million other things to finish that afternoon, so I got in and out as fast as possible." She paused and I waited to see if she had anything more to add.

"Truly, that errand annoyed me. Why should I go traipsing around art galleries, buying paintings for Nick Villardi? But then, what could I do? He's the boss."

"Nick Villardi sent you to buy the painting?"

"Oh, he wanted it in a big hurry, too, but he didn't have time to go for it himself. I don't know why he just didn't call them and order it or something." She shrugged and shook her head. "Anyway, he buzzed me just before five thirty that afternoon and asked me to run over and buy it, the show opened at six. He said he thought it would be a nice gesture, in memory of Warren and Julia, to have one of her paintings."

"Did he specify which painting?" I asked.

"Oh yes, he described it as the best of the bunch, a little different and therefore more interesting than the others."

"Is it hanging in his office? I didn't see it in the reception area."

"Beats me. I haven't been invited into his office since then," she said with clear disappointment in her voice.

I stood up to go, assuring Kelly that I could find my way back to the reception area on my own. Instead, I continued past the front desk and headed down the hallway to Nick Villardi's office. The door stood open and the office appeared empty so I poked my head in, crossed the threshold, and took a quick look around. Nick belonged to the clean desk club, no papers anywhere, just a computer humming away on the side table. I looked at the screensaver and smiled—a slide show of the Mariners' last season. I knew I liked this guy. The art on the walls were black-and-white photos of street scenes, possibly taken in Europe, kind of edgy. Satisfied that Julia's painting was not around, I stepped into the hall and nearly slammed right into Nick himself.

"Hey, Ann Dexter!" Nick looked puzzled but pleased as his eyes swept over me and I felt myself blush. "Kim didn't tell me you were here. What a pleasure." He looked as if he meant it.

"Yeah, hi! Sorry. Actually I came to talk with Kelly Long about one of your corporate donations, a project I happen to be working on at the *Times*, and then thought I'd pop in to see if you were in. Do you know about the School in the Woods on Bainbridge?" I rambled on, talking way too fast.

"Come on in and tell me about it. I'm glad you took a detour to my office."

He smiled again and I felt the heat lingering on my face.

"Come, sit down. Can I get you some water?"

"Ah, no, I mean, sure. Water would be great, thanks." I sat down in one of the leather chairs around the small table in the corner of the room while Nick opened up a cabinet exposing a small bar well stocked with bottles.

He handed me a plastic bottle of sparkling water, and sat in the facing chair. "So, tell me about the School in the Woods. I hope we're being good citizens?"

I explained the project to him as briefly as possible and ended with, "And, yes, Comvitek seems to be donating a large sum to this very worthy cause for the Seattle school kids, future leaders of the city." I smiled, recovered from my momentary embarrassment and went on. "You know, it's funny. It turns out I'd seen Kelly Long before and remembered it just before I left her office. I went to the Giordano Gallery for Julia's opening and saw her buy Julia's red painting. I thought maybe you had it hanging in here."

Nick leaned back in his chair and lifted his arms above his head in an exaggerated stretch before continuing.

"Well, well. No, I have that painting at home right now. I'm not sure where I'll hang it. I thought it would be a nice gesture. To buy one of Julia's paintings, I mean." He leaned forward again, put his elbows on the small table, and winked, or maybe he just had something in his eye.

"So, are you having any luck in your investigation?" he asked, looking at me closely.

"A little. Remember Sylvia Carter?"

Nick presented a complete poker face, so I continued.

"The person who showed up at Julia's house after her death, posing as Victor Lloyd's assistant?"

"Oh, right, I remember."

"I have a sketch of her, although she doesn't look familiar to anyone at Nirmala, and not to Lloyd. He swears she never took one of his workshops."

"You have a sketch?" he asked, raising an eyebrow. "Where did that come from?"

I explained that Maria had seen her on the day Julia died, and how she had worked with the sketch artist to produce the likeness.

"Do you have it with you? The sketch?"

"I don't. I left it at the office. But you know, I think the face in the painting you bought looks a lot like the sketch. Did that face look familiar to you? Is it anyone you recognized?"

Nick's eyes locked onto mine for a long moment before he replied, shaking his head.

"There was something about that face, I'm not sure. I think she seemed familiar, in an idealized artistic way. You know, like angels in religious works: perfect features, pleasant expression, none of the flaws and imperfections of real life."

"You never met her then," I pressed, just to be sure.

"No. I never met her."

"I'm thinking this woman, whoever she is, has to be key. Maybe she knew something about the circumstances of Julia's death that she didn't want anyone to find out. She's scared. So she disappeared."

"Death frightens people." He said, looking down at the table. I waited for him to continue. "I've been thinking quite a bit about Julia's death. And I think it's possible that Victor Lloyd didn't have anything to do with it. Maybe we're all just grasping at straws here, trying to find an excuse for her. No one wants to think Julia's unhappiness drove her to suicide. We all feel guilty, responsible, like we could have prevented it in some way." His voice cracked.

"Sure." I nodded, trying to gauge the sincerity of his words. "I'm just trying to find some answers for Caroline. There are still questions out there."

"Life is filled with questions. This is one of them. All I'm saying is that maybe it's time to move on."

The phone on his desk buzzed and he got up to grab it. "Right. Okay. Tell him I'll be out in a minute." Nick looked over at me and shrugged as I stood up. "I've got a guy I need to meet with. Sorry. I'll walk you out."

I headed to the door but he stepped in front of it. "You know, I'd love to see you again. You could bring that sketch by and we could have lunch?"

"Sure, Nick, I'll give you a call," I said.

He put his hand on my shoulder. "I hope you do. Please do."

Back at the *Times*, I studied the sketch of Sylvia Carter and wondered about Nick Villardi's apparent change of heart and why he appeared so interested in taking me to lunch. I knew I'd have to get a look at that painting, even if it wouldn't get me closer to finding the mystery woman. I'd take the sketch to the Villardi's house after work, show it to Liz and Nick together. Lunch was not a good idea.

I pulled up in front of their house at around five thirty, thinking Liz might be playing the role of perfect wife, making a gourmet dinner for her hardworking hubby. The thought nauseated me somehow. With daylight savings time a dim memory, darkness descended early in Seattle and the Villardi's front steps were wet with rain despite the current "period of partial clearing." I climbed them carefully, counting twenty-five, and reached the front porch slightly winded. I rang the bell even though the house had that empty feel to it. No answer. After a few minutes, I walked around to the back, where a small guesthouse sat just off the alley, a walkway of stepping-stones connecting it to the main house. Maybe someone there could tell me when Liz might be home.

As I approached the door, a pair of motion-sensitive outdoor lights flashed on and practically blinded me. No doorbell. I grabbed for the old-fashioned door knocker when I realized that the guesthouse was a miniature of the Villardi's main house. Cute. With the entire yard bathed in light now, I looked around, idly appreciating the landscaping and how, from the street, the house had looked much smaller than its actual size, tucked into the hillside.

When no one answered the door, I wandered toward the alley, wondering whether the guesthouse had once been a garage. They must have to park their cars somewhere. Continuing through the alley, I noticed the garage was on the other side of the house connected by yet another walkway. More motion-sensing lights turned on and I hoped the alarm system wasn't next. I saw the garbage and recycling neatly set out for pick up and headed back toward the walkway and main house when I spotted it, leaning up against the green plastic garbage bin.

22

I pulled the empty frame from between the two bins. It looked as if someone had sliced out the canvas with a razor knife. Maybe this wasn't the frame from Julia's painting at all. Maybe they were just cleaning out their garage. Maybe. All sorts of thoughts whirled through my head as I lifted the garbage can lid and peered in. Reaching between two white plastic bags, I dislodged the canvas and unfolded it while shifting out of the shadows to get a closer look. My stomach tightened. Whoever cut the painting from its frame had also slashed it diagonally, cutting straight through the face in the corner: Sylvia Carter's face.

I stood there gaping at it when headlights flared into the alley—a car, heading straight at me. Ducking behind the garbage bin, I listened over the pounding of my heart as the Villardi's garage door opened and a car turned in. Folding the canvas into a bundle and tucking it under my arm, I ran around the side of the house as fast as possible and headed down the stairs. I hit the first landing and slipped, taking the last few steps on my butt.

"Goddamn shoes!" I cursed my fashion choice, jumped into the car, and waited for my breath to return to normal, vowing to wear only sensible shoes from now on. With the canvas stashed in the backseat, I considered walking back up the treacherous stairs to the front door and having a chat with Liz Villardi. But then, it could be Nick who had just driven in. Plus, I was a mess.

Considering my options, I rummaged around the glove compartment for the emergency pantyhose I usually kept in there, struggled into them and checked my face in the rear view mirror—

tolerable. I pulled a brush through my hair, put on some lip-gloss and grabbed my cell phone. Liz answered on the second ring. I told her I was in the neighborhood and wanted to come by to drop off a sketch for her and Nick to look at.

"A sketch?" she asked, waiting for an explanation.

I told her it related to Julia's death, I'd explain more when I got there, that I'd talked to Nick earlier in the day and he'd suggested I drop it by. I didn't tell her he'd suggested lunch.

"Okay, I just got home but I'm in for the night. Nick has a business dinner meeting. Sure, come on over."

I started up the car and drove around to kill some time, down to Lake Washington Boulevard, through Madison Park and through the Arboretum, then back to the Denny Blaine neighborhood. I pulled up in front of the house fifteen minutes later and got out of my car. This time I held the railing in a death grip as I climbed the stairs to the front door.

Liz opened the door the moment I rang the bell. She didn't offer to take my coat and she seemed distracted. She released her long blonde hair from its bun and ran her fingers through it as she led me through the living room and into the kitchen where she poured herself a glass of white wine and offered me a glass. I declined. She shrugged and sat down at the antique French table, gesturing for me to do the same. She was wearing a deep emerald-green silk jacket over black silk pants. The color brought out her eyes and I had to admit she was striking, in an ice queen sort of way.

"So, you said something about a sketch?" she asked, appearing bored.

I reached into my purse and pulled out the sketch. As I handed it to her, we both spotted the dirt and scrape on my hand from my tumble down the stairs. I decided to ignore it and she snatched the sketch out of my hand to avoid any possibly contagious contact. She glanced at the sketch briefly and discarded it on the table in front of me.

"Doesn't look familiar. Who is she?"

"I'm not sure. She called herself Sylvia Carter and said she was Victor Lloyd's assistant when she showed up at Julia's house the day she died."

"Right, I remember hearing something about that. So, how did you get it?"

I explained and she nodded, finished off her wine, and got up to pour herself another glass, not bothering to offer me any this time.

"Are you sure she doesn't look familiar to you?"

"Oh, I'm sure."

"Because I thought she looked familiar and then I remembered the painting that Julia did with a face kind of floating in the background. I think it's this person, Sylvia Carter, in that painting. The one Nick bought at Julia's gallery show. Do you have it here?"

Liz looked confused momentarily, then forced a quick laugh. "That painting! Really?" she scoffed. "I couldn't believe it when Nick brought that thing home. I mean, I suppose he thought he was being kind but I'll never hang it in our home. You can't even call it art. It's terrible, belongs in the garbage." She waved her hand dismissively and took a deep intake of breath as if shocked at her outburst.

"May I take a look at it—satisfy my curiosity?" I asked.

"Oh, it's not here." Liz locked eyes with me as she went on, "I sent it off to be reframed. Maybe a new frame will help, though I doubt it. Nick can hang it in his study if he wants. I never go in there." I looked away first and knew I was in the company of a practiced liar.

"You didn't like Julia very much, did you?"

She readjusted herself on the chair and tapped her manicured index finger on the rim of her wine glass before looking back at me. "No, I didn't."

"I can imagine your frustration. Here you are, wife of the number-two man at Comvitek, setting up the Foundation, staffing it and doing all the footwork while Julia sat in her big house in the

Highlands messing around with paints."

"Yes, well, you're right about some things but very wrong about others. First of all, Nick was never 'number-two man' at Comvitek." She punctuated the word "never" by raising her voice, throwing me a look of pure loathing and shaking her head before continuing in a more even tone. "Warren and Nick were always equal partners. They took the same salary, had the same stock options. They were CEO and CFO. Nick the visionary, Warren the number cruncher. Oh no, there's nothing second-rate about Nick Villardi!"

I detected loyalty but not warmth in her voice. "Okay, I didn't mean to imply—"

"Good. You're right that I do all the work for the Foundation, but I enjoy it and I'm good at it. The thought of Julia taking any responsibility for it was quite ludicrous. She could barely take directions herself, let alone give them. I involved her in a charity event once. What a disaster!"

"Really, what happened?"

"Besides the fact that she wore blue to the black and white ball?" Liz chortled viciously before explaining, "I had an unavoidable conflict, which meant I couldn't get there until an hour or so after the event started. I asked Julia simply to arrive a little early and mingle, make sure that as many people as possible knew she represented Comvitek, a corporation that supports the arts in Seattle. When I arrived, there was Julia standing off in a corner talking to one of the waiters. I couldn't believe it! What an idiot! Instead of mingling with the Who's Who of Seattle, she preferred talking to the hired help. Turns out she had gone to art school with this guy and now he waited tables at the Westin to support himself. I'd say it's just where she would have ended up too if Warren hadn't married her. No, it's a good thing she didn't have much to do with the Foundation—she was useless."

Just then we heard the low rumble of the garage door opening and Liz looked at her watch. "What's Nick doing here? I thought he had a dinner meeting."

We stopped our conversation and listened as a distant door opened, footsteps approached, keys jangled, and Nick called out, "Liz?"

"In here, Nick."

Liz stood up as her husband walked into the room. "Hi, honey, I thought you had a dinner meeting?" She kissed him perfunctorily on one cheek as he cast a puzzled look in my direction.

"I do, but I thought I'd stop by to change. Ann Dexter!"

I got up and the three of us stood there awkwardly, like teenagers who'd arrived at the dance too early and couldn't find any of their real friends to talk to.

"Yes, Ms. Dexter stopped by to show us a sketch of Victor Lloyd's—" she searched for the correct word, "—accomplice, Sylvia somebody. We were just talking about Julia. Do you have time for a glass of wine before you go?" Liz made a move toward the counter where the wine stood in an ice bucket but stopped and turned as Nick replied.

"Sorry, no. I'm due at Wild Ginger in half an hour. So, let's have a look at Sylvia Carter."

I picked up the sketch from the table where Liz had discarded it and handed it to him. He sat down, examined it closely while rubbing his forehead. Shaking his head, he looked up at me. "Well, I can't place her, but she does look a *little* familiar to me. How about you Liz? Do you recognize her at all?" He glanced over at his wife with a grimace, as if expecting a slap.

"Not at all." Liz said, with the dismissive hand wave I'd seen earlier.

Nick appeared to relax and forced a smile. "She is very pretty."

"Really, I'd say kind of mousy," Liz said, glaring at her husband. I could feel the tension between the two of them.

"Sorry to rush off, but I'd better change and get to my dinner." Nick reached over to shake my hand. "Good luck, Ms. Dexter. Sorry we couldn't help you out here."

"Uh," I stammered, chagrined by the change in his demeanor from this afternoon, calling me "Ms. Dexter" as if he had caught his wife's frosty persona just by walking into the same room with her.

"Not a problem, I should be going too, but there's just one other thing, Mr. Villardi." Two could play this game. "The more I look at this face, the more familiar it looks to me too. I'm pretty sure it's the face in Julia's painting, the one you bought. You do remember that, don't you?"

Nick looked a bit startled, then shot another glance at Liz who moved to the ice bucket and busied herself pouring another glass of wine. She stared at the liquid in the glass as if it might produce the answer she was looking for.

"Whoa, I think you're right. Liz, go get the painting so we can take a look."

"Too late, Nick," she said putting down her glass and grinning at him. "I'm afraid I sent it to Williamson's for a new frame. It'll probably be there for a long time. You know how busy they are." Liz pressed her lips tightly together as if to keep a laugh from escaping.

"How about I give them a call tomorrow, see if I can stop by and look at it there? Aren't they just across from the art museum on Second?" I asked.

"I don't see what difference it makes," Liz snapped. "So what if Julia painted a picture of this woman? We still don't know who she is." Liz started biting her bottom lip, looking from me to Nick and back again.

"You're right. I'm just curious is all." I smiled.

"I really do have to run. Let me know what happens with the painting," Nick said, as he walked toward the staircase.

I grabbed my raincoat from the back of the chair and moved toward the front hall. "I will, and I should go, too. My poor dog's been home alone too long." Nick disappeared up the stairs while Liz walked automatically to the door and held it open for me.

Nicole sat snuggled up on the couch with Pooch when I walked into my living room a half hour later. The dog jumped off the sofa and stretched in my direction, her tail expressing joy at my arrival, though her eyes looked sleepy.

"Hey, Nicole, what's up? Did you need a little break from Mommy Dearest?"

"You have no idea. The woman is psycho! She acts like I'm sixteen. 'Nicole, when are you going to get a real job? Why can't you find a nice young man to date, one with prospects? Turn down that music.' Christ, I'm twenty years old! Okay, I'm still living with my mom, but not for long. How about I move in with you and Pooch?"

"And have your mother over here all the time? Forget it!" We laughed.

"What's that?" she asked, following behind as I carried the wrecked canvas into the other room.

"Modern art. Although the slashing was not intended as a statement by the artist." I unfolded the canvas on the dining room table, fitting the pieces together to get a better look at the face.

"What do you think, Nicole? Is this the same face?" I put a copy of Sylvia Carter's sketch next to the painting.

"It sure looks like it to me. What happened to it? Someone doesn't like this woman very much."

23

Nicole took off, leaving me with only Pooch for company and a refrigerator almost as empty as my stomach. I scrambled up a couple of eggs and buttered some toast for dinner, then flipped through my mail. Amidst the solicitations for credit cards and bills, the unmistakable "save the date for our wedding" card glared at me. Jeanine from work had finally decided to make it official with Dan. They were planning a New Year's Eve wedding—very romantic. I hadn't been to a wedding in a while and I wondered if I could pull it off without wallowing in self-pity.

Images of my own wedding ran through my head; indelible, apparently, since I'd long since packed away all of the photos—reminders I didn't need. The beautiful Discovery Park bluff, how unseasonably hot it was that September, the Shakespeare sonnet Ben read to me, his eyes full of love and happiness. I felt the familiar sting of tears and knew I couldn't do it yet. I'd have to tell Jeanine I was planning to be out of town on New Year's: skiing in Colorado or sunning in Hawaii; I'd think of a plausible excuse. I usually did.

I dropped the card into the recycle and picked up my notebook on the Comstock investigation, trying to refocus. After rereading my last entry on Sylvia Carter, I scribbled, "Julia/Sylvia/Liz connection?" and added the details of my interactions with Liz and Nick tonight, trying to make some sense of it all.

I scanned Julia's most recent journal, including the end of May and early June, searching for any entries about Victor Lloyd's workshops. I discovered a note she made after Liz attended a workshop with her.

Terrible night with Liz. At dinner she drank too much AND flirted with the bartender. Insisted on going with me to Victor's workshop. Bad idea. Says Comvitek is having financial trouble and Warren would want me to lend Nick enough to get him over this crunch. I don't know. I think the church needs the money more than Comvitek.

I wasn't surprised that Liz was hitting up Julia for money. But it must have been tough for Julia to turn her down. Something bothered me about this scenario, something I couldn't put my finger on. After an hour, I came up with nothing more interesting so I threw in the towel and headed for bed. Often I did my best thinking while asleep.

Tom Hill called me at work the next morning. He had a lead on someone, a former cult member who'd known Nancy and was willing to talk about her. He'd set up a meeting with her for the following day in Portland.

"Who is this woman?" I asked. "Does she know where Nancy is, Tom?" The lump in my throat made it difficult for me to come out with the other questions stuck in my head.

"Her name is Hanifah Griffin. She saw Nancy about two years ago and got a card from her last summer. It sounded like things were going well for her."

"Okay, good. Will you call me after you meet with this woman? As soon as you have any news at all?"

"Will do."

I spent the rest of the workday trying to focus on the details of my real job while the Comstock investigation, Victor Lloyd, and my sister continued to intrude. My mind wandered back to my last conversation with Nancy. Those angry words I hurled at her, the words I'd spent years wishing I could take back. They were vivid, brutal, the memory as intense as if it happened yesterday.

I had tracked her to Maupin, Oregon, where the cult had bought some land—an old ranch. She seemed happy to see me at first, or maybe just happy—kind of blissed out. I accused her of being high. Nancy laughed at my suggestion, told me The Circle C Ranch was a totally drug-free community. They were committed to remain that way. That was why security had asked permission to search my bag when I arrived. No, she explained, she wasn't stoned; she had just finished her "dynamic meditation" for the day. It always left her feeling joyful. She tried explaining the technique to me, but it sounded like hyperventilating until you felt lightheaded and giddy. Then you were supposed to yell out whatever came into your head. It struck me as a weird form of therapy—oxygen deprivation masquerading as enlightenment.

I remembered how the change in Nancy's appearance had shocked me at the time. Solid and athletic as a young woman, she now weighed little more than a hundred pounds. She had chopped off most of her hair and wore an orange robe with a picture of the cult's favorite guru on a chain around her neck. She seemed agitated and laughed at almost everything I said. Finally, I begged her to come home with me. She shook her head sadly.

"This *is* home, Ann. It's the most supportive community I've ever known. Circle C is a refuge from helplessness and obscurity. We all think alike here. We're simply not interested in the outside world—a world gone crazy. Just look around, can't you see how we're getting stronger every day?" She gestured at our surroundings and smiled broadly at me. "You'll see. Stay for a while and learn about us."

I told her I learned all I needed to know from the media coverage. She called it "paranoid propaganda" and urged me to judge for myself. Finally, we argued about how she'd given all her money to the commune. Money meant nothing, she said. The community would always take care of her. My anger boiled over then. I called her an idiot for giving away half a lifetime of our parents' hard-earned money to some charismatic asshole who thought he was God. I told her I couldn't stand to hear any more. I couldn't even stand to look at her. And then, the words that came back to me so often, "You are *not* my sister."

At four thirty, I decided to call it a day, a fairly nonproductive day, in fact. I rounded up my notes and shoved them into my bag with the good intention of working over the weekend. I stared at my copy of the Sylvia Carter sketch for a while, then slid that in along with the rest of it, thinking about the journal entry I'd read last night, about how Liz Villardi had gone to one of Victor's workshops with Julia. Rather than heading straight home, I decided to stop off at the church to see whether Victor had any luck with the sketch, whether he remembered anything about Liz Villardi.

By the time I got to West Seattle it was after five and the church was closed, the front door locked. I should have called ahead. I knocked a few times, then called Victor's direct line. As always, he answered on the first ring and said he'd be right out. I took a deep breath and waited.

A few minutes later the door opened and Victor smiled in that disarming way he had. "I'm glad you caught me. I just came by to pick up some things for a workshop this weekend."

I looked around the entryway. "I don't see that sketch I gave you. Weren't you going to post it?"

"Yeah, well, Bob wasn't so keen on that idea. But I have Rose showing it around some. Come on back."

I followed Victor down the quiet hall.

"Where is everyone? Do they all hit the door at exactly five o'clock?"

He laughed. "We have odd hours around here. No one actually works nine to five."

Victor's office reminded me of a more masculine version of the therapist's I'd spent some time in years ago: comfortably neutral with soft leather overstuffed furniture. A substantial old desk piled with books and papers took up the far end of the room and the wall of bookshelves behind gave it a serious, almost academic feel.

I shrugged out of my jacket and draped it over the back of the sofa. Victor's eyes swept over me but his expression remained neutral. Either he liked what he saw and was keeping it to himself, or I had succeeded even more than I'd hoped in choosing completely non-provocative business attire. I returned his gaze and wondered what he'd been doing before he stopped by. His slightly damp hair gave him a just-out-of-the-shower appearance and he smelled clean and delicious, like hot sun on freshly cut grass, with a hint of spice. He hadn't shaved and I liked the five o'clock shadow look he had going—very sexy. I sat down on the sofa and he plopped into the facing chair and stretched his long legs out in front of him.

"Did you come all the way over here to ask me about the sketches?"

"That and I also wanted to ask you about Liz Villardi."

"Who?"

"Liz Villardi, wife of Nick Villardi, Warren Comstock's business partner."

"Liz Villardi." He shook his head. "What can I possibly tell you about a woman I've never met?"

"Apparently she came to one of your workshops with Julia and I hoped you might remember her or anything about that particular night."

He sighed. "When was this?"

"Last June."

Victor stared over my head for a while, concentrating. "Sorry, I got nothin'. What does she look like?"

"She's blonde, striking, kind of severe." I searched my brain for other adjectives to capture Liz. "Rich. Bitchy," I said.

Victor laughed. "I see. Well, I can't be sure. I see a lot of women in my workshops. I don't remember Julia ever introducing me to anyone, or bringing a friend with her."

"This woman would be hard to forget."

He shook his head. "Sorry. Is it important?"

"I don't know." I shrugged. "Maybe not." Something held me back. I'd come all this way and yet I wasn't ready to confide in him. I decided not to tell him about the damaged painting or Julia's journal entry.

"Anything else you want to talk about?" he asked.

"I guess not. But thanks."

I stood up to go, grabbed my coat, and looked past Victor to the bookshelves. A framed photo caught my eye, two guys in baseball uniforms. I crossed the room and picked it up.

"Oh my God! Is this you with Edgar Martinez?"

"Yeah," he said.

"Just 'yeah'? Want to tell me how you happened to have your picture taken with one of the all-time great players?"

"I used to play a little, pitched, until I blew out my arm. I thought I mentioned it."

"You said you played in college. But you pitched? Like, in the majors?"

"No, no, never got there. Just Triple-A."

"Just Triple-A!" I gushed, "That's amazing. And you played with Edgar! That must have been Calgary, right?" I knew I sounded like a baseball groupie but I couldn't help it. I'd never gotten close to a real baseball player except for the time I got some Mariners' autographs through the fence while at spring training with Ben. "I'd love to hear about it."

He laughed. "Sure. I'll tell you all about Edgar and me, but not here. Baseball stories go much better with beer. And I know a great place nearby. What do you say?"

We drove the few minutes to Alki Beach Bistro without any real conversation, except Victor giving me driving directions while I tried to reimagine him as a former baseball player. Certain things fit: his relaxed gait, large hands, quiet intensity. But I couldn't reconcile the two. There is nothing more down-to-earth than baseball and nothing more out there than conversing with the dead. I remembered the story he told me about his friend, the pitcher who died. As I pulled into a parking place around the corner from the restaurant, I gave up trying to analyze it all and decided to simply enjoy myself.

We got out of the car and I turned up my collar against the stiff breeze blowing off the Sound and quickened my pace to keep up with Victor's long stride. I'd never been to Alki at this time of year and was struck by how few folks were out and about on a raw October night. In the summer this place was a scene, Seattleites of all ages arriving via car, bike, roller blades, and water taxi to hang out at the public beach and admire West Seattle's version of the Statue of Liberty.

We pushed our way into the small bistro jammed with happy hour revelers and I headed for the bar with Victor following behind. Squeezing myself into a small space, I tried without any luck to get the bartender's attention so I gave up and looked for Victor to help. He was no longer behind me. I searched the crowd and spotted him talking to a couple at one of the tables. They got up to leave and he gleefully waved me over.

"Hey, how'd you do that?"

"I lead a charmed life." He grinned. "Actually, I recognized them from the church. They were just leaving."

We looked over the menu and I ordered a Mirror Pond. Victor opted for an ESB and suggested we share some mussels steamed in white wine and garlic. I nodded, handed the waitress my menu, and began my baseball interrogation.

"So, what's Edgar really like? Is he the nice guy everyone says he is?"

He laughed. "Edgar is a great guy. Even back in Triple-A everybody loved him; he was a real force in the clubhouse." Victor offered several stories about Edgar as a humble and sincere guy and mentor to the younger Latino players just coming up.

"When Edgar first came up from Chattanooga he was skinny and optimistic—eager. The coaches were impressed with his catching ability and his arm but no one talked about his hitting—he hit under 200 back then. By the time he made it to the majors he had put on twenty-five pounds of solid muscle and raised his batting average to over 300."

"Steroids?"

"Never! Not Edgar." He shook his head. "I never saw a player work harder at improving his game. He always said he got his work ethic from his grandparents who raised him in Puerto Rico. When he got his first major league contract, I heard a reporter ask him how he planned to spend the money. He said first he would buy some medicine for his grandma who had been very sick."

I was glad to know the PR was right on with Edgar. When I asked Victor about the best game he'd ever pitched, he smiled broadly and his eyes lit up.

"No-hitter through the eighth. I was throwing a ninety-mile-an-hour fastball and couldn't miss. Two outs against the heart of the batting order. Catcher called a slider inside. I left it over the plate. Guy got a hold of that pitch and ripped it into left. Stand-up double. Damn. Still pisses me off! Should've stayed with the heat." Victor laughed at himself and shrugged. "We did win. 1-0. Whatever. Can't go back."

Victor was quiet for a while so I switched the subject, asked him about his family. I learned that he grew up in Northern California, that his parents were "down-to-earth folks." His dad was a pharmacist and his mom worked part-time for a nonprofit. He had one sibling—an older brother who worked in Los Angeles in television. He'd been trying to get Victor to sign on to a psychic network.

"Why not do it?" I asked.

"No way. I'm not at all interested in television—too much hype.

Frankly, my brother and I couldn't be more different."

"I know what you mean. It's the same way with me and my sister, Nancy." I stopped abruptly, hoping he'd let it go, wouldn't mention the workshop or the spirit connected to Nancy.

He looked at me quizzically at first, then closer, in that way he had that made me think he could see into my soul.

"You're not reading my mind, are you?" I asked nervously.

"No, no, there's a difference between clairvoyance and what I do. But hey, I wish I *could* read your mind, then I'd know how to answer those questions you've been afraid to ask me." He searched my face, then settled back in his chair. "Want to tell me about Nancy?"

I told him I had a sister but that, like his situation with his brother, we were very different.

"Does she live in Seattle?"

"No. I don't know where she is right now."

Victor nodded but remained quiet, thoughtful. A moment later he stood up and excused himself.

"What's wrong?" I asked, recognizing the faraway look he got on his face when he was about to move into psychic medium mode.

He shook his head. "I'll be right back."

Victor headed to the bar and I watched him walk away while I played with my cocktail napkin and cursed myself for mentioning Nancy. I'd been having such a great time. I liked Victor the former baseball player so much more than Victor the psychic medium. He'd just reminded me they were the same. After a few minutes he returned with a glass of water, sat down and smiled at me, his face back to normal.

"You okay?" I asked.

"Sure."

Suddenly tongue-tied, we sipped our beers and pretended not to notice the large gray elephant that had joined us at the table. I knew Victor thought he had some message for me from the spirit world, something about Nancy, but I didn't want to hear it, couldn't make the leap. I felt his sincerity and his attraction but I was wary of it. Scared of the emotions that would surface. I would find out about Nancy in my own way. From Tom Hill, not Victor Lloyd.

"I know you're afraid, Ann."

"What? I—"

"You like to be in control, you're highly rational, you need *proof* before you would ever believe in something as irrational as messages from the other side."

"But you *can't* prove it. That's just it."

"No, but what if I could show you how it works in a setting you control?"

He had my attention. "Go on."

"You find someone totally unknown to me, a friend of yours, and that person works with me in a private reading. That way you know that I haven't picked up any information about your friend beforehand."

"I thought you said you couldn't just turn it on."

"Right. And sometimes I can't turn it off either." he said, staring straight into my face. I glanced down at my beer, took a sip.

Looking up, I asked, "Why would you do this? What's in it for you?"

"It has more to do with you. I'd like to help you and you won't let me. Maybe a reading of a close friend will help convince you."

"No. I don't think so."

"I think it's important, Ann."

I finished off my beer and set the glass in front of me. "Okay, I'll think about it. I will."

"Fair enough. Want another?"

"No, I'd better go. But thanks. Next time I want to hear more baseball stories. And how you made the switch from baseball to psychic medium."

"Ah, next time," he said with an amused smile and a raised

eyebrow. "You'll call me then?"

"I will."

"Good. I'll walk you to your car."

We hit the sidewalk and headed down the street with the icy wind in our faces.

"Not exactly the night for a stroll on the beach."

"No kidding."

"I live over there, by the way." Victor gestured to a row of apartments past the public beach area on the water side.

"Really?" I wondered if it was a veiled invitation as I squinted towards the low-rise buildings. A gust of wind blew my jacket open and I stopped to zip it up.

"Hey, you're freezing," Victor put his arm around me and briskly rubbed my upper arm. Shocked by his touch, his warmth, I pulled away, hugged myself against the cold and kept walking.

"Here's my car." I unlocked the door, turned back to say goodbye. "Thanks for the beer."

"Sure." Victor opened the car door for me and I got in. He closed the door, then leaned down and said something I couldn't hear through the window. I touched the button to open it.

"Think about what I said. Okay?"

I smiled up at him. "Okay."

He continued to hold me with his eyes. "Call me," he said.

Heart pounding, I nodded and closed the window. Victor smiled, stood up, tapped the car's roof, and headed back toward the beach.

24

I woke up Saturday morning with the sun shining through my window and a hyperactive retriever. The dog ran a couple laps around the front yard and into the living room. She lapped that room too, then jumped onto the sofa, tail wagging and a smile on her furry face—a clear case of cabin fever after a rainy week. And yes, Pooch definitely smiles.

"Want to go out?" I laughed at her enthusiasm for the sunshine. It mirrored my own. "Discovery Park?" When I pulled out my hiking boots from the front hall closet she gave me her most joyous bark, the one that always ends with a howl. The dog clearly understands the correlation between footwear and outdoor activity.

Discovery is the largest park in Seattle, over five hundred acres of rolling hills, wooded trails, tidal beaches, and sand dunes—and all only ten minutes from downtown. What began as Fort Lawton, a chronically underused military base, is now a unique area for hiking, beachcombing, family fun, and, of course, weddings. Jeanine's announcement and the memories it triggered probably drew me but I wasn't planning on getting too close to the Daybreak Star Cultural Center where my wedding took place. Instead, Pooch and I would keep to the three-mile loop trail around the park's perimeter.

I pulled into the northeast parking lot and let Pooch out of the backseat. She ran to the visitor's center and slurped water from the doggie bowl set on the ground next to it. While I filled up my water bottle from the drinking fountain, Pooch bounded to the trailhead and sat waiting for me. She knew the drill. We hiked through the woods for about a half-mile to where the trail passes the military cemetery. I looked at the rows and rows of white grave markers on the hill, each one representing a young life cut short. Passing this place always twisted my gut—since Ben's death I'd avoided it. I didn't need a grave to remind me that Ben is gone. He is everywhere and nowhere. I only have to feel the wind on my face to remember the day we scattered his ashes on Puget Sound, how the wind blew the ashes back at me, into my face, how I tasted them. I felt the tears welling up and stopped to blow my nose. Pooch whimpered and pulled at her leash.

"You're right, Pooch. We need to keep moving."

I thought about Victor's description of "the other side," a place where these young soldiers might exist in some way without pain, where Ben might exist. But it seemed as unlikely as the place I'd heard about in my Lutheran elementary school: filled with love and angels playing harps. And that place had a pretty strict entry fee: not everyone was invited. No thanks. No wonder Victor's idea was so appealing—there were no strings attached. I considered how dealing with death was part of his everyday life, how he'd invited me to observe it, how it might help me find Nancy. As the path ascended up and away from the cemetery and out of the trees, I couldn't wait to get to my favorite spot on the bluff overlooking the Sound and clear my head.

Pooch tugged impatiently at her lead, hurrying me along and threatening to pull my arm out of its socket. I dropped the leash and let her run ahead to the sand dunes where she romped with abandon around a young family playing in the sand. I plopped down to catch my breath and watched the toddler clap his hands and laugh, squealing, "Doggy run! Doggy run!"

"Could my son pet your dog?" the dad asked. "He loves dogs, but we're not ready for one of our own." I smiled at the man's very pregnant wife.

"Sure." I told Pooch to sit and stay while the boy vigorously patted her head.

"Gentle, Max." The dad said, demonstrating by softly stroking Pooch between the ears.

"She can shake," I said and Pooch presented her paw. The boy giggled but backed away. The dad thanked me and I stood, grabbed Pooch's leash, and walked across the meadow where a couple of teenagers were playing catch. It reminded me of Victor's Triple-A Calgary experience, which made me smile. No doubt the man was attractive, maybe even a catch, if it weren't for his annoying day job, which he clearly had a hard time leaving at the office. I thought about his suggestion of a blind psychic reading and wondered whom I could persuade to help me out with that, if I decided to do it. By the time we got to the parking lot, I'd convinced myself that I had nothing to lose by giving it a shot. If it went well, if I thought Victor might tell me something about Nancy, I could go for it; if not, I might get some good material for a Halloween article instead.

I wracked my brain to think of someone I knew who would be willing to be a guinea pig for Victor Lloyd. A man would be better than a woman. Victor had way too much sexual energy going with most women, including me. As I pulled out of the parking lot and headed home, the light bulb went on. Mike Porter would be perfect. I could even stop in on my former neighbors on my way home.

It amused me to think of Mike Porter and Victor Lloyd together. Mike was one of the nicest people you'd ever meet: married with two young boys, Little League baseball coach, the neighbor I could always call on to help with a leaky faucet or car problem. If Mike couldn't fix it, he knew who could and for the best price. Professionally, Mike divided his time between holding together the family business after his dad died— something to do with large machinery—and singing in the Seattle Opera chorus. Toni has her own computer graphics business and is one of my favorite people—no-nonsense, slightly outrageous, and very active in local liberal politics. Mike would probably find the prospect of a psychic reading with Victor Lloyd amusing and bring a healthy dose of skepticism to the process. In exchange for spending an hour or so with Victor, I'd offer to cook dinner for them. Cooking was not Toni's forte so dinners around their house were usually grilled on the barbeque by Mike or came home in those little white boxes.

As I turned onto the quaint winding street on top of Queen Anne Hill, fond memories of my time in this neighborhood came flooding back to me. Old folks and young children lived here, couples and singles and extended families, just the kind of mixed bag that keeps a neighborhood vital. The houses were owned by entrepreneurs—computer businesses operated out of two of the basements—and young professionals: one dentist, a pharmacist, and a couple of lawyers. The woman who had lived next door to me owned a fledgling bakery, now quite well-known. I saw her on television a few weeks ago baking with a famous international chef. The neighbors still invited me to their annual summer picnic and let me know when a house went on the market. Too bad I couldn't afford to buy one: two-bedroom bungalows in Queen Anne now sold for around three quarters of a million dollars—the Californication of Seattle some people called it.

I rang the bell and heard the Porters' two Scotties yipping like crazy and Toni hushing them on her way to the door. When Toni spotted Pooch in the car she insisted I put the dog in the backyard with Teddy and Toby, guaranteeing that Pooch would enjoy the visit as much as I would. Once the dogs were settled Mike joined us and we got caught up on each other's lives: the latest opera Mike was learning, Toni's new clients, how the boys were faring in school and in sports, and my current project at the *Times*. As a Little League coach, Mike enthusiastically endorsed the baseball/math connection. "It might even get David interested," he said.

"Hey, how's that church article you're working on?" Mike asked, explaining to Toni that I had begged off having a beer with him after the opera the other night, saying I had to go to church the next morning.

"What? You going to church? No way!" Toni laughed.

I gave them an abbreviated version of my involvement with Nirmala and then got to the point of my visit.

"So, actually, I'm hoping you might be willing to help me out, Mike. I want to have someone I trust, someone who Victor Lloyd doesn't know, take part in a regular psychic reading." Mike's eyes widened so I kept talking before he could object. "I'm trying to figure out what caused Julia Comstock's death and it would help to know how a psychic experience might affect someone as fragile as Julia was at the time." I left out my personal interest in Victor's talent.

"Ha!" Mike slapped his knee and smiled. "Sure, I'll do it. I couldn't be more skeptical, although Toni might be even better. What do you think?" I explained that Victor had a certain effect on women and while I doubted that Toni would be enamored with him, I just wanted to see him work with a man for a change. Mike gave me his schedule for the next week and I jotted it down in my notebook. I told him I'd call him the next day to set it up. As I got up to leave, the door opened and their two boys burst into the living room. Mike went to the door to wave at tonight's soccer carpool driver and asked the boys how practice had gone.

The boys grunted noncommittally, hung their coats on the hooks in the front hall, threw their shoes into a heap, and said they were starving.

"All right, all right, go see what's in the fridge but say hello to Ann first, you guys. Where are your manners?" The boys paused for a quick hello, then charged past me into the kitchen.

"I was meant to be the mother of quiet girls, how did I end up with these big boys who are always making noise and eating me out of house and home?" Toni shook her head. "It gets worse every day."

We laughed and I collected Pooch from the yard, promising to have them all over for dinner after the Victor Lloyd reading.

When I called Victor later that afternoon he was happy to hear from me and said he could make some time available for the reading the following night.

"Does that work for you?"

I checked the calendar on my phone and read, *Jazz alley, Jack @ 7:30*. "I'll need to rearrange a few things, check with my friend, and get back to you," I said, vaguely noticing how quickly I'd ditched Jack for Victor.

"One more thing, Ann." He paused. "I ran into Rose earlier this afternoon at the church."

"Did she have some luck with the sketches?"

"It's not about the sketches. I just thought you'd like to know that she's pretty upset with you right now."

"Because I lied to her."

"Yeah. She's hurt that you weren't up front with her about investigating Julia's death. You might consider going over there, talking to her in person."

"I do feel bad about lying to Rose. She's been great to me." I filled the void in the conversation by silently beating myself up about it.

"Don't worry too much. Rose will forgive you. Forgiveness is part of her belief system. But you'll have to ask for it."

We hung up and I thought about his comment for a moment—and the concept of forgiveness—then tried to shake it while I called Mike. He was ready; said he couldn't wait to "beat this guy at his own game."

I had no response to that. "Pick you up at seven?" I asked. "We can drive to West Seattle together." Then I called Jack, left a brief and apologetic voicemail, saying a work thing had come up. I'd talk to him when he got back from Houston.

25

I drove to the top of Queen Anne Hill to pick up Mike just before seven. Waiting outside while he put the dogs into their run, I looked up into the sky. The moon, high and almost full, shone brightly. A few stars blinked on. The temperature had dropped ten degrees since yesterday but I didn't mind. Give me dry and cold over wet and miserable any time.

During the twenty-minute drive to West Seattle, Mike asked me how I wanted him to play it with Victor Lloyd.

"Just be yourself, Mike. And don't give him anything to work with. I mean, don't give him even the slightest hint about your personality, your work, your marriage, your family, your past, or your goals. Answer 'yes' or 'no,' and when he asks you something, like, 'I'm getting a name that starts with a "b" sound,' don't fill anything in for him. Just nod or shrug, unless he comes up with a complete name, then go from there."

"Okay, I see. So if he says, 'I'm getting signals from your cousin, it sounds like "b,"' I shouldn't say, 'I don't have a cousin whose name begins with a "b" sound, but there is my cousin Matt whom I always refer to as that bum?'"

I laughed. "You got it. See, it'll be easy. He knows nothing about you and so he can't fake anything unless you let him."

We pulled up to the church at 7:25. The front foyer was empty but well-lit. A whiteboard set up on an easel described the night's events: "7:00, Meeting Hall, J. Robert Waters speaks on the great Oneness of existence, readings from the Upanishads and New Testament. 7:30, Room 136, V. Lloyd, private reading." Underneath the second listing Lloyd had written, "Ann, Room 136 is down the hall, first door on the left. Come on in!"

As we passed the meeting hall door, I opened it tentatively and saw Reverend Waters at the front of the room holding forth while a packed house of listeners gave him their rapt attention. It sounded more like a lecture than a meditation session and, thankfully, the noxious odor of incense was absent.

Mike touched my arm. "Come on, let's do it."

The sounds of the lecture faded as Mike and I walked down the hall to room 136. Victor sat in an overstuffed chair absorbed in a book he was reading as I tapped on the open door to signal our presence. He stood, smiled broadly, and reached for my hand while placing his left palm on my shoulder, drawing me closer—not quite a hug.

"Ann, come in! Good to see you and your friend." Victor turned to Mike and they shook hands.

"I'm Mike Porter. Nice to meet you."

Unlike Victor's office, this room lacked all personality and felt a bit like a conference room in a hotel or real estate office. The beige walls were bare except for a large photograph of a waterfall. Subtle New Age touches broke the monotony: ivory pillar candles of varying heights were displayed together on a glass tray filled with white sand and seashells and placed on the coffee table, plush velvet sage-colored pillows were tossed onto the grouping of upholstered chairs clustered around it, a small fountain burbled in the corner. I spotted a box of CDs next to a small stereo system against the wall and hoped Victor wasn't into playing New Age music during these sessions.

Victor gestured to the chairs and we all three sat down facing each other. He offered us water or tea, filled our requests, and then settled back in his chair. After the obligatory discussion of Seattle weather, Victor explained to Mike how he expected the session to go.

"First off, I don't want you to tell me anything about yourself. Just answer yes or no. My job is to fill in the details. That will happen later, as I get to know you and any of your spirit guides who show up."

Mike looked a bit nervous at first but Victor's straightforward manner and self-confidence began working its magic on him.

"I assume Ann has filled you in a little bit about how I work."

Mike nodded.

"Basically, I communicate with spirit guides, or as some people like to picture them, angels without the wings. Everyone has them, these guides, even though most folks never meet them. Spirit guides are souls who occupy the light around us to help us through our lives."

"Uh-huh," Mike said with a smirk, "Sort of like Clarence in *It's a Wonderful Life?*"

"Yes, you can think of it like that if it helps you, Mike." His serious response to Mike's flip comment charged the air somehow, and he went on.

"We know that our lives here on earth are temporary. It's what happens after death that is uncertain. Over the years, the spirits have given me a glimpse into their world, shown me that after death we are liberated, free in the comfort of light and love."

I noticed the quality of Victor's voice, how it changed when he explained his work and his belief system. I felt calmer as he talked, almost hypnotized by his serene and soothing manner. A few moments passed. Victor's voice, the rhythm of it, became a pleasant humming in my ears, the words blurring together. I glanced at Mike and saw him relaxing as well. He had uncrossed his legs and arms and tilted his head to one side as if to hear Victor more clearly. Mike's eyes focused on Victor's face. He occasionally nodded, showing he understood. After a brief pause, the next words out of Victor's mouth startled both of us.

"Two of your guides are here in the room with us, Mike: your grandmother and your father. One of them, your maternal grandmother, I think, is telling me that you are quite the skeptic and that you will need very clear proof that she is here."

Mike and I exchanged a brief glance.

"She is giving me a long list of names. They are people to the side of you, that usually means cousins or, no, these are slightly above, maybe aunts and uncles: Donna, Sam, Kathy, George, and another one that sounds odd like Blitz or something. Is that right?"

Mike inhaled sharply and looked over at me.

"Ann, is this some kind of joke? You gave him the names of my relatives?"

"No, of course not. Do I know the names of your relatives? Well, I recognize the crazy one you sometimes talk about, Donna, but, do you have an aunt named Blitz?"

I chuckled nervously while Victor waited patiently looking from Mike to me, his focus clearly internal, a look of concentration on his face.

"Yes, those are all names of my mother's siblings, my maternal grandmother's children," Mike said to Victor. "But not Blitz. That's my Uncle Samuel—for some reason everyone called him Fritz."

"Don't fill in the missing details, Mike. I confused that last name." Victor went on, explaining to Mike the same things he had told me the other day about how he receives information from the spirit world: through symbols, verbal cues—often unclear sounds, like a radio with static—and sometimes physical sensations, pain in a part of his body.

"Emotions, though, come through just the same, as feelings. Right now your grandma, Anna, is it? She's sending some happy feelings to me, congratulating you on some new business venture, I think. Something to do with a vehicle."

Mike looked over at me for further explanation. I shook my head.

"I'm getting a picture of white flowers being scattered around a truck. But I don't think it has to do with travel, it feels more like business, there's an abundance involved, possibly money."

Mike was shaking his head. "Ann, did I tell you about the dump truck I bought, as a little side business?"

"No, Mike, I hadn't heard about that." It would have been funny if Mike hadn't been so obviously blindsided. I knew there was no way Victor could know this stuff, and yet, he did.

"I didn't think so, I haven't even told Toni about it yet. I figure she won't be too excited about it. But I got a great deal, and I'm hooking up with a nursery in Kent, delivering compost and dirt."

"Your grandma thinks it's a great new venture," Lloyd said, smiling at Mike. Then, "Mike, there's another guide here, your father."

Mike stiffened and sat rigid in his chair. "I'm not sure I want to hear from this one. Can we skip it?"

I knew what a bastard Mike's dad had been most of his life. How, as an old-school authoritarian, he ruled the family and the family business with an iron fist. He despised Mike's singing career, sabotaged it as often as he could.

I looked from Mike back to Victor. His eyes were filled with emotion, concern.

"Your dad is saying how sorry he is for the pain he caused you and your mom. And he wants you to know how proud he has always been of you." Victor's eyes were shining now. "He's showing me a room full of people, an audience, applauding. I'm feeling it's you they're watching. I'm getting music, singing. Are you a musician, Mike?"

Mike sat back in his chair shaking his head and pressing his lips together tightly. I thought he might burst into tears or an angry rage at any moment. He looked from me to Lloyd and said, "Okay, okay, I really don't want to continue this. It's too much, coming in here and hearing this from a total stranger. I don't know how you do it, but it's too much. Ann, I think we should go now."

He stood up and Victor and I did the same.

"Wait, Mike," Victor said quietly. "Don't leave yet. Please sit down. Let's talk a while longer. I understand how bizarre this is. It's hard enough for people who come here hoping to hear from their loved ones, believing it's possible. It's always emotional. Over the years I've learned that it can be quite a shock to the uninitiated. I'm sorry you were unprepared." Victor looked at me as if reading the astonishment I felt, before he went on.

"Ann, I offered this blind reading tonight because I wanted you to understand the integrity of my work. I never imagined how difficult it would be for Mike. I'm sorry." His eyes reflected his sincerity.

Mike sat down and I followed his lead again. "I understand. Or, well, I don't really understand but I appreciate what you're saying."

"Often when someone dies with unfinished business, as I suspect happened with Mike and his dad, that's when the spirits are most adamant about getting their message across. They can be quite desperate. Let me tell you about my strangest experience with a resolute spirit."

Victor launched into a story about his experience with a spirit so determined that it came through to him while reading a woman only vaguely connected to the spirit's family. According to Victor, it seemed as if the spirit knew his own family would never contact a psychic medium and this was the only way to get through. So Victor urged his client to call her acquaintance and deliver the message, which she did. After the initial shock, the woman herself came to see Lloyd, greatly comforted to hear from her son who had died as a teenager in a car accident.

While Victor's story didn't exactly help Mike or me understand what had just happened, it succeeded in shifting the focus from Mike's painful relationship with his dead father to more neutral ground. Sensing we had reached a good stopping point for our session, I stood, thanked Victor, and told him I'd be in touch. Mike and I walked back to the car in silence.

"Jesus, Ann, what the hell happened back there?" Mike asked as soon as he got into the passenger seat. I was wondering the same thing as I noticed a silver Lexus SUV pull out from in front of the church. I couldn't get a good look at the license plate number, so I put the car in gear and sped after it, telling Mike, "Hold that thought."

I wove through the traffic on Fauntleroy Way, trying to catch up with the silver Lexus. I lost sight of it pretty quickly when a car cut me off and turned left onto a side street.

"Damn," I muttered under my breath.

"What was that all about?" Mike asked. "Now that you're an investigative reporter, you're into car chases?"

"Sorry, Mike, it's a long story. Let's get back to what happened back there with Victor Lloyd."

"Whoa, that was weird. At first I thought it was a joke—that you'd told this guy some things just to pull my chain. But I knew you wanted to nail him, so it didn't make sense. Then the stuff about the dump truck—wow! And my dad, I can't even go there. What the hell?"

Mike's confusion mixed with my own and hung heavy around us. I opened the car window a crack, hoping that clearing the air might clear my head, that together we could make sense of this.

"There must be some explanation, but I'll be damned if I can find it right now, Mike."

We drove the rest of the way without much conversation, caught up in our own thoughts. As I pulled in front of Mike's house, he invited me in. "I can't wait to talk to Toni about all this. Why don't you come in? You could have a beer—I know I could use one. Besides, Toni will never believe what I'm going to tell her happened tonight."

I declined, explaining that I needed some time to work this through myself. "Tell Toni to call me. I'd love to hear what she has to say."

I turned on the radio and listened to jazz as I drove north, a soothing backdrop for the chaos in my head. *How does Victor know those things about Mike? Does he know something about Nancy?* Nancy! I'd forgotten about Tom Hill's interview with Nancy's friend. While stopped at a red light, I dug around in my purse, pulled out my phone, and turned it on. One missed call. I pressed the "retrieve messages" button and heard Tom's voice.

"Ann, it's Tom. I've got some information for you about Nancy. Nothing earth-shattering. Here's the deal: the last time Hanifah saw Nancy, she had a line on a job teaching yoga at a health spa in Mexico. Thought she might move there. I've got some other leads to follow up. I'll get back to you."

Teaching yoga at a spa? The yoga sounded plausible but not the spa part. I couldn't imagine my anti-establishment sister involved with any corporate money-making venture. She'd railed against capitalistic corporate greed as a teenager. Money meant nothing to her, she'd said, and she'd meant it, too, giving it all away to that cult leader. Maybe now, as she approached forty, she felt the need for some financial security. Funny how that works.

26

After work the next day I called Caroline to bring her up to speed on what I'd learned over the past twenty-four hours and she suggested I stop by on my way home so we could talk in person. Turning off Greenwood and driving past the black expanse of the golf course toward the gatehouse reminded me how isolated the Highlands neighborhood felt at night. No wonder they needed security. It seemed the perfect environment for random acts of violence. With these cheery thoughts in my head, I smiled at the gate guy who returned it with a frown, like I'd pulled him away from his favorite TV show. Roger didn't work the evening shift. Bernie (according to his name tag) let me pass.

Caroline met me at the door and we walked back to the living room, an oxymoronic tag for the huge formal space I hadn't entered on my previous visits. Caroline gestured toward one end of the room where two wing chairs flanked an imposing marble fireplace. We sat down and I felt uncomfortable until Maria came in with a welcoming smile.

"Hello, Ms. Dexter, may I get you anything?"

"Hey, Maria, thanks, but couldn't you call me Ann? You know, I've had quite the day. I'd love a glass of wine. What about you, Caroline? I'd rather not drink alone."

"Sure. I discovered some wonderful bottles of pinot noir while cleaning out the wine cellar. How does that sound?"

"Perfect." While Maria went off to get the wine, I gave Caroline the update on Julia's painting, Nick and Liz Villardi, and my experience with Victor Lloyd. She shook her head.

"You're telling me you believe in his psychic powers? Seriously? I thought you were trying to expose the scam, find out his connection with Julia's death. You sound more smitten than skeptical right now."

"No, no. I don't necessarily believe he's for real. I just wish I could explain it, is all. But what do you think about the painting?" I asked, shifting the focus away from Victor. "Why would Liz Villardi trash the painting, then lie about it? Do you think there could have been something between Julia and Nick?"

"You mean an affair? No! I had the feeling that Julia didn't like those two very much. She did her best to distance herself from them pretty early on. I can't imagine Julia and Nick having an affair. Although I have met Nick Villardi: very good looking, quite the ladies' man too, I'd say, given how he came on to me the first time we met."

I felt a slight twinge at her comment, realizing the chemistry between Nick and me was obviously nothing extraordinary. And her suggestion that I was smitten with Victor was embarrassing. But, Julia and Nick? Maybe.

"Maybe that's it. Even if Julia and Nick never had any kind of romantic relationship, maybe Liz suspected them. She is the jealous type, and there wasn't much warmth between her and her husband, I'll tell you that."

Maria came in with two crystal wine glasses, a bottle of Napa Valley pinot, and a small dish of Spanish almonds on a silver tray, which she set down on the coffee table between us. Caroline handed me a glass and picked up one for herself. She tipped it back and forth a couple of times, watching the ruby-colored liquid swirl around before she inhaled its aroma, then smiled and looked at me. "Santé, Ann," she said, raising her glass in my direction.

I lifted my glass to hers and took a sip, relishing the warmth of the wine and its immediate calming effect. I kicked off my shoes and tucked my feet under me, feeling more relaxed as I looked around the opulent room. Now that we were sitting next to the fire, the room seemed less imposing, some trick of decorating I guessed. All this wealth and comfort every day, I wondered how it would affect a person's psyche and how, if you had a taste, you'd be hard-pressed to relinquish it.

"What's happening with the lawsuit? What are your chances of getting some money?"

She shrugged.

"Nirmala's lawyers are offering me a settlement. If I drop the suit, they'll split the bequest sixty-forty. They get the sixty percent, naturally. My lawyer is stalling, waiting to see what you come up with, actually." She spoke about it so nonchalantly now, as if Julia's death were a distant memory and the money not much of an issue. But then, I figured forty percent of Julia's estate might be worth more than anything Caroline could expect to make on her own as an accountant.

"Any idea what Warren's interest in Comvitek totaled at the time of his death? You did work as an independent auditor for the company, right?" I asked, a hazy thought passing through my mind.

"Yes, but several years ago, back when dot-coms were flying high. Their net worth at the time figured right around twelve million. I imagine they took a bath like everyone else in the last few years. The lawyers are still working up the accounting of the estate. To answer your question, I don't know whether I'm likely to get forty percent of millions or thousands at this point, although this house and all the furnishings are worth probably close to six million. Of course, there's a mortgage and the estate will have other outstanding debts as well. It's quite complicated with Warren and Julia's deaths occurring within the same year. I thought you were going to talk with Richard Jarndyce, my lawyer?"

"I am. I hope to see him sometime over the next few days." I hedged, realizing I'd been so caught up with Victor Lloyd and Nancy that I'd forgotten to make this appointment.

"You think I should tell Jarndyce to settle up? That you're unlikely to find any connection between Julia's death and Victor Lloyd or Nirmala? That's pretty much how it looks at this point, unless you have something new to tell me. Any luck on the sketch or the SUV?"

"No," I replied, surprised by her resignation, and more than a little annoyed at her suggestion of my failure. "And no, you shouldn't tell your lawyer to settle just yet. There are still too many loose ends out there. I'm not ready to give it up and you shouldn't be either."

Caroline raised an eyebrow, but said nothing more as we finished our wine. Feeling suddenly weary of the whole thing, I promised to keep in touch and headed for the door.

Back home, I sorted my stack of mail while playing a halfhearted game of fetch with Pooch. Then I got sucked into an old movie on TV and wasted the rest of the night on it. As soon as I turned off the television, my thoughts returned to Victor's performance and I wondered what he might tell me about Nancy, if I would let him. The prospect no longer scared nor angered me. I had moved closer to curiosity. I decided to call him before I chickened out. I walked into the kitchen and picked up the phone. Then I looked at the clock: eleven thirty, too late to call anyone, except maybe a close relative— or a lover.

The thought startled me and I wondered if it was too late to call Jack, if he was pissed off that I'd cancelled our date. Funny he hadn't even responded to my voicemail. It was just as well. Now I wouldn't have to explain that my "work thing" involved Victor Lloyd. Jack would probably ask me why on earth I kept on with this investigation—an interesting question. I no longer believed that Victor had anything to do with Julia's death. Not really. But I needed to get to the bottom of it and, if I was honest with myself, I needed something from Victor. I thought about his interaction with Mike, his deep conviction, his sincerity, and his sensitivity. I'd never known a man so unafraid of his emotions, or so complex, so fascinating—and a baseball player too. I smiled, thinking about that and thinking I should leave these thoughts alone.

First thing Tuesday, I put in a call to Jarndyce and Maxwell. According to his assistant, Mr. Jarndyce had meetings most of the morning but would return my call before lunch. Next, I called Victor to see when we could get together, talk about the other night, possibly about Nancy. Victor sounded busy but enthusiastic, suggesting we meet right away, before I got cold feet. We settled on five thirty at the church.

I hung up the phone and stared at it. The sound of Victor's voice unnerved me, brought back the scenes I'd so neatly put away yesterday—all the impossible things he knew about Mike's relatives, his relationship with his dad, and the emotions it brought out for both of them. I wondered how Mike was feeling about it now and vowed to get in touch with him later. In the meantime, I pulled out the sketch of Sylvia Carter and the workshop rosters I'd lifted from Nirmala's files, trying to make some connection between the name and the face—anything.

I was still staring at them ten minutes later when Richard Jarndyce returned my call. Happy for the interruption, I explained my relationship with Caroline, and asked if he could spend some time talking with me about Julia's estate. Jarndyce came off as all business and formal. He said he'd checked with his client and, since she was amenable, he could see me early in the afternoon. His one o'clock conference call had just cancelled.

I ate some yogurt at my desk, heading out the door for Jarndyce and Maxwell around twelve thirty. The law firm was on Fourth Avenue, in a structure we Seattleites fondly refer to as "The Darth Vader Building," a daunting black glass box in the middle of the high-rent district, filled with established law firms, brokerage houses, and the Bank of America. I didn't want to walk that far and was too cheap to drive and pay the ten bucks or so to park in one of the uptown lots, so I hopped a bus. Buses run frequently along Third Avenue from Belltown, near the Space Needle, all the way to Safeco Field at the south end of the city.

I took a seat at the front of the bus and immediately regretted my choice. While most of the riders were business types moving through the city to appointments, a very drunk thirty-something guy sat behind the driver ranting about his plight. He needed to get to an appointment with his probation officer for a urinalysis, which he referred to as "piss in a cup." He railed on incoherently about the unfairness of the system as everyone else avoided eye contact with him but couldn't avoid his smell. Perhaps they could simply take a sample of his pants and skip the cup completely.

Relieved when the bus finally stopped at Madison Street, I hopped off and walked one block uphill to the lawyer's office. I rode the elevator with three suits and two blonde secretaries gossiping about some new employee. The doors opened into a large reception area where the supermodel who was doubling as a receptionist looked up as I approached the dark mahogany fortress of her desk. I gave her my name and sat on the formal white sofa waiting for Jarndyce's assistant to appear. Amy walked up the internal spiral staircase to meet me, pleasant and friendly, making small talk about the weather and offering me something to drink as we made our way back down the stairs and around the corner to our destination. She tapped lightly on the doorjamb and introduced me to her boss before closing the door quietly behind her.

Richard Jarndyce was in his mid-fifties, portly, fairly bald, with a round face and an incongruous large graying mustache. His eyes appeared tired but friendly and he gave me his full attention as I explained my interest in the Comstock estate and particularly the bequest to Nirmala.

"I believe Caroline has told you that we are in the process of negotiating with Nirmala's lawyers?" I nodded and he continued.

"I'm fairly pleased with their latest offer and have strongly encouraged Caroline to accept it. However, as you know, she holds the church responsible for her sister's death and, therefore, any amount of money going to Nirmala is repugnant to her. While I can appreciate her emotional investment with respect to the church, I have been in this business long enough to also appreciate just how tenacious an organization can be when it comes to the kind of money we're talking about here."

"Can you tell me how much that is, and how it breaks down? I'm particularly interested in Warren's interest in Comvitek—just a ballpark dollar figure."

"I don't have that figure locked down yet. You see, Comvitek took quite a hit just about the time of Mr. Comstock's death, when his partner began to spend large amounts of borrowed money to expand into foreign markets. Just a few months later, at the time of Julia's death, the stock was worth substantially less than when she first inherited it." He paused and waited for me to take in his comments.

"And what about the stock now? Is it still in the tank?" I asked.

"Actually, it seems to be coming back out of the tank, as you so aptly put it. Of course, Mr. Comstock had other resources—the money from those is more substantial than his interest in the corporation at this point."

"You mean he didn't put everything he had into Comvitek?"

"He couldn't. His parents had set up a trust for him and he received a prescribed amount from the trust annually. Each year he invested the maximum allowable amount into the corporation, but was prohibited from dissolving the trust until he reached the age of forty-five. Apparently his parents had an inkling that he might go through their old family money quicker than fire through an oil field, so they effectively made that impossible."

"Okay, I think I understand. Warren's estate was still worth big bucks when he died, but most of that money was inherited from his parents. Comvitek is kind of like Amazon.com in its early years, all glitz but little substance. The church is as greedy as anybody and unlikely to give up its big piece of the pie."

Jarndyce's eyes sparkled. "That's correct."

"And what about the church? What will they do with such a large chunk of change? My cynical side says they're not giving it to the poor." I sat forward in my chair and noticed an article on Jarndyce's desk, "Estate Planning for the Terminally Ill." It gave me the shivers.

"You raise a very interesting question. I have taken the liberty of investigating the church's financial structure and discovered something a bit irregular."

27

"Irregular, in what way?" I asked, noticing a look of amusement cross his face.

"As a religious organization in Washington, Nirmala has been granted tax-exempt status under 501(c)(3) of the Internal Revenue Code. However, the church is currently embroiled in a lawsuit in Idaho over a large tract of land they are developing there as a retreat and meditation center."

"Why a lawsuit?"

"In a nutshell, the state of Idaho assessed property taxes against Nirmala's development, claiming it does not fit the definition of a religious organization under Idaho State law. Nirmala refused to pay the tax and promptly filed a lawsuit against the Idaho tax assessor, claiming that the actions of the assessor violated numerous state and federal laws, including the First and Fourteenth Amendments of the US Constitution and the Exercise of Religion Act of the state of Idaho." Jarndyce paused to let that sink in.

"Aren't they likely to prevail? Nirmala, I mean? If they've been granted tax-exempt status by the US government, how can Idaho say it's not a religious organization?"

"In Washington, Nirmala has a church, worship services, pretty recognizably religious activity going on. This development, on the other hand, appears more like a spa, a resort where they might have a few meditation and yoga classes, hardly 'religious' by mainstream standards. Presumably Nirmala will collect large fees from the individuals vacationing at its 'retreat' center. The State just wants them to share the wealth."

"What if it were some fundamentalist Christian retreat center?" I asked. "Would the state be more likely to grant tax-exempt status? I mean, Idaho, the state of neo-Nazis and fundamentalism, seems an odd choice for Nirmala."

"Perhaps. You raise another interesting point. Nirmala is unlikely to have many advocates in the Idaho courts or legislature. I must say, it is a beautiful piece of property." Jarndyce opened the low file cabinet behind his desk and pulled out an expandable file labeled "Nirmala" and then a full-color glossy booklet advertising Satya Retreat Center in Sandhurst, Idaho, complete with photos of the site and artist renderings of the proposed buildings.

"Sure looks like a health spa, doesn't it? I can't see anything religious about it from this brochure."

Jarndyce nodded, smiling more broadly now. "That's just what the State hopes the Court concludes. In terms of our probate contest, this puts us in an excellent position. Nirmala needs lots of money, and pretty darn quickly, in order to complete this development, especially if it turns out that they will be required to pay property taxes on it."

"I see. Nirmala is more likely to settle for something now rather than risk the chance of getting less after a long, drawn-out court fight, yes?"

"Exactly."

"But wait a minute. How can the church use the money for anything besides Victor Lloyd's work? I mean, the bequest gives the money to the church with the caveat that it be used to further the work of Victor Lloyd, right?"

"That's how the will reads, Ms. Dexter, but there's no way for the Court to enforce that language unless, of course, Mr. Lloyd brings a lawsuit at some future date, claiming the money was not used for his benefit."

"Sounds like a poorly written will, if that were Julia's intent, doesn't it? Why didn't she just leave it outright to Victor Lloyd?"

"I would agree that it could have been made more clear. However, I believe Ms. Comstock's other intent was that Mr. Lloyd not get saddled with the tax consequences of such a large inheritance. This way, the church—the tax-exempt organization—inherits the full amount and presumably passes it on to Victor Lloyd for his work."

"On the other hand, the church wouldn't have to give Victor a thing, would it?"

"Oh, the church is certainly obligated to use the money to further Mr. Lloyd's work, but just how they interpret that instruction remains to be seen."

"Right. And how would the church make that decision? I mean, who would decide?"

"I expect the distribution would be voted on at a meeting of shareholders called for that purpose."

"I see," I said, thinking that Julia was pretty naïve to trust her intentions to an anonymous group of shareholders.

"Now, what about your investigation, Ms. Dexter? Caroline tells me that you've made very little progress connecting the church and Julia's death." Jarndyce clasped his hands together and placed them on his desk as if in prayer, waiting for my answer.

"I'm afraid that's true." I gave him the abbreviated version of my investigation so far.

Jarndyce nodded and said he would continue negotiating with the church and contact me when they got close to making a deal.

I stood up to leave and asked if I could keep a copy of the retreat center brochure.

"Sure, sure. I have another." He shook my hand. "Pleasure to meet you, Ms. Dexter. I hope you'll keep me informed of your progress."

I agreed and he buzzed his secretary to show me out.

This time the bus ride was uneventful, just a handful of ordinary folks making their way through downtown.

Jeff was sitting in my cubicle exuding bad vibes when I got back.

I walked around him, dropped my purse next to my desk, and sat down in the chair facing him.

"Hey, Jeff, what's up?"

"That's my line, Ann. We missed you at the meeting with the Mariners' reps at one."

I looked at my watch—it read two thirty. "Oh, shoot, Jeff, I forgot. I—"

"You've been distracted a lot lately, investigating the Julia Comstock death." It was not a question. "I hope you found something newsworthy today because you're finished with this thing."

"I haven't come up with anything conclusive yet, Jeff. But I have some excellent leads. I'm sure with a little more time—"

He was shaking his head. "You're out of time. You went ahead with it even though I believe I discouraged it from the get-go. Look, I need you here working on projects that have deadlines, projects that have potential readers. Do I make myself clear? No more suicide investigations, no more psychic mediums. Got it?"

"Let me tell you what I've come up with so far."

He cut me off. "Not now. Now, you need to talk with Jeanine and the rest of the crew. Find out what happened at the meeting you missed."

Feeling pissed off and slightly mortified, I made my way to Jeanine's cubicle and got up to speed on the meeting and the project. I spent the rest of the afternoon dutifully working on the math and baseball connection.

I watched as the clock hit five. By 5:05 I was out of there and heading for Nirmala, apprehensive and yet excited to speak with Victor about Mike—and possibly about Nancy. Twenty minutes later, I turned onto Fauntleroy Way looking for a parking space and spotted a red Jaguar pulling out in front of the church. I wheeled into the space, smiling at my good luck but annoyed that I'd have to pay for a half hour of parking. I decided to risk not feeding the meter and headed for the church.

At the front desk, Rose was in the process of packing up for the day, turning off the computer and copier. She turned as I moved toward her, frowned, and appeared busy collecting her things.

"Victor Lloyd has been trying to get a hold of you," she said, avoiding eye contact. "Something came up and he has to reschedule your appointment. He'd like you to call him."

I must have looked disappointed because she followed up with, "Reverend Waters is here, though, if you'd like to see him instead. He doesn't have any more appointments on his schedule for today."

"Hi, Rose." I said, thinking Yogi Bob was about the last person I wanted to see. "No, thanks, I don't want to see Reverend Waters, but I would like to talk with you. Can I buy you a coffee?"

"I'm just leaving," Rose said, finally looking directly at me. "I have nothing to say to you, Ann. I guess Ann is your real first name?"

"Look, I'd really like to explain things. I'm sorry I wasn't straight out with you before but I thought—" I stopped mid-sentence, remembering Victor's admonition. "I was wrong, Rose. Can you forgive me?"

I watched that settle in and saw her eyes soften. "Please? It would mean a lot to me."

"Okay. I'll just let Bob know I'm leaving."

While she moved down the corridor to Reverend Waters' office, I snooped around, expecting to see Sylvia Carter's sketch displayed somewhere. Maybe there was a copy on her desk but I didn't see it anywhere.

Rose suggested we try a small coffee shop a few blocks away instead of the Starbucks nearby since, she said, "I figure it's only a matter of time before they lose all their business to The Man. Do you mind the walk?"

As Rose locked the front door, I looked up the street and caught a glimpse of the dreaded small white vehicle of Parking Enforcement moving toward us.

"Hey, let's get out of here before I get a ticket." We jumped into my Camry just in time. Glancing into my rear view mirror, I saw the disappointed frown of the officer as I pulled away from the curb.

Lighthouse Coffee occupied a converted bungalow. Its cushioned window seats, overstuffed sofas, and almost-antique tables covered with Provençal print cloths gave it a comfortable, homey ambiance. The barista greeted Rose by name and smiled at me. As she made our drinks, I found myself also hoping this place could survive.

Settling into the corner window seat, Rose sipped hot chocolate out of a hand-painted bowl-like cup while I explained how Julia Comstock's sister had contacted me and how I had tried to put myself in Julia's shoes, see how the church—and particularly Victor Lloyd—responded to newcomers.

"You're wrong about Victor, you know."

"How's that?" I asked.

"Victor is the most caring and kind man I have ever met. He is not capable of hurting another human being. I'm certain of it. The whole reason he works as a medium is to help people bear the pain of losing a loved one. He cares deeply about each person he works with. How can you think he would harm anyone?" Her eyes flashed angrily at me as she put down her cup, crossed her arms, and shook her head. "Victor would never hurt anyone."

I knew I needed to choose my words carefully now or Rose might walk out of here. "Okay. I admit that the more I've gotten to know Victor, the more unlikely it seems that he intentionally had anything to do with Julia's death."

"It's not just unlikely, it's impossible."

"Okay, let's say he had nothing to do with it."

Rose nodded, picked up the bowl of chocolate, and took a sip.

"Did you know he used to play baseball?" I asked.

"Of course, but he doesn't talk about it much. I think the injury was the biggest disappointment in his life. But then, it meant he could turn his full attention to psychic work."

"Right." There would be no convincing Rose that baseball was more important or at least more natural than what Victor was up to now, so I moved on. "What about Reverend Bob? Did he have any interactions with Julia?"

"No, I don't think so. Bob is more concerned with the administration of the church. He keeps things running smoothly, deals with the money end, stuff like that."

"What about the development in Idaho? Is Bob involved with that?"

"Absolutely—Satya is his brain child. He's pretty worried about that right now, actually. I guess there's a lawsuit."

"Hmm," I said, thinking about my conversation with Caroline's lawyer but not wanting to get into that. "You know, the only lead I have to go on now is the sketch of the woman who showed up at Julia's house after she died, claiming to be Victor's assistant. Called herself Sylvia Carter. Have you seen it?"

"Yes, I have." Rose looked like the cat that swallowed the canary.

"And?"

"And, I think I've seen her at the church—I'm pretty good at remembering faces. But I can't remember the context. I mean, did she show up for a workshop, attend a service or a lecture? I don't know. I know we have no record of anyone by that name in any of our data bases because I checked them personally." I nodded, thinking about my own foray into Nirmala's records.

"But there is another name, kind of similar to that one."

I snapped to attention. "How similar?"

Rose leaned closer to me. "I've been looking through every workshop roster, class registration, sign-in sheet, everything we have. When the exact name didn't come up, I started looking at initials that matched." She shrugged and smiled. "I saw some crime show on TV where they talked about aliases? It turns out most of them are a variation of their real names or they use the same initials."

I nodded, so she continued. "I found that someone named Sienna Curtis took one of Victor's workshops last July. It was not a class that Julia attended so I guess they couldn't have met there, though."

"Can I get her address or phone number from you, Rose? It's a long shot, but it's something anyway. I'd love to meet with her, see what she looks like."

"Well, I called the number she listed on the registration form but I didn't get anywhere. I got that recording, you know: 'the number you have reached is no longer in service.' I could give you the address, though. I'd never have the nerve to go there. What would I say?"

Planning what I would say, I drove through heavy traffic from West Seattle to the Southwest slope of Queen Anne Hill in half an hour. Sienna Curtis lived on West Olympic Way, a street that wound around the bottom of the hill, past Kinnear Park, and became Tenth Avenue West, before turning north a few blocks later. The address matched one of three apartment buildings just across the street from the park. From the sign above the locked mailboxes in the lobby, I understood that the apartments were now the "Olympic Hills Condominiums."

It took me a moment to figure out the perplexing security system. Eventually I discovered that I could scroll through the alphabetical listing of residents by repeatedly pressing the number three for A-L and the number six for M-Z—not exactly intuitive. There were fifteen units. No resident had a last name beginning with the letter C. Discouraged, I stood there staring at the mailboxes when a well-dressed middle-aged woman approached from behind the locked glass door.

"May I help you?" she asked, with a slight English accent. "The security system is terribly hard to manage," she said, opening one of the mailboxes with a key. "Half the elderly residents here have a miserable time when their friends come to visit. They can't see to read the instructions." She began to explain how it worked when I interrupted.

"Thanks, I appreciate your help. Actually I'm looking for a friend of mine. Her name is Sienna Curtis. I haven't seen her in a couple of years. We used to work together. This is the address I have for her, but I don't see her name on any of the mailboxes. Do you know her?"

"Oh no, I don't think so. But then, I'm just here for the week visiting my brother. Shall I call up and ask him? I'm sure he'd know. I believe he's the treasurer of the condominium association." The woman picked up the security phone and punched in the appropriate code. As she explained my dilemma to her brother, she looked me over, smiled, and said yes into the phone a few times, then handed me the receiver.

"Why don't you talk to him yourself? It seems as though your friend sold her unit and moved away last summer. Sorry."

Picking up where his sister left off, I told him I was in town for a few days; I had lost touch with Sienna but thought I'd pop in for a visit. I didn't know she'd moved. Did he have a current address? He believed that he did, but sounded slightly annoyed, as if interrupted by a telemarketer.

"At the moment I'm in the middle of preparing dinner. Could you ring back tomorrow? I'm afraid you won't be able to visit her tonight anyway. You see, Ms. Curtis has moved to Mexico."

He let that sink in, and then rattled off his phone number, suggesting I call after nine tomorrow. He expected to be home most of the day. I scribbled the number onto the back of a receipt I found tucked into the back pocket of my purse, thanked his sister for her help, and stepped out onto the sidewalk.

28

Frustrated that I didn't get any real information on Sienna Curtis, I drove home thinking I'd do some Internet research on her later. First, I needed to attend to my empty stomach. I stopped at the Central Market to pick up something already prepared for dinner and just a small carton of Ben & Jerry's. When I placed my purchases on the express checkout conveyor belt, my favorite checker, Jim, smiled knowingly and winked as he picked up and scanned the pint of Karamel Sutra. I laughed remembering our recent conversation about Ben & Jerry's—how Jim decided to stop eating it cold turkey once he recognized the warning signs of obsessive behavior. It was bad enough, he'd said, that he bought a pint every day he worked, but when he found himself eating it with a plastic spoon on his way home, he knew he was out of control. As he dropped the carton into my grocery bag he deadpanned, "Do you need a spoon?"

Pooch demanded immediate attention as soon as I walked through the door, so I put the ice cream in the freezer, leaving the rest of the groceries on the counter and ran her around the block, then spent a few minutes throwing a tennis ball in the front yard. It was a clear night with a chilly edge; three days without rain in October—amazing. Back inside, I listened to my voicemail, including one from Victor apologizing for missing our appointment.

I set out one of my favorite hand-painted Portuguese plates and yellow cloth napkin on the kitchen table, a ritual I follow whenever I feel particularly stressed, lonely, or just plain out of sorts. I zapped the fish taco in the microwave, poured a glass of pinot grigio and flipped through my mail. I couldn't put off paying bills any longer; at least I could do it online.

I clicked off my bank's website, then rewarded myself with ice cream and a little internet sleuthing around the name Sienna Curtis. With Google, I just might pick up some scrap of information about her. My search yielded several hits for Sienna Curtis, but only one exact match. Her name appeared in a list of speakers at a Seattle Sheraton conference of corporate marketing representatives, nearly two years earlier. She'd worked for Princess Tours, a subsidiary of a larger cruise line based in California. Excited to be getting somewhere, I quickly typed in "Princess Tours, Seattle" and their corporate home page popped up a few seconds later filled with colorful photos of various cruise ships and a feature on their latest addition: a luxury cruise to Alaska. I jotted down the number of their Seattle office and the name of another marketing representative on the list and planned my call for first thing in the morning.

The phone rang as I was brushing my teeth and I tripped over Pooch running into the kitchen to pick it up.

"Ann, it's Victor. Am I calling too late?"

I smiled into the receiver and felt my heart racing more than warranted by my brief jog to the phone.

"Not at all. I'm glad you called." I said, hoping I didn't sound quite as enthusiastic as I felt. He was apologetic, but vague about why he couldn't meet me earlier, suggesting we reschedule for the next day, same time, same place. It worked for me.

"So, instead of seeing you this afternoon, I spent some time with Rose," I said. "She's forgiven me, and possibly given me a lead on Sylvia Carter."

"That's great." He sounded tired and only moderately interested. "Why don't you tell me all about it tomorrow."

I hung up, feeling hyped from the ice cream and slightly miffed at Victor. So I called Jack in Houston. He answered on the first ring, his voice at first groggy from sleep, then worried.

"Ann, what's wrong? Why are you calling me at one in the

morning?"

I'd forgotten about the two-hour time difference. "Oh, Jack, I'm sorry. I wasn't thinking. It's just that I'm wide-awake and wanted to hear your voice. Go back to sleep. Call me tomorrow if you get a chance. Goodnight, Jack."

I called Princess Tours from my cell phone at 8:35 a.m. while stopped at a red light on my way into work. Yes, I was technically violating the law, but what could I do? I couldn't call from the *Times* with Jeff watching me like a hawk.

"Good morning, Princess Tours."

I asked for Sienna Curtis.

"I'm sorry, Ma'am, there's no one by that name on the company roster. Are you sure you have the right number?"

"Well, yes, I met Sienna at a marketing conference in Seattle a couple of years ago. I know she worked for Princess then. I've been out of touch for a while—on maternity leave. Now that I'm back working and visiting Seattle, I hoped to look her up."

"I see. I'll connect you with human resources." I listened to canned music interspersed with ads for cruise vacations for a few minutes before someone picked up. Again I gave my spiel about maternity leave and the marketing conference.

"Sienna left about a year and a half ago to work for some high-tech company. We haven't heard from her since," the woman said, with an edge to her voice.

"Do you remember the name of the company? I'd love to track her down while I'm in Seattle."

"Sure. It's, ah, Com-tech, something like that."

"Comvitek?"

"That's the one. Sounds like you know it. Is there anything else?"

The guy behind me laid on his horn. Still holding the cell phone to my ear, I hadn't noticed the light had turned green. He sped around me and yelled out the open window of his Geo Metro, "Hang up and drive!"

I pulled into the nearest parking lot just as the sky opened up and began to pour. I punched in the number for Comvitek.

"Sienna Curtis, please."

No response.

"Hello?"

"Sienna Curtis? Sorry, she doesn't work at Comvitek. I just checked the directory to be sure."

"Well, I know she used to work there. She left Princess Tours to take a job with Comvitek about a year and a half ago."

Again, I was connected with the human resources department. Someone picked up on the first ring.

"Gina Turner."

I gave Gina my story about meeting Sienna at the marketing conference and asked when she left Comvitek.

"I'm afraid our personnel files are confidential. I can't give you any information about Ms. Curtis. Sorry." She clicked off before I could protest. I pulled back into traffic and headed for Olympic Hills.

It was just about nine when I entered Dean Merriwether's code on the condominium's security system.

"Yes? Who's there, please?" I recognized his sister's voice.

"Sorry to bother you two again, but it's Ann Dexter. I came by last night looking for my friend Sienna Curtis."

"Oh, yes. One moment." I heard a muffled conversation before she returned to the phone. "I'll be right down while my brother looks up your friend's address."

True to her word, she appeared at the door in a few minutes, held it open, and gestured me in. "Why don't you come right on up? That will be more comfortable than waiting here. Who knows how long it will take Dean to find the address? He's terribly slow and my tea's getting cold." I followed her around the corner to a small elevator. She pressed five and shrugged. "We're on the top floor.

Sorry he didn't give you that address last night. I told him he was quite rude." She held out her hand. "I'm Gillian Merriwether."

The condo had an ordinary layout: entry into a narrow hallway, bedrooms and bath on one side, small kitchen on the other. Dean rummaged around in one of the rooms, set up as an office and guestroom from the looks of it, and called out "Be right there," as we passed by the open door. I followed Gillian into the living room, taking in the southwest view over the park and Elliott Bay. French doors opened to a small terrace.

I declined the offer of tea and commented on the view as we sat facing each other.

"Well, it's lovely when the sun is shining. You should come back in August."

I chuckled at the ubiquitous Seattle weather joke as Dean walked into the room.

"Here it is," he said, handing me a small piece of notebook paper on which he'd written an address in Mexico, along with a telephone number.

I thanked him and tucked it into the side pocket of my bag while removing the sketch of Sylvia Carter. I had to find out if Sienna and Sylvia were the same person. I handed the sketch to Dean and said, "I've been carrying around this sketch of Sienna for years."

He looked at the sketch and then back at me.

"Are you a police officer? Is Sienna Curtis in trouble?"

"Do I look like a cop?" I laughed.

"No, but this looks like some sort of police sketch. I wondered why your 'friend' left town so fast—something fishy about it. What's really going on here? You're not some old friend."

"You're right, I'm not Sienna's old friend, but I'm not a cop either. I'm a newspaper reporter and Sienna Curtis is a lead I'm following up on for a story. She's not in any trouble, not yet anyway. I just want to make sure this is a picture of the person who used to live here before I make my way to Mexico to track her down."

"Oh, it's her! What did she do? I doubt that your boss would send you all the way to Mexico if it wasn't pretty newsworthy." He sat forward in his chair, placing his hands on his knees, while his sister looked my way as well, teacup poised a few inches from her lips, eyebrows arched.

"I can't go into the details, confidentiality and all. But Dean, I do appreciate your help. I'll be sure to let you know if I come up with anything." I got up and made my way to the door while he asked for my business card.

"I'll be in touch." I waved and grabbed the doorknob with my other hand. "I can find my way out."

I drove the ten minutes to the *Times* with my windshield wipers on high, thinking about how much I would enjoy a trip to Mexico. Once at my desk I logged on to Expedia and looked at airfare to Cabo San Lucas. Not bad, Alaska Airlines advertised a fall special: book before November fifteenth and save fifty percent off the regular fare. I was watching the little airplane graphic—"Expedia is processing your request"—when Jeff poked his head into my cubicle.

"Are you planning a vacation, Ann?"

"Oh, hi, Jeff! Not a vacation really. I'm so glad you popped in. I need to talk to you about this." Thinking fast, I continued. "I'm having a family crisis. I have to go to Mexico." It was mostly true.

"If by 'family crisis' you mean, 'I can't possibly stand the thought of three more months of rain,' I'm with you."

The pained look on my face must have convinced him of my seriousness.

"I'm sorry, Ann, I thought you were joking. What's happening? Do you want to talk about it?"

"You know my sister Nancy has been missing for several years?"

"The one with the religious cult?"

"She's the only sister I have, so yes. I hired an investigator who has a lead on her. She's in Mexico. I have to go there, talk to her personally. I want to do it now before she disappears again."

He looked thoughtful, then nodded.

"I figure I can finish up my part of the math/baseball project and get it to Jeanine tonight. I'll miss only a couple days of work. I'll be back by Monday. I do have some vacation time coming; of course, I hadn't planned on using it so soon. What do you say?"

"I say, 'go for it,' but in the words of Ebenezer Scrooge, 'Be here all the earlier on Monday morning.'" He laughed and stood up, heading back to his desk.

"Thanks, boss. You're the best."

Before booking my flight, I left a message on Tom Hill's cell phone. I needed to know if he had any more information about Nancy, if she really worked at this Rancho La Puerta Spa. I could fly to Cabo, talk to Sienna Curtis, then fly back to Seattle with a stopover in San Diego. According to the spa's website, guests were picked up at the San Diego airport and transported to Tecate where the ranch sprawled over several acres of high desert. Unlike traditional spas featuring massage and all sorts of beauty treatments, this one highlighted early morning hikes on Mount Kuchumaa, all manner of yoga and meditation classes, and vegetarian cuisine prepared by their renowned chef and mostly grown on the ranch property. I began to imagine Nancy there, then realized I was getting ahead of myself, caught up in the idea of some idyllic reunion with Nancy when the reality might be very different.

I willed myself to switch gears: I would make one more phone call about Sienna Curtis, then focus on my work for the rest of the morning. I put in a call to Kelly Long, Comvitek's Assistant of Corporate Giving and purchaser of Julia Comstock's painting. She was surprised to hear from me but agreed to meet for lunch when I told her I'd buy and suggested Etta's at the Pike Place Market.

I arrived at Etta's a few minutes early, took a quick glance at the menu, and decided to check with the waitress. Experience told me everything would be good, but she could recommend the most outstanding item of the day. I sat back and watched the people walking by. Some were clearly headed to the Seattle Athletic Club: gym bags in one hand, cell phones in the other. Some appeared to be shopping on their lunch hour— toting bouquets of flowers, paper-wrapped fish and bottles of wine. Others looked like they were simply enjoying themselves, strolling rather than walking. I wanted to join them.

Kelly arrived and smiled my way as the hostess pointed to my table.

After preliminary niceties, Kelly said her curiosity was killing her. Exactly why had I invited her to lunch? What was the "important matter" I wanted to discuss outside of the office?

"What do you think of Nick Villardi?" I asked.

She flushed and I followed up on my hunch.

"He is pretty hot, isn't he? But what's up with his wife? I just don't see those two together."

"So, you've got your eye on Nick Villardi? Forget it! He's a flirt but I don't see him leaving his wife any time soon." We commiserated about how all the good men were taken and then I asked her about Sienna Curtis.

"I don't know the name, should I?"

I pulled the sketch out of my purse and set it in front of her. "This is Sienna Curtis, also known as Sylvia Carter. I know she used to work at Comvitek and that she left town in a big hurry about six months ago. No one at Comvitek will talk about her. I think there's some connection between Curtis and the Villardis. I hoped you might have an idea since you bought the painting with Sienna's face in the corner. For Nick. I also sensed that your relationship with Nick was more than boss-employee."

Kelly's face registered surprise, possibly fear. "Look, I don't understand what you're doing here. You work for the *Seattle Times* writing articles about education. You interviewed me about our corporate donations to support Seattle school programs. And now you're asking all about paintings and missing former employees. What's going on?"

While I explained my understanding of the facts and my role in the situation, Kelly looked confused, then scared.

"Why are you telling me this? I'm not involved in any way. Nick and I—oh, I regret that, but it was the proverbial one-night stand, working late, out for dinner, too much wine. Oh, shit. I'm in it now, aren't I?" I waited for her to continue. Instead she just sat there, distraught.

"Look, Kelly, you couldn't have known everything going on at Comvitek—most of this happened before you got there—but you could help me out now, do a little legwork."

"Well, I'm screwed anyway. This is my first job out of grad school. I violated the cardinal rule in my first year: sleeping with the boss. What an idiot! And not just any boss! From what you're telling me, he might be some kind of criminal."

"I don't know that Nick Villardi is a criminal, Kelly, but I do need some questions answered, to prove he isn't. You could help."

Her eyes cleared and she focused on me again.

"What could I do?"

"Look through Sienna Curtis's personnel file. Find out the circumstances of her resignation, or firing—anything unusual."

"What if there's nothing weird about it? What if Sienna Curtis is just someone who worked at the company and left? Maybe Julia Comstock saw her at some corporate function and remembered her face. That's why she put it into a painting. There's nothing wrong with that."

29

I left Kelly at Etta's, headed back to the *Times* and called Victor to see if we could push back our meeting time—I still had hours of work to clear up before I could leave town. As usual, he was accommodating.

"Just call me when you're finished," he said. "We'll take it from there."

At eight thirty, I finally packed it in and drove to West Seattle. Finding the front door locked, I rang the after-hours bell and waited a few minutes before Victor appeared, all smiles. I smiled in response and thought about his appeal as I followed him down the hall to his office. Not only was he physically attractive in the conventional sense, Victor exuded warmth. He had an ease about him that struck me as different, as genuine. And there was something else. Maybe it was his intensity that intrigued me, or, honestly, it might just be his baseball background.

I sat on the sofa and Victor on the facing chair.

"So, how's Mike doing?" he asked.

"He's still pretty weirded out about the other night. According to Toni, he's been reading everything he can get his hands on about psychic phenomena."

He chuckled and nodded. "That's good. And you? How are you doing? Are you ready to hear from the spirit world?"

"I think so. But first I want to ask you some things."

"Shoot."

"Did you know that Rose recognized the sketch of Sylvia Carter as someone she'd seen at the church?"

"She mentioned it to me but I guess I didn't pay too much attention to it. I mean, Rose reads a lot of mystery novels." He shrugged. "I thought she might be trying too hard to find a connection."

"Well, she's a great amateur detective as far as I'm concerned." I told Victor I was on my way to Mexico to track down this mystery woman and he seemed surprised. I also told him I'd learned a bit about Julia's bequest and asked him if he knew how the money would be used to "further his work."

"Have you heard about Satya?"

"Yes."

"The plan is that I will spend most of my time there, in Idaho, leading workshops, seeing individuals like I do here, but also that it will evolve into a kind of state-of-the-art center for psychic mediums. Eventually, I'll work with well-known psychics from around the world, develop a training program, and a network of the most highly regarded international practitioners." Victor's eyes sparkled with enthusiasm. "It's pretty heady stuff."

I nodded. "I guess. But will they have a baseball team?"

Victor laughed. "Hey, anything's possible."

"So, you're not worried that you won't personally see any of Julia's money."

He scowled at me. "The money is for my work, not for my personal use."

"Okay, I'm just asking, wondering if there has been any tension about it."

"No, not at all."

"Good."

"Okay. So, do you want to try to connect now?" His matter-of-fact tone made me smile, as if this were a normal everyday sort of question, like, "Do you like broccoli?" But it was a nervous smile.

"I guess."

"Let's go next door. It's a more serene environment."

It was the same room where Victor had done the reading for Mike but it felt different. Instead of overhead fluorescent lights, Victor switched on a small table lamp and lit the candles flickering in their sandy tray. He noticed my discomfort immediately.

"I can see that you're tense, Ann. I thought the low light might help you relax. Please, sit down."

I sat on the small loveseat and Victor sat across from me, fixing me with that intense soul-searching look he had. I met his eyes and a sense of warmth washed over me, a feeling of vulnerability tinged with fear. As he leaned in closer I felt drawn toward him, then overwhelmed.

I pulled back. "Whoa, wait. I should go." I stood up. "You know, I have no idea why I'm doing this. I need to let it go."

"Ann, from the first time you walked into my workshop, there has been a persistent spirit trying to get through to you. I think you're very close to being open to it. Of course you're wary of what might happen here. It's natural. Let's start out with some relaxation meditation. Go from there. Don't worry! I'll behave." Victor smiled and I felt myself relax.

I nodded and sat back down. Victor began taking me though some meditation exercises: focused breathing to shut off what he described as "mind noise;" thoughts like, "I need to call Mark back," and "Did I turn off the coffee pot before I left the office?"

"See these random thoughts as beach balls, let them bounce off, float away, and disappear out of your sight."

He continued the beach theme and I visualized lying on a white sandy beach. I felt the warmth of the sun seeping into my pores from the sun above and the warm sand beneath me.

"Look up and see the clear blue sky, feel the warm breeze blowing across your body, inhale the clean refreshing air. You feel secure, united with the universe. Let the feeling of joy flow through your body. You are completely relaxed, free of meaningless thoughts and ready to invite all messages from the other side. Open your eyes,

Ann."

When I did, Victor took both of my hands in his and searched my face. He seemed to see what he wanted. He nodded, released my hands, and sat back focusing inward.

For a long time we were both quiet. Then Victor spoke softly.

"I'm getting the name Laura." He paused another moment. "One of your guides is here: your mother, I believe."

"That's my mom's name."

"I'm feeling some pain in my chest. She had a painful death, difficulty breathing."

"She died of lung cancer, yes." The memories of her final weeks in the hospital came back to me: her labored breathing, the oxygen, the painkillers, the tears.

I looked up at Victor. His face changed and he smiled. "She's showing me some kind of a bird. A chicken, I think."

"Oh my God," I gasped, remembering the day toward the very end of her hospital stay. She'd stood up, needing help to get to the bathroom. I couldn't hide my shock at the sight of her emaciated body, how the flesh hung loosely on her bony arms. She tried to make light of it. She kept her sense of humor even then.

"Don't look so shocked, Annie," she'd said, "I know I look like a chicken."

The tears streamed down my cheeks and I grabbed a tissue from the box in front of me.

"Your mom wants you to know that she loves you, that she's feeling very good now, on the other side."

I nodded, unable to speak.

"She's showing me the name Nancy. She's to the side of you. Is that your sister?"

"Yes."

"I'm feeling some pain. Has she crossed over?"

"I don't know, I don't know. I've lost track of my sister. Is she alive? Can my mom tell me? Can you?"

Victor concentrated hard, perspiration appearing on his forehead. He ran his fingers through his hair. "I'm seeing white along with bright light. Sometimes this means health care, a holistic approach. Is she into holistic medicine?"

"Probably. She's into lots of things I don't understand. Victor, my sister disappeared several years ago. I'm trying to find her now. Is she sick? Can my mom say where she is?"

"I'm being shown the same symbols, Ann: white, health care, a door. I think you should go to her."

"Is she in Mexico? She has been there, I think. Is she still there?"

Victor sat staring into middle distance for some time before he spoke. "Your mom is quiet now. I'm losing the thread. I'm sorry."

I nodded, trying to collect myself.

"Wait. There's something else. Another spirit."

"No," I whispered, my thoughts racing. "I can barely process this." I sat quietly avoiding his eyes for some time. When I finally got the courage to look up at Victor, I saw that his face had changed again.

Beaming at me, he said, "I'm getting an overwhelming sense of love here."

At first I panicked, sure he was going to tell me this spirit was Nancy, that she was dead. "Stop! Please!" I begged.

Victor nodded, waited, watched me closely. I met his eyes and felt that warmth wash over me again, flowing somehow from him to me just as a vivid image of Ben entered my mind. It was a well-loved memory: the day we decided to get married, just the two of us on the beach at Golden Gardens that warm June evening, the glorious sunset. Ben's words, *Ann, I don't want this to end. Us to end. What I mean is, why don't we get married?* He'd pulled me close and I'd tensed up, clung to him, not knowing what to say. Loosening his embrace, he'd whispered, *Hey, you don't have to answer right now. Just don't say no*, while his hands worked their way up my back, slowly massaging all of my apprehension away. I didn't want it to end either.

Yes, I'd said, relaxing into his arms.

Yes? This is the right spot?

Yes, it's definitely the right spot. And yes, we should get married.

"Ann?" Victor's voice pulled me back and I struggled to return to the here and now. As he studied my face I wondered if he'd felt Ben's presence too. He simply smiled and asked gently, "Do you want to talk about it? Where you've been?"

"Uh. Where I've been?"

He nodded, waiting. When I didn't respond, he said, "Okay, let's move on then. What about your sister? Do you want to tell me about her?"

And I did. I wanted to tell him everything, starting with Nancy. "I need to find her, Victor. I need to know that she's okay."

"How did you lose touch?"

It all poured out then, how Nancy had left in her second year of college to follow a guy she met camping, how they'd traveled to India on a spiritual quest, how they'd become two of the earliest disciples of a notorious guru. How Nancy had moved to north central Oregon and become part of the inner sanctum on the cult's ranch, a close friend of the guru's right-hand woman. How I'd visited Nancy back then, witnessed her pride in every aspect of the ranch, even while it began to deteriorate into a power struggle. How I'd disowned her, frustrated at what I saw as her stupidity, how she had given up everything for this very flawed utopia. How I'd looked for Nancy when it all came apart in Oregon and her friend fled the country under threat of federal indictment, with the guru blaming his former right-hand woman for everything gone wrong. How I'd discovered only that Nancy escaped with her boyfriend under cover of darkness in one of the ranch's patrol vehicles.

Victor listened closely, occasionally shaking his head. When I finished Nancy's story he said, "I understand now why you were so quick to blame Nirmala for Julia's death. Your sister's experience, the result of her religious quest, was so extreme, so negative, so disillusioning. It's not always that way. As human beings, we do the best we can to make sense of this world, to find the right path. I've known other disciples of your sister's guru who now work in the human potential movement. They're still seeking. They've taken the positive from his teachings and moved on."

I sat quietly, processing his comments. Then he spoke again.

"Have you forgiven your sister? Forgiven yourself?"

I stared at him, dumb, turning the word over in my mind. A few moments passed. I looked at Victor, recognized the fatigue in his face and my own exhaustion.

"I need to get home now, figure out what I can do. Thanks." I stood up and Victor walked me to the door.

"This has been difficult for you," he said. "You'll do what's right. I'm sure of it."

We stood at the door awkwardly, neither of us knowing quite what to say. As I grabbed the doorknob, Victor touched my shoulder.

"You're so tense. Let me take care of that." Victor began to slowly, expertly massage between my shoulder blades. I relaxed into his touch, then turned to look up at him. He held my gaze for a long moment, then pulled me close.

"Don't go." His soft voice in my ear raised the hair on the back of my neck. "I don't want this to end."

I looked up at Victor and he took my face in his hands, touched my lips softly with his, and then looked into my eyes, waiting for me to make the next move. I returned his kiss lightly at first, then pulled him close, pressing my mouth on his. He gently nibbled my upper lip, teased me with a brief taste of his tongue. When his playfulness moved into a kiss so deep and intimate that a low moan escaped from me, I pulled back again, gasped.

"Wait. I think we should wait."

Victor raised his arms, palms up in front of him, as if he'd just been arrested.

"Okay. Sorry, I—"

"No, I'm sorry. I don't know what I was thinking. I'm very confused right now. Good-bye, Victor."

30

Somehow I managed to get to my car and point it toward home, images of Victor and Ben wrestling in my head—Victor's solid presence, Ben's words on his lips. I couldn't deny the chemistry: my intense physical response to Victor or that I wanted more. But this could never happen. It was ludicrous, or maybe really basic—a need I had to make a connection, to feel something real again. I drove on in a fog. I couldn't figure this out now—it would take time, lots of time.

What I could do was deal with things within my control, like finding Nancy. I grabbed for my cell phone, found Tom Hill's number in my directory, and pressed the call button. When he didn't pick up, I left another desperate-sounding message asking him to call me back tonight no matter what, since I'd be on my way to Mexico in the morning.

At home, I called Nicole and arranged for her to take care of Pooch, then logged onto Expedia to finalize my reservations. That done, I wandered into the living room, lit a fire in the fireplace, then walked back into the kitchen, filled the teakettle, and set it on the stovetop. Waiting for the water to boil, I decided to call Victor, to talk about what happened between us. I picked up the phone, easily touching the correct numbers on the keypad, only slightly surprised that I knew them by heart. When I heard ringing on the other end, I thought better of it, pressed the off button, and dropped into the chair. "Crazy," I said to the wall.

The kettle whistled and I got up, finished the tea-making ritual, and picked up my notebook on my way back to the fire. I made some notes and, when my mind wasn't wandering back to Victor, I outlined a strategy for approaching Sylvia Carter, aka Sienna Curtis, wondering just how hostile she might be. I realized that I must have dropped off to sleep only when the distant sound of ringing roused me from a twisted dream involving a Mercedes Benz ride with Liz Villardi driving Nancy, Victor Lloyd, and me through the Circle C Ranch.

"Ann? It's Tom Hill." He apologized for not getting back to me sooner. He said the shit had hit the fan in his other case in Portland; he'd only now come up for air. "Do you have a pen? I have a name and address for your sister."

My stomach tightened as I wrote down the name she had taken, "Leila Morgan." According to Tom, Nancy/Leila lived and worked at Rancho La Puerta, where she taught something called "Iyengar Yoga" as well as clinical hypnotherapy and massage. I thanked Tom and asked him for the phone number of Nancy's friend, Hanifah Griffin. I needed to talk to this woman personally, to find out if Nancy was well when she last saw her. Victor had definitely gotten some things right: holistic health and a door. Even I could translate "Rancho la Puerta."

I hung up and began packing with my usual system, throwing everything into my suitcase. Pooch got nervous, understanding somehow the significance of my packing. She wouldn't let me out of her sight, following me around the house, driving me crazy.

"Stop stalking me, Pooch!" I snapped. The dog cocked her head and stared at me, confused by my tone. "Oh, never mind, you big baby." I sat down and scratched behind her ears. "I'll be home soon enough and Nicole will be here to play every day! Way fun!" I spoke in a high voice and Pooch wagged her tail, reassured.

Next I made a copy of my itinerary for Nicole and emailed a copy to Jeff at the *Times* in case he needed to get a hold of me. Out of habit, I sent one to Jack. Jesus, Jack! I couldn't even fathom how he fit into the craziness of the past few hours. At least with him in Houston, we wouldn't have to talk about it right away. By the time he looked at my email, I'd be traveling. I would have to explain things to him soon, knowing it would hurt both of us. Maybe after a few days and some distance, I'd be able to explain it to myself.

First thing in the morning, I called Hanifah Griffin. Hesitant to talk to me at first, she warmed up quickly and seemed to appreciate my genuine concern for Nancy. I explained that I was on my way to Mexico on a business trip, and that I planned to travel to Tecate to see Nancy afterwards.

"I'm especially concerned about my sister's health. How was she when you saw her last?"

I listened to Hanifah breathe into the other end of the phone. Finally, she said, "Nancy was not well. That's one of the reasons she decided to go to Mexico. She didn't go into the details with me except that she'd been diagnosed with something serious by a doctor in the States. She didn't have much faith in Western medicine, you know. She'd been trying some herbal treatment instead, knew of a shaman who consulted at the spa, so she went there."

Hanifah's voice trailed off and I heard Victor's in my head, *I'm seeing white, a symbol for holistic medicine, a door.*

She continued, "But I got a card from her last year, from Rancho la Puerta. She said she felt fabulous. The high desert agreed with her."

I thanked Hanifah, hung up, and tried to hold on to her last words, *she felt fabulous,* as I made one last check of my bag before leaving.

The trip to the airport seemed longer than usual—rush hour traffic, a wait for the shuttle from the parking lot to the Alaska Airlines gate, tight security at SeaTac, endless lines. As the plane took off, I felt lighter—both excited and apprehensive, determined to leave behind the emotional turmoil of the past several hours and figure out the puzzle of Julia Comstock's death. I thought about my last trip to Cabo, over ten years ago, a fun trip with my good friend and former college roommate, Molly. Back then, it was a sleepy Mexican town with a few upscale hotels on the Playa el Medaño and around the marina where middle-aged marlin fishermen coexisted happily with the younger college crowd during peak spring break weeks. I'd heard that Cabo was the fastest growing resort area in Mexico, so I expected it had changed quite a bit.

I got a chance to see the changes during the bus ride from the airport. The corridor between San Jose del Cabo and Cabo San Lucas, some eighteen miles long, was lined with a full array of high-rent resorts. The address I had for Sienna Curtis—the Westin Regina— was the most upscale of all. According to Jorge, our Mexican tour guide, the Regina was the most expensive resort ever built in this country, designed by the famous Mexican architect Javier Sordo Madaleno. When I asked about it, Jorge pulled out the hotel's brochure and suggested I take a tour of the property during my stay. If I took the tour and mentioned his name, Jorge Escoban, he would get a commission and I would get a free champagne brunch at the Westin and a coupon good for dinner in one of three restaurants in town, my choice. He would even arrange for free transportation from my hotel to the Westin.

"A great deal, no? When would you like to go?"

"Sounds too good to be true. What's the hitch?" I asked.

"No hitch, as you say, pretty lady, as long as you bring a major credit card. Do you have one?"

"It doesn't sound free."

"Oh, yes, completely free," he said. "Only a half-hour of your time is required to hear about opportunities to buy a time-share. The credit card is just so they know you *could* buy a time-share if you wanted to."

When I declined, Jorge frowned and moved quickly down the aisle to hit up the young couple a few seats behind me.

After checking in at my hotel, the Melia on the Playa el Madeño, I chatted up the concierge and we commiserated about how much the area had changed. He shook his head, said Cabo had been overbuilt in the last few years. Now there were too many vacant resorts. In fact, the Melia had a new property out in the corridor. Did I want him to arrange a tour? I didn't. Instead, I asked about getting a cab to the Westin Regina. Not a problem, he could have one for me in a moment at a small cost, about thirteen dollars for the trip. I nodded and headed up to my room.

I dropped my bags and looked around the room. They'd done a good job of creating an "old Mexico" ambiance: warm and inviting terra-cotta-tiled floor, bed linens and drapes in sunny yellow and orange tones, paintings of Catholic missions on the wall. I crossed the room, stepped out onto the balcony and inhaled the warm, fragrant air. Looking down at the pool, the tables in the outdoor restaurant, the garden, and the ocean beyond, I longed to kick off my shoes and wander out for a swim and piña colada. Instead, I picked up the phone and dialed the Westin Regina.

"Hola, Westin Regina."

"May I speak with Sienna Curtis, please?"

"Ms. Curtis is with a tour right now, may I take a message?"

"Oh, a tour," I said, thinking fast. "I'm a friend of hers. From Seattle. I'm here in Cabo on a little vacation and thought I'd surprise her. When is her next tour?"

"She finishes up for the day between four and five—the time varies. And she'll be leading the first breakfast tour tomorrow morning at nine. Shall I leave her a message for you?"

"Not necessary. I'll come by and see her in person."

I decided to call Jorge after all. He could get me a free ride to the Westin and I'd try to sign up for Sienna's tour. I hoped they wouldn't confiscate my credit card, though, or check on the limit.

The sounds of happy hour in full swing drifted up to my open balcony and tugged at me. I threw off my Seattle jeans and pulled on my swimsuit and all-purpose sundress. The light clothes felt foreign and wonderful next to my skin. I made my way past the rowdy crowd at the swim-up bar and headed for the stairs to the beach. A hotel employee, manning the steps like a security guard, greeted me and I shook my head absently, thinking how superfluous he seemed standing there. A few minutes later I changed my tune. I'd stopped briefly to look at some silver jewelry laid out for sale by a young woman and immediately found myself in the middle of four vendors, all holding out their wares. I shook my head and started moving down the beach, like the Pied Piper leading a merchandising throng. It didn't take long for me to feel more harassed than refreshed, so I hurriedly made my way back up the hotel steps and into the protection of the Melia grounds thinking that, with money and privilege, it's just a matter of degree.

Selecting a lounge chair that caught the last bit of slanting sun, I dropped my bag and slathered on sunscreen. Jeff might have a little trouble believing in my family crisis if I got back to the *Times* with a sunburn. My family crisis—I couldn't let myself think about Nancy just yet. Instead, I forced myself to consider how I would approach Sienna Curtis in the morning. I closed my eyes and awoke when a shadow passed across my face.

"Is that a good book?" Looking up at the obviously drunk and too-young guy peering down at me, I picked up the copy of Scott Turow's latest page-turner and said as evenly as possible, "Yes, thanks for waking me up so I can finish it. You can go now."

He went scuttling off to a nearby table where his friends were laughing loudly and taking full advantage of the two-for-one drink deal. I moved my stuff to a chair closer to the pool and jumped in, swimming a few laps to get my blood moving before approaching the bar. I ordered a piña colada and looked around at the other late-afternoon patrons while munching on a pineapple spear. Besides the table of rowdy college boys, there were two families with young kids, one Mexican and one American. In both families the dads were reading and the moms were in the water, playing with their progeny. Apparently, resort behavior bridged cultural if not economic gaps.

I filled the rest of my night with a quick dinner in the hotel's outdoor restaurant trying to avoid contact with all the happy-looking couples, which reminded me too much of the chaotic nature of my own love life. Good thing my cell phone didn't work in Mexico or I'd surely make a fool out of myself by dialing up Victor right now. I couldn't get him out of my head. I'd forgotten how the replay of a kiss could be almost as sensual as the original experience and how it triggered the longing for a repeat performance. I took my book to bed instead and fell into a deep, dreamless sleep.

31

Jorge appeared as promised at eight thirty sharp the next morning, waving at me as I walked into the lobby.

"Miss Dexter, hola! My cousin is here to drive you to the Westin. Have a good time and remember to give them this when you arrive." He handed me a coupon with the Westin's logo, on which he had written, "9:00 tour, Ann Dexter." His signature and an identification code of some sort appeared in the lower corner. Just then, a van pulled up and Jorge opened the door for me and spoke in rapid Spanish to the driver, who smiled and said, "We have one more stop. We get there in no time."

I settled in to enjoy the scenery as the van turned onto the highway. A few moments later, we pulled into the Pueblo Bonita's drive and picked up a young family, who, I quickly learned, hailed from Ohio. The, "Hi, I'm Doug" dad kept up a steady stream of conversation all the way to the Westin—I knew his life story by the time we arrived. Relieved when I finally saw the Westin sign set up away from the highway, I craned my neck to get a look at the resort itself. Doug helped me out here, too.

"Oh, the Regina is right on the beach, a long way off the main highway, it'll be a few minutes yet." He then filled me in on the famous architect who designed the resort at tremendous expense. Doug sounded so proprietary already that I guessed he'd be easy pickings for this morning's hard sell. As we rounded a bend in the road, the resort sparkled into view. It was gorgeous: a cluster of modern curvilinear buildings in vibrant colors—magenta, bright yellow, deep blue, and emerald green—rose out of the Sea of Cortez set off by large cliffs behind. We pulled into the drive and were met by two smiling Westin employees, each in a different brightly colored shirt, echoing the palette of the buildings. They ushered us into a courtyard where other smiling tourists stood chatting with each other, and a barista handed out complimentary bottled water from her espresso cart. Two young women stood behind a desk busily checking in arrivals for the nine o'clock tour. I gave them my name and asked how the tours worked. "Will we tour in a group?"

One of the women, Anita from Guadalajara, according to her nametag, looked up and smiled. "Oh, no, ma'am, we like to offer personal attention to our guests. Each family or individual guest will have their own tour guide." She looked down at her notes, then over my shoulder. "Stan will be showing you around the property today."

I looked around to see a middle-aged guy wearing a Hawaiian shirt smiling and heading in our direction: Stan from Idaho.

"You know, I think I'd feel more comfortable with a woman. I don't mean to be picky, it's just . . ." I bit my lip and affected, I hoped, a worried look. A cloud passed momentarily over the young woman's expression as she shook her head at Stan.

"Hmmm, I believe I've paired up all of our female tour guides already. Let's see." She ran her index finger down the list on her clipboard.

"I'm from Seattle. Anybody from there?"

"Just a moment, please." Anita picked up the telephone on her desk and spoke in rapid Spanish. I thought I heard her say the name "Sienna."

She turned back to me and asked to see a major credit card: Mastercard or Visa.

"Is there a charge for the tour? Isn't it complimentary?"

"Oh, no charge, ma'am. We need the card only if you decide to purchase today. Many guests use their credit card for a down payment."

"I see." I forked over my Visa. Anita glanced at it and handed it back, asking me to wait on the lower terrace. "Your tour guide will find you in a few moments."

I complied and sat on the steps, watching the folks milling about, searching for Sienna Curtis in the mix and hoping there weren't two female employees from Seattle signed up to lead a nine o'clock tour. I saw Stan cross the terrace and approach a young couple and their Westin guide. He gestured to me and the woman turned. From this distance I could see only that she was petite, with short brown hair. As she got closer, any doubt vanished.

"Hi, I'm Sienna." She shook my hand and made small talk while we checked each other out. Wearing a snug white tank top and khaki pants, Sienna Curtis looked like any other upscale resort-goer. Italian designer sandals hugged her small feet and set off the hot-pink color of her recent pedicure while the sun glinted off the Rolex on her wrist. Prada sunglasses tucked, resort-style, into the V of her top completed the look—just the sort of girl to make potential time-share buyers feel at ease when plunking down their Visa cards. Pleased that I'd paid some attention to my own outfit, and hoping I didn't stand out as someone whose main motivation was the free breakfast, I listened to Sienna Curtis launch into her spiel.

"Here's how the tour works," she said, as she began walking away from the hotel proper. "First, we'll look at the condominium units. They're set apart from the main hotel and have their own amenities, which we'll pass along our way. Besides three swimming pools and tennis courts, we have a top-notch fitness center."

All business, Sienna recited from her practiced script and I had to step lively to keep up with her. We made our first stop on a terrace filled with pots of flowers, a breathtaking view of a swimming pool, and three curved buildings in bright shades of eggplant, terra-cotta, and aquamarine. As I took in the sight and smells of jasmine and bougainvillea, Sienna asked me how often I vacationed at destination resorts and if I was married. She seemed pleased at my answers, then asked me which hotel I'd chosen in Cabo and the room rate. Impressed with my Internet deal, she told me that these condominium units went for anywhere from three hundred to fifteen hundred dollars per night. I must have gasped since she asked, "So, are you here for the free breakfast or are you at all interested in the time-shares?"

Taken aback by her bluntness, I responded in kind.

"Actually, I'm here to talk to you."

Sienna looked closely at me for the first time since we met. "Excuse me?"

I noticed another tour guide walking onto the terrace with his guests in tow at the same time she did. "We need to keep moving the tour along. We'll go directly to breakfast and you can explain yourself there."

We walked rapidly past the fitness center and down a corridor to a large ballroom set up with a buffet breakfast and over thirty small, round, linen-covered tables. One other family and tour guide sat at the far end of the room.

"Go ahead and fill your plate. It's quite good," Sienna said. I selected some fruit and a muffin and poured a large glass of orange juice from an iced pitcher. A waiter arrived with a coffee pot just as I sat down. I nodded and he poured coffee for me and Sienna.

"So, who are you and what do you want?"

"I'm a friend of Julia Comstock and I want to know how she died."

All the color drained out of Sienna's face and her eyes widened. I detected a slight tremor in her hand as she picked up her glass of water and took a sip. Choking on it, she coughed; the color rose in her cheeks and perspiration appeared on her face. She went from ghastly pale to looking like she'd just had a long workout at the full-service fitness center.

"Should I know her?" she asked, regaining some composure.

"Oh, you know her all right, Sylvia. Let me tell you what I know. I know that you attended workshops at the Nirmala Church of Self-Actualization where you met Julia. I know that you and Julia were good buddies for a couple of months before she died. I know that you appeared at Julia's house the day she died calling yourself Sylvia Carter, and that you left Seattle in a big hurry shortly after that, selling your Queen Anne condo. I know that you worked at Comvitek and were close to Nick and Liz Villardi." I watched as my revelations registered in Sienna's face.

"Does Liz know I'm here? Who are you? Are you a cop? I don't have to listen to you!" She stood up and I grabbed her arm.

"Wait!" I said loudly enough to attract some attention. The other tour guides and employees cast worried glances in our direction. "You'd better sit down and talk to me or your employer will wonder what you're doing right now. Aren't you supposed to be selling me a time-share?" Sienna looked around, smiled at the onlookers, and, composing herself once again, sat back down.

"I can tell you that there are at least two people in Seattle who are certain that Julia Comstock did not commit suicide without a little help from her friends. I think it best if you told me your side of it, before I call my friends at the Seattle PD." I opened my purse and handed her the sketch of herself. "They'd be interested to see this sketch of the woman who had an appointment with Julia on the afternoon of her death, according to the Comstocks' housekeeper."

The unmistakable pop of a champagne cork and loud applause punctuated my statement. I turned and saw Doug from Ohio smiling broadly as his tour guide announced, "Doug is the first guest this morning to become an owner of the Westin Regina! Congratulations, Doug!" Doug waved at me from his table where his wife and two blonde children beamed their approval. When I turned back, Sienna Curtis was gone.

32

I jumped up and ran toward the closest door, weaving my way through the tour guides and guests converging on their free breakfasts.

"Miss, the tour heads out the far door."

I waved and kept going, picking up my pace to a jog, through the corridor and past the fitness center. On impulse, I turned and ducked into the center's reception area where a good-looking muscular guy wearing a sleeveless shirt stood folding towels.

"Have you seen Sienna Curtis?" I blurted out. "I thought I saw her come in here."

"Yeah, she just headed into the locker room in a big hurry." He gestured to a doorway beyond.

My eyes swept the huge room, rows and rows of lockers with wooden benches between, more lockers lining the back wall. The sound of running water suggested shower stalls through a doorway on my right. I moved quickly along the rows of lockers, looking for Sienna. The few women standing about in various stages of undress ignored me as I passed. I spotted Sienna close to the shower room, emptying a locker and stuffing things haphazardly into a large gym bag.

"Going somewhere?" I asked softly, startling her as she spun around, swinging the open bag at my stomach. Doubled over, more from shock than pain, I grabbed the bag and pulled, wrenching it from her grasp and knocking her on her butt while some of its contents went skittering onto the floor: shampoo, hairbrush, t-shirts, and a small spiral-bound notebook. We both watched it slide across the floor and land at the feet of a middle-aged woman in a skirted swimsuit and hot-pink swim cap.

"Whoa, here, let me help." The woman said as she bent to pick up the notebook. I lunged, grabbing it before Sienna could pick herself up off the floor. Springing toward it, she met my open palm instead as I thrust it upward making solid contact with her chin. She flew back against the lockers.

"Hey, what's going on? No fighting in here, I'm calling the attendant."

Sienna picked herself up and turned to the woman in the swim cap. In a reassuring voice, she said, "No, no. It's okay. We're just practicing for my self-defense class later. We're leaving now."

Sienna glared at the sight of Julia's notebook, clutched tightly in both my hands. She picked up her bag and snarled at me, "Let's go someplace where we can talk."

The woman in the swim cap mumbled something under her breath, shook her head, and walked toward the pool.

Once again, Sienna led the way past the sparkling swimming pools and across the tiled terraces, back through the open reception area and courtyard to a parking lot behind the resort. Only this time she remained silent. She pulled out a set of keys and aimed them at the row of cars as we approached. The lights on a small BMW convertible flashed in response and the locks popped up.

"You must be good at selling time-shares," I said, as I got into the passenger seat. "Or was this part of your payoff for Julia's death?"

"I didn't cause Julia's death. They used me in the twisted game they were playing with her. I didn't know they would drive her to suicide. You'll see from her journal. I kept it to protect myself. So I don't end up like she did."

I flipped open the cover and ran my fingers over the familiar handwriting while Sienna steered out the long drive to the highway and back toward town. I read the final entry dated August 16, the night before Julia went off the bridge.

I'm excited. Soon Warren and I will be together. Charlotte will send me a sign and I will know when the time is right.

"Charlotte? Another one of your aliases?"

"No. Let's stop here where we can talk."

We pulled into a gravel parking lot next to a small, bright-yellow house doing double duty as a restaurant. As we entered, Sienna spoke in Spanish to a woman behind the bar who smiled, recognizing her, and pointed us toward a vacant table. We sat down and the waitress appeared with a pot of coffee and a plastic laminated menu, which she placed on the table in front of me. I turned over my coffee cup and nodded but shook my head at the menu.

"Order something! They need the money," Sienna said.

Surprised at her concern, I suggested she order for me, confessing my ignorance of the language. The proprietress nodded as Sienna ordered, then disappeared behind the bar and into the kitchen beyond.

"Why don't you start at the beginning and tell me about your relationship with Liz Villardi. And about the deadly game you two played with Julia Comstock."

Sienna stared down at her coffee cup and took a deep breath before she spoke. "I first met Liz at a corporate function, the Comvitek spring retreat at Harrison Hot Springs Resort. I was rounding out a golf foursome. We hit it off, talked about our work. She suggested I mention the Foundation in the new brochure I was putting together since Comvitek wanted to enhance its image as a top high-tech firm and good citizen. We got together that next week and I incorporated several of her ideas into the marketing plan. Over the next few months, we played golf once in a while, I'd see her at the Seattle Athletic Club, things like that."

"Did Liz have an office at Comvitek?"

"No, she worked from her home mostly, stopping by Comvitek's office from time to time. But she stayed on top of everything going on in the corporation, that's for sure. I had the sense that Nick confided in her and she stood behind him all the way."

"Tell me about the 'twisted game' you and Liz were playing with Julia."

"That was much later. At first, Liz was just friendly, and she seemed genuinely interested in my career at Comvitek. She started telling me about new projects coming up, suggesting ways for me to get involved. Pretty soon I started getting all the plum assignments, bypassing some of my coworkers who sat much higher on the corporate food chain. I knew Liz must have intervened on my behalf."

"But she wanted something in return."

"I didn't figure that out right away. At first I felt pretty lucky. I mean, I knew I could handle the work and enjoyed the old 'it's not what you know but who you know' kind of thing. Looking back, I'd say shortly after Warren Comstock's death, something changed in Liz. Or maybe I just never noticed that side of her before."

"What do you mean?"

"You probably know that Warren Comstock died at a really tough time for the firm. Comvitek borrowed heavily to finance the European expansion. When it was in full swing, the stock tanked, the lenders got nervous, and Warren died."

"Was there ever any suspicion around Warren's death?"

"No. He was the classic type A kind of guy. Everyone figured the stress finally caught up with him and caused a massive heart attack." Sienna shook her head and I steered the topic back to Liz.

"You were talking about how Liz changed."

"Right. I had a conversation with Liz a few weeks after Warren's death. I told her how sorry I felt about it. I asked how Nick was holding up, as well as about the professional hole that Warren left in the company." Sienna paused and shook her head. "Liz laughed and said Nick could easily handle the company on his own. She even suggested that Warren's death might turn out to be the best thing that happened to Comvitek. She went off about Nick's brilliance, how Warren held him back with his conservative ideas, how the company would now make more money than ever."

Her words struck a familiar chord as I recalled Liz's harangue to me about her "first-rate" husband. Sienna went on. "Liz told me that she would tell Nick to promote me to work on the European team. She asked me if I would like to spend some time in Italy. Of course I said yes."

"And you got it?" I asked.

"Yes." Sienna looked pensive. "About a month later, Liz suggested lunch. She talked about her latest pet projects and asked me how I liked the Italy team. We were setting up an office in Milan. I'm sure I gushed on and on about it. She said she knew I had the talent for the job. During that same lunch, she told me she'd been seeing Julia Comstock at Nick's suggestion that she reach out to her. She described Julia's newfound interest in the Nirmala church and how she had been seeing this psychic medium, trying to contact Warren."

"Did she mention the psychic's name?" I asked.

"Yes, Victor Lloyd. Apparently Julia was disappointed because this psychic guy had failed to connect with Warren. I told her I thought it was sad and that I hoped Julia would get over it." Sienna stopped talking and stared past me into middle distance.

"How did Liz respond to that?"

"She laughed and said she didn't want Julia to get over it. She said she had plans to make sure Julia connected with Warren and I would help her. First I took it for a joke, and tried to laugh it off. Then I told her she could count me out. That made Liz furious, she went off about how she much she had done for me. All she wanted was one small favor. She said, 'I thought you liked the Italy project, your job at Comvitek.'"

"She threatened to fire you if you didn't cooperate."

"I was terrified. The woman went completely psycho. I mean, she recovered quickly but I couldn't look at her the same way after that. I kept flashing on the pure hatred I'd seen on her face. She convinced me that her plan would be best for everyone involved. I convinced myself that Liz had Julia's best interests at heart after all. If Julia thought Warren spoke to her from beyond the grave, it would be comforting."

"So you and Liz started having your own private séances with Julia? Wait. Julia detested Liz. I can't imagine the two of them getting together on this. How did it work?"

"Right. Liz didn't want Julia to know she was involved in any way. That's where I came in. Liz worked with someone at Nirmala, someone who knew how these things were supposed to go." Sienna shook her head, sipped her coffee. "Basically, they gave me a script. I started meeting with Julia at the church, pretending to be getting through to Warren."

I felt the heat rise in my face and began to perspire. In a voice I hardly recognized as my own, I said, "Victor? Liz was working with Victor at the church?" My mind began racing. I thought about Caroline's comment, that I'd let myself get sucked in just like the rest of them, including Julia. No, it couldn't be Victor, I told myself, remembering Rose's comment, *Victor would never hurt anyone.* He appeared genuinely upset that he hadn't been able to prevent Julia's death. I couldn't be wrong about him. Trying to control the full range of emotions that ricocheted around in my head—shock, disbelief, hurt, anger—I took a deep breath and refocused on what Sienna was saying, though her voice sounded a long way off.

"What? Who? Oh, I never knew who it was. I wasn't supposed to know."

"Did you ever meet Victor Lloyd?" The anger in my voice brought the owner out from the kitchen and over to our table apologizing, I supposed, that our food wasn't ready yet. Sienna shook her head reassuringly, said something in Spanish, and turned back to me.

"Our breakfast will be here soon, and yes and no to your

question. I never met him personally, but I saw one of his performances at the Red Lion at SeaTac. Liz wanted me to see how he did his readings so I could pattern my meetings with Julia in the same way. Then I read his book. I found it surprisingly easy to mimic his style. He's so down to earth." She grimaced. "Sorry, I guess I can't really describe some woo-woo psychic as down-to-earth, but he's, you know, confident. He seems so sincere."

"Oh, I know. Believe me, I know."

"I think I almost convinced myself that there were people who could connect with the dead or, as Lloyd says, those 'on the other side.'"

"But you were getting a script from Liz, and Liz wanted Julia dead."

"I never realized that until our last session. I went to Julia's house that day to confess, to warn her. I felt terrified by then, sure her days were numbered." Her voice faltered. "Liz sent her off the bridge that morning without my help."

Sienna started crying and our food arrived at the same time. The owner put the plates on the table and then put her arm around Sienna, saying something comforting to her in Spanish while giving me the stink eye. A couple of middle-aged fishermen walked in and, sensing female distress, moved to the table most distant from us. We were left alone while our hostess waited on them. The distraction helped Sienna pull herself together. She looked down at the plate in front of her and began to eat as if on automatic pilot.

"What scared you about your last session, Sienna?"

"In earlier sessions, Julia talked about joining Warren, how she would rather be with him on the other side than living without him. I usually let it go, saying something about how there was a right time for everything and it wasn't her time yet. The script gave me symbols for Julia—you know, the way Lloyd refers to symbols—and together we tried to interpret them. In earlier sessions I'd given her a hillside, a church, Mt. Rainier, water, a sensation of flying or falling. The script for our last session suggested I give her the image of a bridge." She shook her head. "I refused to give her that last sign."

The picture came together in my head. "If you're on the Aurora Avenue Bridge, you see all those things, St. Mark's Cathedral on Capitol Hill, the east side of Queen Anne Hill, Lake Union, and Mount Rainier in the distance. You were not only telling her to jump, but from where."

She nodded grimly. "Instead, that night I told Julia that Warren loved her, that he was happy on the other side but that she had more things to do here on earth, that those signs he'd been giving her were signs of life. Liz raged at me afterwards, fired me from Comvitek, and assured me that if I said anything about these sessions to anyone I'd be the one joining Warren."

"She couldn't actually fire you."

"Oh, but she could. The next day Nick Villardi called me into his office to say he'd put the European expansion on hold. He blamed it on Comvitek's tremendous financial pressures; he said he needed to downsize."

"Do you remember the date?"

"How could I ever forget it? August eighth. I wrestled with what to do. I was worried that Liz would find a replacement for me, worried what Julia might do. A few days later, I called Julia at her home and told her I needed to see her. She was surprised to hear from me directly. She said someone from Nirmala had called and told her I'd been called out of town unexpectedly for a family emergency and that someone else was covering our weekly session."

"Did she tell you who made that call?" I asked, thinking about Rose, knowing it couldn't have been her. It crossed my mind that Sienna might be making up this story as she went along, covering her ass. But she seemed sincere.

"No. The name didn't matter. I knew Liz had found someone to replace me, someone who could easily and even unwittingly push Julia off the edge. If only I'd insisted on seeing her right away instead of waiting, she might be alive."

I filled the silence with a question. "What happened on the day she died?"

"I heard about it from my neighbor. He'd been driving north on Aurora that morning, on his way to the DOL to renew his driver's license and complained about how the Aurora Avenue bridge was closed. The rumor was that someone had jumped. I turned on the radio but they weren't reporting it. I guess they never report suicides. I felt sick. Somehow I just knew Julia had jumped. Frantic, I went to her house. And my fear was confirmed."

"That's when you stole her journal. Why didn't you go to the police?"

"Right, and get arrested for being an accessory to murder? Isn't that what they call it? The journal is clear. I'm the one Julia worked with. She didn't know about what happened behind the scenes. Liz obviously paid off someone at the church. They would deny any connection to me. Nope, I was a sitting duck. I had to leave."

"But who sent her off the bridge? Does the journal describe the final session? Can we connect that with Liz?"

"I've read the thing over and over. In it, Julia says Charlotte, the name we used for Julia's 'spirit guide,' showed her a bridge and Warren calling out to her."

"But she doesn't say who Charlotte came through?"

"No."

"And why didn't she jump the next day? Why did she wait a week?"

"I think she was waiting for a sunny day. Only on a sunny day can you see Mount Rainier from the bridge deck."

I let her comment sink in while I tried to put all the puzzle pieces together in my mind. Something was missing. Why did Liz want to kill Julia? Nirmala got all the money.

"Sienna, we're going back to Seattle. I've got to find the connection between Nirmala and Liz. I want to know if Victor Lloyd was writing that script for you. We'll contact the police and you'll tell them what you know. You're likely to get a favorable deal if you testify against Liz and Nirmala."

Sienna slowly shook her head. "No, Ann, I'm not going back. Even if you do find some way to connect Liz and Nirmala with Julia's death, any 'favorable' deal might mean jail time. I can't do it."

"But I have the journal. It implicates you."

"Maybe. I've thought about that. But I doubt the police will want to reopen this case. They won't go through the trouble of extraditing me from Mexico based on the confused writing of an unstable woman. No, I'm not going back. I can get pretty lost in Mexico, live pretty cheaply."

I knew she was right. Julia had jumped off the bridge. The "push" was purely psychological. Still, I wasn't about to give up. Liz Villardi and whoever else was behind this would have to pay.

33

Sienna dropped me off at the Melia and I went up to my room to make some phone calls. I forced myself to look at the situation rationally. If Victor was involved with Liz Villardi and Sienna Curtis, he might try to put me off his trail by sending me to look for my sister. He might pretend to have messages for me, feelings for me. I cringed thinking about how easily I'd been seduced—the memory fresh in my mind, so thrilling, even now. Maybe that was his usual M.O. It's what Jennifer Dixon told me early on.

No, I refused to accept that, couldn't believe I'd been so wrong about him. I cast about for other possibilities. I decided to call Erin Becker to see if she'd gotten any information on that license plate, then I'd call Rose to see if she ever saw Liz Villardi around the church.

Reaching for the phone, I saw I had messages waiting. My stomach reacted before my head, with that sinking sense of dread I get whenever the phone rings in the middle of the night. I carefully followed the instructions for picking up voicemail, imagining Jack calling to say he missed me, or Jeff with some ridiculous work-related crisis.

"Ann, Kelly Long." Her voice sounded shaky, worried. "Call me as soon as you can. It's about Sienna Curtis. Shit. I got caught snooping, and, uh, mentioned you. Call me." I wrote down her cell number and retrieved the next message.

"Ann, it's Nicole." Her voice cracked and I could hear her struggling not to cry. "I'm so sorry." There was a long pause. "It's Pooch, oh God, she's been poisoned, Ann. She's at the vet right now.

Call me!"

I had difficulty controlling my fingers on the phone pad with the buzzing that had started inside my head. After two unsuccessful tries to place the long distance call, I gave up and asked the hotel operator for help. Nicole's number rang four times before going into voicemail. I left a frantic message, then tried my home number. My own voice startled me as the machine picked up on the first ring. Nicole must be on the phone. The vet. I'd call his office. I fumbled through my carry-on bag and found my planner but I couldn't remember if I'd written the number under V for Vet, O for O'Malley, or G for Greenlake Animal Hospital. I finally located the number. Becky, the ever-cheery receptionist, answered on the first ring, patiently listened, and reassured me that Pooch was resting now. The next twenty-four hours would be key as to whether or not she would make it.

"Luckily your dog sitter got Pooch here right away."

The buzzing in my head got louder and Becky sounded farther away.

"She might not make it?" I asked in a small voice. After a few minutes I managed to ask the questions running through my head.

"How did it happen? What kind of poison did she get into? I don't know anything. Please tell me what you know."

"I'm sorry, Ann. I'll have Doctor O'Malley call you back with the details. He's in surgery right now. If you hold, I'll take a look at Pooch's chart and see if I can find out anything for you."

I sat there on hold listening to canned music, vaguely annoyed to hear the Beatles transformed into Muzak. I stared blankly at the wall while images of Pooch ran through my brain: Pooch greeting me at the door, Pooch following me around the house, Pooch chasing a tennis ball, Pooch swimming in Puget Sound. My tears overflowed, running down my cheeks and dripping onto my sundress. I reached behind the phone for a tissue and wiped my face while the minutes passed with agonizing slowness. Finally, Becky's voice,

"Ann? I've got the chart." I could hear papers shuffling as she searched the file. "Nicole brought Pooch in around eight thirty this morning. It says Pooch got into something when Nicole first let her out around seven thirty. The dog vomited, had diarrhea, and seemed disoriented; she was bumping into things. Her symptoms are consistent with poisoning and the doctor is treating her for that. We'll know what kind of poison when traces show up in her urine. That can take from three to six hours post ingestion. Should be within an hour. We're lucky she got to us so quickly. The prognosis for successful therapy is usually excellent, depending on the type of poison, if treatment is started within a few hours. As I said, Pooch is resting now. She's not in any pain."

Those last words rang in my head: "not in any pain" as in, "at least she was not in any pain when she died." *Pooch can't die!* I couldn't stand it.

I thanked Becky and told her I'd come in as soon as I got back to Seattle. Somehow I managed to call the airline, pack up my stuff, pay my bill, and get a taxi to the airport. The next flight left at two, getting me back to Seattle around seven.

Sitting in the waiting area at the airport, I flipped through a magazine, worried about Pooch, wishing I could get home sooner. As I headed for the bank of pay phones to call Jack, hoping I could reach him, I heard my name announced from the overhead speakers: "Ann Dexter, please return to Alaska Airlines, gate number fourteen, for a message."

I ran for the desk, dreading more bad news about Pooch.

"You have a call on line three, Miss. You can take it on the courtesy phone there." The airline employee gestured to a phone in a small alcove to her right.

"Ann, it's Sienna Curtis. I'm so glad I caught you before you left."

"What's wrong?" I asked.

"When I got back to my place, it had been torn apart."

"You were robbed?"

"I don't have anything of value, really. Nothing's missing as far as I can tell. But I'm scared. One of the hotel employees said a guy showed up at the Westin late this morning, asking about me. He said he was my brother. I don't have a brother, Ann."

"Did you get a description?"

"Yeah, American, sandy hair, tall and big and muscular, with a tattoo of a snake on his arm. It doesn't sound like anyone I know. Or care to know."

"But maybe this guy showing up is just a coincidence. Maybe some guy you sold a time-share to got his Visa bill and had a change of heart." Another thought entered my head as I glanced at my carry-on bag. "What about the journal, Sienna? Does anyone know you have it?"

"I don't have it, do I? Liz knows about it, but surely she would have come looking for it before now, if it worried her. Wait! Does she know you're here?"

"Yeah, I think she figured that out," I said, thinking of Kelly Long's message. "I guess I don't have to tell you to watch your butt. You know, you might reconsider talking to the cops before you get hurt."

"Talking to the cops will only bring me trouble, Ann. I don't think so."

"Look, Sienna, I have a friend in the Seattle PD whose husband is a lawyer. I'll talk to him when I get back. See what he says about your involvement and what your testimony might be worth. If it will nail Liz Villardi and Nirmala."

"Right." Sienna hung up abruptly. I still had a few minutes before boarding so I enlisted an airport security guard to help me place a long distance call, cursing myself for not getting an international chip in my cell phone before I left. Kelly Long answered on the first ring.

"Oh my God, Ann, you have no idea what's going on around

here. They fired me!" I held the phone at arm's length to keep from damaging my eardrums as Kelly yelled incoherently into the other end.

"Kelly, slow down! Listen to me. I'm sorry about your job, but you know you're better off out of there." I hoped my words didn't sound as self-serving and hollow to her as they did to me. I kept talking to fill the silence on Kelly's end.

"Kelly, what did you find out about Sienna Curtis?"

"Not much, that's the bizarre part. Comvitek gave her a healthy severance deal and there's no forwarding address in the file. The way Liz went off, though—it was unbelievable. She came into Comvitek right after Nick let me go. I hadn't even finished packing up my desk. She shut the door to my office and asked me who put me up to snooping in the files. She said she could make life pretty difficult for me if I didn't tell her. She scared me, Ann. I honestly thought she might mean physical violence, not only that I would never find another job in Seattle, which she also promised."

"So you gave her my name. Never mind about that now, Kelly. You need to stay out of her way. Go visit a friend somewhere. Can you do that?"

"What are we talking about here, Ann? What did you find out about the Villardis, are they dangerous? Like murderers?"

"Let's just say it would be best for you to steer clear of them for a while, that's all. So, think about where you might go for a few days and let me know."

After more worried questions, which I answered as best I could, Kelly gave me the name and number of an old college friend of hers, living in Portland now. She would call me if she went anywhere else.

I had the entire flight from Cabo to Seattle, with a stop in LA, to figure out my next move, but I felt like I was operating in slow motion, or underwater, my worries about Pooch constantly in the forefront. Only one thing was certain: if Victor was involved in any way, I would make him pay. I took out my notebook to write down the facts as I understood them, already considering how I could use them in an article exposing Nirmala and Liz. I flipped open the notebook and the Satya Retreat Center brochure fell into my lap. I studied it, noticing the names of the developer, a list of donors, and the partnership for the project on the back page. There it was: Comvitek—the connection between Liz and Nirmala. I slipped the brochure back into my bag and began to write.

When a flight attendant came by offering beverage service, I closed my notebook and ordered a Corona, relishing the tart tang of lime on the bottle's lip as the cold bitter drink rolled across my tongue. I licked my lips and drank down the twelve ounces in a few long pulls. The beer went straight to my head, dulling my worry while sharpening my anger. I got up and moved toward the rear of the cabin to stretch my legs. Standing behind a sunburned young mom with whining preschooler in tow, I reminded myself that my childless state was not without its benefits, while idly glancing around at my fellow passengers stuck in their impossibly small airplane seats.

Responding to that sense of being looked at, I turned and caught the man staring at me. Our eyes locked for a long moment before he looked away. He appeared to be in his late twenties or early thirties and quite tall, considering how his knees jammed up against the seat in front of him. He wore his thick, sandy-colored hair cut short. Dismissing my thoughts as paranoid, I reminded myself that scores of tall, blonde, buff guys spend time in Cabo. Just then, he reached over with his left hand and began rummaging through the seat-back pocket in front of him. Large biceps strained the fabric of his short-sleeved polo shirt and I noticed the dark smudge of a tattoo appear briefly from beneath his sleeve.

The bathroom door swung open, sending mom and toddler into my face and momentarily blocking my view of the cabin. I wedged myself and my carry-on bag into the closet-like toilet, slid the latch to "occupied," and waited for my pulse to return to normal. I looked in the mirror and didn't like the fear I saw staring back at me. I took a deep breath, searched my bag for a hairbrush, and pushed Julia's journal to the bottom. Dragging the brush through my hair, I told myself that no matter how big and menacing this guy might be, he couldn't hurt me on a crowded airplane.

Somewhat reassured, I opened the door and walked quickly through the cabin to my seat, planning to take a closer look at Mr. Universe as I passed his row. Even though he was now wearing a straw hat with a green "Cabo-Wabo" band pulled down over his forehead and a pair of Ray-Bans, the guy remained conspicuous. He looked out the window and appeared oblivious to me, so I plugged into the headset and watched the in-flight entertainment, relieved to have a diversion.

34

As we touched down in LA I fired up my cell phone, got through to Nicole, and asked her exactly what had happened with Pooch. She launched into the story.

"When I let her out first thing this morning, she took off around the house and into the backyard. She didn't come when I called so I got my jacket and went looking for her. There she was chowing down on something—I couldn't tell what—so I yelled, 'Leave it!' She gobbled it up instead."

"Typical," I said.

"Right. So I took her in and fed her—she inhaled her food as always—and I went up to take a shower. When I got out, I heard noises coming from the living room. I ran downstairs and found Pooch on the floor twitching."

"Oh, God."

"It was really scary. She'd thrown up most of her dog food onto the rug. I called her and she struggled to get up. She walked around like a drunk, bumping into the furniture, falling down again. Oh, Ann, it was horrible. I had to get my mom to help lift her into the car. She couldn't even jump into the seat."

I imagined the scene, how painful it must have been.

"But, Ann, the vet's pretty sure she'll be okay. The tests identified the poison as slug bait, not antifreeze. That's good since antifreeze is pretty much always deadly, but slug bait can be purged if you get the process going right away. Dr. O'Malley pumped her stomach and he's giving her some fluids and is keeping her overnight. We can get her in the morning."

I thanked Nicole and told her I'd be in touch, then called Erin Becker. She wasn't in so I left her a message asking that she get back to me with any information on that partial license plate as soon as possible. I hung up, hoping for a break. The few passengers who were continuing on to Seattle stood in the aisle stretching their legs—no Mr. Universe in sight. I laughed at my earlier trepidation and checked my watch—plenty of time before takeoff. I headed into the terminal for some frozen yogurt, stopped at a newsstand for a *New York Times*, and got back to the gate just in time to reboard.

A middle-aged, balding, and talkative man now occupied the seat next to me. Before the plane even lifted off, he told me he'd been in Los Angeles for his niece's wedding and that he worked for Boeing. I wasn't up for listening to the rest of this guy's fascinating life story, so I smiled, nodded, and opened the newspaper, hoping it might work as a "Do Not Disturb" sign and idly wondered why strangers so often engage me in these one-way conversations on airplanes. Maybe I look like a shrink.

After landing in Seattle, I made my way to the third floor of the parking garage looking for a shuttle van to long-term parking. I stood shivering in my light raincoat, as the biting wind and rain whipped through the waiting area, while all the wrong courtesy vehicles slowed and moved past me. Just as I flagged down the Doug Fox van, my cell phone rang and I managed to retrieve it from my bag while handing my suitcase to the driver.

"Ann, it's Erin Becker. I've got that report you wanted from the DOL. The best they could do with a partial number is a list of similar plates in Washington. That's what I've got here. You want me to scan and email it to you?"

"Sure. Wait—how long is it? I mean, could you take a quick look at it now? Check for a couple of names?"

"It's a few pages. Sure, what am I looking for?"

"Check for the Nirmala Church or Liz Villardi. Maybe Victor Lloyd."

I listened to papers shuffling as Erin paged through the list, occasionally mumbling, "Nope, nope, nope" into the phone.

"I think you're out of luck, Ann, I don't see any of those names here. But I'll email it to you so you can take a better look. Oh, here's something."

My heart thumped as I waited for Erin to go on. "What is it?"

"Well, it's not a church, but there is someone listed here with a prefix, R-e-v, Reverend, in front of his name. It's Waters—Reverend Robert Waters. Does that help?"

"Yup, that's perfect. Thanks so much."

"Ann, is there something you should be reporting to the police?"

"I don't think so. Not yet, anyway. Believe me, you'll be the first to know when I do," I said as the shuttle pulled up and stopped next to my car.

I sat behind the steering wheel and punched in Victor's cell phone number, waiting for the heater to kick in. No answer. I wasn't leaving a message. Frustrated, I dialed up the church and got the after-hours message. Okay, Plan B. I hit 411 and waited until I got an actual person, then asked for Victor Lloyd's home phone number and address. As I jotted down the numbers, I remembered our night at the Alki Beach Bistro, how Victor had pointed out his apartment across the street.

I drove to West Seattle and found a parking place one block from the public beach and close to Victor's address. His apartment was on the second floor at one end of a white clapboard building with its own exterior staircase. I climbed the stairs and stood shivering on the small covered landing searching for a doorbell while the sound of the waves crashing onto the seawall and the noisy wind chimes from the apartment next door rang in my ears. Rain pelted the deck. I knocked on the door's window and waited. Light from inside the house leaked out at the edges of the blinds. When I heard footsteps approaching, I felt my stomach flip and took a deep breath, imagining how Victor would react to my unannounced appearance, to the accusation I'd have to make.

The door opened and Victor stood there looking at me, his eyes registering surprise, then delight as he flashed one of his most inviting smiles. Taking a closer look at me, he rearranged his expression into one of concern. He reached for me but I backed up fast, losing my balance for an instant before my hand found the railing.

"Ann, what's wrong? Come in. What happened? Did you find your sister?" He held the door open for me and I stepped into the small entryway.

"Please, sit," he said, gesturing to the brown leather sectional that dominated the living room and faced the fireplace. I sat and avoided his eyes, looking instead at the large vintage photograph of a baseball stadium—Candlestick Park maybe—hanging on the wall.

"Tell me what's going on. Your face is scaring me," he said, sitting on the edge of the sofa, his eyes riveted on mine.

"I have some pretty scary things on my mind. And no, I didn't find my sister, but I did find Sylvia Carter, now living in Mexico. Her real name is Sienna Curtis."

He reacted as if I'd slapped him—a mix of shock and puzzlement crossing his face.

"She told me some interesting things about Julia Comstock's death. Like, Liz Villardi and someone else, someone from the church, sent Julia off the bridge that day. They gave Sienna a script. She pretended to be a psychic medium, getting messages from Warren. Her technique was a lot like yours."

Victor slowly shook his head. "What are you saying?"

When I didn't reply, he stood up, looming over me. "You think I'm in on it!" he said, his voice echoing the disbelief in his face. "Have you been to the police?"

"Not yet. I . . ." I couldn't sit still any more, nor could I control my own voice, rising in volume and pitch. I stood to face him. "Tell me what you know about this, Victor, and don't mess with me anymore." I squeezed my hand into a fist and slammed his chest.

"Someone poisoned my dog!"

Lloyd backed away from me and raised his palms out in front of him. "Whoa, now whoa, wait a minute! What's your dog got to do with this? Please sit down, Ann. Start at the beginning and tell me what happened in Mexico." His voice—low, even, and filled with concern—calmed me.

I sat down on the sofa's edge and told him everything I'd heard from Sienna Curtis. The longer I talked, the more doubt crept back into my head. "Can you honestly tell me that you knew nothing about this, Victor?"

He sat motionless, the question hanging between us.

"I'm as shocked as you are," he said softly.

I registered his sincerity and looked away, my head a jumble of competing thoughts and emotions.

"Did you even *consider* it might be someone else and not me?"

"I think it might be Reverend Bob," I said in a small voice, realizing that I believed Victor—had wanted to believe him all along. "But I needed to be sure, needed to hear you deny it."

"Okay, I'm denying it." Victor abruptly stood up and walked to the far side of the room, staring out the French doors at the Seattle skyline shimmering in the distance over Elliott Bay, before turning back to me. "Why Bob? I mean, I've always thought of him as a flawed human being. He's used to getting what he wants. But I've always considered him to be genuinely spiritual—serious about his work with the church."

"Oh yeah, he's serious all right, serious enough to kill someone to finance his business venture, all in the name of religion, no doubt." I told Victor how Bob ran me into a ditch and followed it up with a threatening phone call. I also told him what I had learned from Caroline's lawyer about the church's financial dilemma and the lawsuit in Idaho.

"Incredible," he said, returning to the sofa and shaking his head. "I mean, Bob was obviously desperate for money, but the idea that he could kill someone . . ." Victor's voice trailed off and he sat there pensively, processing the whole ugly mess.

"What are you going to do now?" he asked.

"I'll have to call the police."

"You can't go to the police! It's too dangerous! Think about it, you don't have anything solid on Bob, nothing connecting him to those meetings with Julia."

"True." I nodded. "But I can't let him get away with this."

We stared at each other for a while.

"Maybe I could poke around the church. See if something turns up."

"I don't know," I said, suddenly exhausted. "I need to think this through. I should head home. I'm pretty wiped. The last couple of days have been unreal." I stood up.

"Wait. You never told me about your dog. Is she okay?"

"She's doing better. Thanks."

"I'm glad to hear it. Hey, you really don't need to run off. Have you eaten? I could put something together. How about a beer? A glass of wine? Baseball stories?" Victor looked so eager that I had to smile.

"I'll take a rain check," I said, heading for the door. Again the awkward moment, as I stood holding onto the doorknob, trying to figure out the right way to say good night to this man.

"Ann, wait," he said, touching my shoulder. "I know we didn't exactly meet in the usual way. And I know you're still a little wary about me. But I'd like to have a chance to prove you wrong. I mean, I'd like to get together outside of this mess. I'd like to . . ."

I let him fumble through his speech, a little surprised that his usual confidence failed him right now. But then, there was nothing usual about this whole thing.

"Yes?" I smiled. "You'd like to . . .?"

He smiled back.

"I'd like to do *this*," he said, pulling me close and stroking my hair. I relaxed into his embrace and held on, just listening to him breathe, to his heart beating. I needed the comfort and it felt so right.

Reluctantly, I let go and looked up at him. As he bent down to meet me, his kiss was tentative at first, then deeper and more passionate, easily moving beyond where we left off the other night to kisses so intense and filled with desire that every nerve ending in my body stood at attention. I focused on Victor's tongue as it slowly moved from my mouth to my neck, then lower. He reached under my sweater to unclasp my bra and I felt an electric zing as he lightly caressed my breast. My sweater was up and over my head in one cooperative moment. Breathless, I moved back against the door, ran my fingers through his hair, and lifted his face to mine.

"Mmmm, nice," he whispered in my ear. "May I show you the bedroom?" His hands inched down my back and he pulled me close, pressing against me so I could feel how much he wanted me. I felt a tingling spread through my body, then realized it was my cell phone vibrating in the back pocket of my jeans.

I groaned and pulled the phone out. Before I could answer it, Victor closed his hand over mine. "Not now. Please."

"But. It could be important. About my dog, maybe. I'll just check."

Victor shook his head and stepped back. I pulled on my sweater and flipped the phone open. One missed call. I pressed "Display." Stunned, I read the name next to the little green telephone icon— "Jack."

"Oh no—I've got to go," I said, and tucked the phone back into my pocket. "I am so sorry."

"Is your dog okay? What is it?"

I shook my head. "It's not Pooch. It's a long story. I really do have to go." I clumsily re-hooked my bra and pulled myself together while avoiding Victor's eyes. I kissed his cheek.

"I'll call you tomorrow," I said, moving out the door, down the steps, and into my car faster than a bat out of hell.

35

I threw my cell phone onto the passenger seat next to me and willed it not to ring while I concentrated on driving home through the rain. As I wheeled onto the West Seattle Bridge, the phone chimed twice, alerting me to a new voice message. I wasn't ready. I'd have to get my thoughts in order before I talked to Jack.

By the time I reached my exit I had decided to tell Jack the truth. Not the whole truth really, not about my feelings for Victor, but the truth about our relationship, that we should stick to being just friends; the benefits had run out. Even in my head that sounded harsh. How was I going to find the right words? And did I have to do that right now? Maybe I should wait until this thing was over.

"Chicken!" I said out loud as I stopped at a light and listened to Jack's voicemail. He sounded worried. He'd talked to Nicole and gone over to my house looking for me. He was waiting for me there now. No putting this off.

I pulled into my driveway with my stomach in a knot. As I reached for the doorknob, Jack opened the door and threw his arms around me.

"Oh, Ann, I'm so sorry about Pooch," he said with so much genuine feeling that I totally lost it. All the tension of the past couple of days poured out in gulping sobs as Jack rubbed my back and murmured soothing words into my ear.

"Hey, hey, it's going to be okay. I'm here. You're okay."

I was *so* not okay. In fact, I was a complete jerk. I'd messed around with this wonderful man, just about jumped into bed with someone I hardly knew and was still mucking around in a murder

258 • RACHEL BUKEY

investigation.

"Just let it all out. You'll feel better."

"I need a tissue," I said, moving away from Jack and into the kitchen. Grabbing the whole box, I used one to blow my nose, then walked into the living room and threw myself on the sofa, trying to get it together enough to talk. Jack followed and sat down next to me.

"I never cry," I said stupidly and Jack smiled, taking my hand in his.

"I know. But you're exhausted, wrung-out. It's not a character flaw, you know. It's probably even good for you, Ms. Tough As Nails."

My turn to smile. Jack could always make me smile.

"Do you want to talk about it? Any of it? Pooch? Your trip to Mexico? Your sister?"

"Not yet. I could use a glass of wine." I walked into the kitchen and Jack followed. Looking for some courage to say what I would have to say, I poured us each a glass of the sauvignon blanc I found in the fridge, took a large sip from mine and sat down at the kitchen table.

Jack sat down across from me and took a sip of wine before he spoke. "You know, Ann, Nicole thinks Pooch will be okay," he said, misreading my discomfort.

"That's not it, Jack. I mean, I'm worried about Pooch—yes—pissed off that someone would do this to her, but I'm so damned confused about everything else."

"Like who's behind it—of course you are. You know you're way over your head here. And I hope you went to the police. Is that why it took you over two hours to get home from the airport?"

"Uh, no, that's not why," I said, looking away.

"Okay, well, I'm pretty much in the dark here. You have to talk to me," he said, waiting.

"Yes, we need to talk," I said pointedly, looking directly into his eyes, figuring he would understand the universal opening for the "I'm breaking up with you" conversation.

"I'm not going to like this, am I?" he asked, recognition dawning in his eyes. "What have you really been doing these past few days?"

I told him everything and he let me ramble on, reacting only with wide eyes and occasional head-shaking before he finally spoke.

"Tell me you're not taken in by this guy," he said, taking my hand. "Tell me you're not falling for him." I pulled my hand away, reaching for the wine glass instead.

"Unbelievable."

"I don't expect you to understand, Jack. I barely understand it myself. I just know that this whole thing has opened me up somehow. I've thought about things I haven't faced since Ben died. Like, what love is all about, how life is short. How I need to get back on track with my life, starting with my sister. And I don't want to jerk you around anymore. I care too much about you."

"Don't say that. You've never jerked me around. I know you care about me and you know how I feel about you. Ben's death brought us together and I've never expected to replace him. I just thought you had room for me too," he said, his eyes searching mine. When I didn't respond, he stared off into space. "Please tell me this has nothing to do with that psychic."

I shook my head. "Look, it's not about Victor. It's about me," I said.

"Oh, Christ, it *is* about the psychic. What's with this guy? He's obviously very good at what he does—it's that he's done it to *you* that infuriates me."

"Jack, it's not like that."

"Right," he said, his anger escalating with each sentence. "I wish you could hear yourself right now, talking about how you're so open to things, how you're contemplating the meaning of life. Next thing I know you're going to tell me that this guy's been channeling your dead parents."

Jack immediately registered my reaction to that one. I hadn't told him about the reading I'd had with Victor but he could see it in my face.

"I know it must sound strange but Victor does have some sort of . . .uh . . . sensitivity, I guess I'd call it. An ability to communicate, understand things about life after—"

Jack cut me off.

"Come on! You sound like someone straight out of one of those bullshit seminars you were laughing at a few days ago. And you trust this guy to help you to investigate this church? His church? First you suspected him; now you're allies. And you still don't see what's going on here?"

"Nothing's going on. Oh, never mind! You just don't get it."

"Oh, I get it all right, but you don't. How about this? You're onto him so he deflects your attention from the truth by seducing you—or whatever the hell has been going on—then offers to help you out. Not surprisingly, his help involves implicating someone else."

"I have other evidence connecting Reverend Waters with Liz and Sienna, Jack. It wasn't Victor's suggestion. Forget it! This isn't productive. Let's not talk about it now. Of course you think the worst about Victor! You're hurt," I said, trying to keep my thoughts straight, to keep the seed of Jack's suspicion from growing in my head.

"Wake up, Ann, and look at what's really going on here! It's all wrong."

I thought about how right it felt less than an hour ago. Encouraged by that memory, I took Jack's hand. "You'll have to trust my judgment, Jack—trust that I know what I'm doing here."

He sat quietly, looking into my face.

"Okay, I'll try. But where does this leave us? I refuse to believe that you don't want to see me anymore. I won't lose you, Ann. Not like this."

"Jack, I . . ." My eyes welled up and I couldn't speak. It was easier when he was angry. I wished he would throw things, call me names, maybe.

"I'm not sure what will happen with us," I said. "I don't want to lose you as a friend, Jack, but I'd understand if you never want to talk to me again."

"Don't be ridiculous. We're adults. We'll work through this. I'll take you on any terms you're offering."

"That sounds terrible. It makes me feel like such a shit," I said, shaking my head.

"No, no, don't worry," he said, his voice lightening up. "I figure you'll come to your senses soon and recognize what a catch I am." His eyes sparkled and he waggled his eyebrows at me, making me smile. "In the meantime, I think I'll head home." He stood up to leave.

"Okay. I'll—"

Jack touched my lips with his index finger. "Don't say it. Don't say, 'I'll call you.' I couldn't stand that."

I hugged him and we walked to the door. I stood there for a long time, staring down the street after he'd driven off, wondering what I'd done. Eventually I closed the door, walked through the room, and slumped onto the couch—Pooch's favorite spot, the one piece of furniture she's not allowed to get up on but always does. I stretched out, sinking into the sofa pillows, and breathed in the dog's scent. "Oh, Pooch," I said aloud, "we'll be okay." Closing my eyes to sleep, I prayed it was true.

I woke up to the sound of a driving horizontal rain pelting the front window. Stretching the stiffness from my neck and legs from sleeping on the lumpy sofa, I walked into the kitchen and glanced at the clock on the microwave, annoyed that I'd slept half the day away. But then, I hadn't fallen asleep until early morning. I went through the ritual of making coffee, searching the refrigerator and pantry for anything edible and trying to remember the last food I'd eaten. It must have been in the LA airport yesterday afternoon.

On automatic pilot, I opened the front door, cursed the rain as it hit my face, picked up the newspaper from the step, and removed it from the double plastic bag meant to keep it dry. I mixed up some instant oatmeal and flipped though the soggy paper while waiting for the coffee to brew. Once the caffeine started to work, I tried to sort through the events of the last twenty-four hours. My head hurt. I took some ibuprofen, poured another cup of coffee, and knew I couldn't do anything until I saw that Pooch was okay. I threw on some clothes and drove to Greenlake Animal Hospital.

Becky had a big smile on her face as I walked up to the reception desk.

"Pooch is going to be fine, Ann. The doctor just checked her. She's had some breakfast and seems to be keeping it down. That's a good thing."

"Can I see her?"

Becky went into the back to check with the vet and returned in a few minutes to say Dr. O'Malley wanted to see me. I followed her down the hall and into an office where I spotted Pooch curled up on a dog bed in the corner.

"Pooch!" I ran over and threw my arms around the dog's big head. She looked up at me and started whimpering, giving me the doggy version of the last twenty-four hours while her tail thumped wildly against the floor.

The vet chuckled. "She's a great dog. I'm keeping her here where it's quiet and I can watch her while I catch up on some paperwork. She's going to make it."

I sat down and let Pooch cram her face into my lap while I scratched her ears. The doctor continued talking while Pooch covered my face with wet kisses.

"Okay, Pooch, enough now. Sit." The dog sat at attention, waiting for the next command while Dr. O'Malley explained that he wanted to keep her for one more night to make sure she could keep her food down. They would keep her hydrated and take some more tests to be sure the poison had worked its way out of her system completely. I nodded, thanked him, and rose to go, noticing that while we were talking Pooch had curled up on the floor and gone back to sleep. It was just as well.

36

I sat in the parking lot and tried to figure out what to do next. There was no need for me to show up at the office—Jeff wasn't expecting me back at work until Monday and I wasn't ready to face him. My head, like the weather, felt foggy and sodden, while the day stretched out before me—a damp gray tableau waiting for me to start the action.

I picked up my phone and called Victor. Both his home and cell phone went straight to voicemail so I drove back to my place for take two of my day. I stood under the hot shower spray, sorting through my options. Maybe I should go to the police. Jack was right—I was in my way over my head.

But then, Victor was right, too: I really had nothing to connect Reverend Bob with Liz and Sienna, nor did I have Sienna available to testify against Liz. But Liz didn't know that. By the time the bathroom was completely filled with steam and the hot water began to run out, I'd decided to confront Liz, tell her about my meeting with Sienna, scare her a little. See if she would give up Bob to save herself.

I dressed quickly and called Victor again. This time I left a message. As I drove to Denny Blaine the wind picked up. It looked like the beginning of a storm—a real howler from the sound of it. Tree branches along Lake Washington Boulevard waved wildly and the wind whipped the lake into whitecaps. The sky turned dark as night. I parked in front of the Villardi's house and thought about Liz. She might be dangerous, but she was a backhanded, sneaky kind of dangerous, the kind of dangerous that can coerce suicide and poison animals, but not the gun-carrying or knife-wielding kind. I figured I could handle her. The stairs up to the house were wet and black and as slippery as I remembered. I held the railing tightly and made my way to the front door as quickly as possible. I saw lights on inside the house and heard music playing but no voices that I could make out. I rang the bell, flipped up the collar of my raincoat, and waited.

The expression on Liz's face was hidden in the shadow of the hallway as she opened the door. Her tone was mocking.

"Look what the cat dragged in," she said. "I expected you a little sooner, Ann. What took you so long? Won't you come in?" Liz backed into the room and made a sweeping gesture to the empty living room.

"Don't worry. We're alone. Nick is a busy man, you know. All work and no play makes Nick a dull boy." Liz weaved slightly as she headed toward the kitchen and I realized she'd been drinking.

"I hope you'll join me in a glass of wine while we have our little girl talk. It must be the cocktail hour somewhere." I declined but followed behind her through the living room and into the kitchen.

The gleaming marble surface of the countertop held an ice bucket from which Liz pulled a half-empty bottle of chardonnay and topped off her glass. She sat at the table, suggesting I do the same.

"I prefer to stand."

"Suit yourself. I know why you're here and where you've been, but you're wasting your time and mine. I have nothing to say and nothing to worry about. Just to be sure, I talked to my lawyer earlier. He confirmed what I already suspected. They'll never go after me for Julia's death. Even if some overzealous prosecutor wanted to pursue murder charges, chances of them being successful are very low. Julia committed suicide, after all."

"That may be true, Liz, but if I were you, I'd be worried about my partner, the good Reverend Bob."

Liz looked stunned for a moment, then charged ahead. "I don't have any idea what you're talking about. Bob has nothing to do with this."

"It's noble of you to defend him. But I can't imagine why you would. Instead, imagine what will happen to your reputation, to Comvitek, once I write Sienna Curtis's story. And think about the will contest—no court will uphold Julia's will after hearing from Sienna."

I let that sink in before I continued. "No, there's no money in it for you. Not now. If I were you, I'd go to the police. Offer to testify against Bob. I'm sure they'll be more interested in convicting a charlatan masquerading as a church leader than you. They'll see that he's much more dangerous, that you were taken in by him like so many other vulnerable women. Now that's a story I can't wait to write," I said.

Liz glared at me with hate-filled eyes, then slowly got up from the table and walked toward the ice bucket. She set her wine glass down on the counter and turned to face me. She shook her head.

"You think I'm stupid, don't you? You come traipsing in here and threaten me? You think I'm worried about you writing fairy tales? What a joke!"

"Oh, it's no joke. Why should you risk jail and ruin your reputation and Nick's, when Bob was the mastermind behind Julia's death?"

"I think you should leave now."

"You could save yourself, Liz. I have a friend who works for the Seattle Police Department. We could go talk to her right now."

"I'm not talking to anybody. Good-bye, Ann."

"Suit yourself. I'd just hate to see Bob walk away with all that money. Once I publish my interview with Sienna Curtis, your good name and that of Comvitek will be history. You'll take the blame and Bob will deny ever having had anything to do with you."

I watched her process my comment and then dismiss it. "You are very wrong. But it doesn't really matter. You'll never get a chance to write your fabricated little story anyway." She turned her back to me, looked out the window, and waved.

The back door burst open and I shrieked at the sight of the man who I thought of as Mr. Universe.

"Leif, I don't believe you and Ann have been formally introduced. Oh, but you have seen each other, haven't you? Lovely." Liz affected a sweet, singsong voice; her hideous smile looked drawn on like the dummy in an old *Twilight Zone* episode. I felt the beads of sweat forming at the nape of my neck and in my armpits. My heart was racing.

Liz kept talking, though her voice seemed distant somehow. "Leif, wasn't it unfortunate how this young woman came sneaking around here this afternoon? How she triggered the alarm and you took off after her? When she didn't respond, you fired a shot, intending to warn her into showing herself. You never intended to kill her."

"That's crazy! Think about it. If you shoot me, they'll never buy your story. And they'll be able to make *that* murder charge stick."

The smile faded briefly from her face. Leif made a move toward me and I ducked, ran around him and out the back door. The motion-sensor lights clicked on as I ran along the path between the main house and the servant's quarters. I'd almost made it to the steps when I heard his voice.

"Hey, you, stop!"

I turned and saw Victor running around the side of the house as Leif closed in on me. Leif turned and Victor punched him in the gut. He doubled over and tumbled a short way down the slope and Victor followed, sidestepping and slipping on the rain-soaked ground to get to him. Leif struggled to his feet and raised his arm. Just as I yelled, "Victor, he has a gun," the shot rang out.

37

I wanted to run but my legs were rooted to the spot. Paralyzed, my heart pounding, I watched Victor kick the gun out of Leif's grasp and the two of them struggle for it, tumbling further downhill beyond the pools of light. I screamed when the second shot exploded into the dark afternoon.

"Ann, call 911! This guy's hurt but he's alive."

"Victor, thank God!" Recovering my mobility, I made my way back to the kitchen. Liz was gone. I found the phone and punched in 911. Waiting for a response, I looked around the room, noticing for the first time the large box of slug bait next to the sink. Rage coursed through me and I swore I'd make her pay. She may have run, but she couldn't hide forever.

The 911 operator came on the line. I explained the situation and gave her the address, then went back outside to where Leif was lying in the wet grass moaning, clutching his shoulder. Victor stood over him, his shaking hand still grasping the gun. He waved it in Leif's direction.

In an unsteady, low voice, he said, "I was trying to get the gun away from him, Ann. It went off. I never shot anyone before."

"You picked a good one to shoot. This is the guy I spotted on the plane from Cabo, the one who trashed Sienna Curtis's room. But what are you doing here?"

"I picked up your message after I had a talk with Bob. I had a feeling you shouldn't be here alone."

"What did he say?"

"He denied everything. I called him a liar and he threatened me.

He said, 'Be very careful what you say, Victor, and to whom you say it. I'd hate to see anything happen to you.'"

"Jesus, the guy doesn't quit."

"He said his association with Liz was strictly business, that she was an investor in the Satya Retreat Center. Hey, where is she anyway?" Victor's question got lost in the sound of sirens coming up the street and the commotion that followed.

After the paramedics drove off with Leif in an ambulance, one of the cops took Victor into the house and another one, Officer Young, according to his badge, asked me if I was the person who'd called 911, and if I knew the whereabouts of the homeowner.

"Yes, I am, and no, I don't. She, uh, that's Liz Villardi, must have left when she heard the gunshot. But she was here just before that. She's responsible—she told that guy to shoot me," I said, hoping I sounded more coherent than I felt.

Officer Young nodded, then instructed two other uniformed men to search the house. Turning back to me, he said, "I'd like you to come down to the police station with me now, Ms. Dexter, to make a formal statement."

As I got into the police car, I saw two cops leading Victor from the house in handcuffs. He looked tired and very alone.

"Hey, you don't need to handcuff him! He saved my life."

"It's just a precaution, ma'am. He fired a handgun, we're taking him in."

"Wait! You need to call Detective Erin Becker. She knows what's going on here."

Officer Young assured me they would get it all sorted out in time.

At the station, I made my one phone call to Erin, who promised that she'd get Matt to recommend a top-notch criminal defense lawyer for Victor. Even so, I knew the criminal justice system worked slowly and I worried that Victor might end up spending the night in jail.

After an initial interview, Officer Young left me at a desk to write out my statement. It was painstaking work, describing everything that had happened at the Villardi's house. But reliving the event strengthened my resolve to make sure Bob and Liz paid for their part in Julia Comstock's death.

When they finally let me go, it was fairly late. I asked Officer Young about Victor.

"He's still being questioned," he said.

"I'll wait for him."

"It will be a while. Why don't you let me drive you home?"

"My car. It's still parked in front of the Villardi's."

"Why don't I have an officer drive it over to your place later?"

"You'd do that?"

"Detective Becker told me to be nice to you," he said with a smile. "And that she'd talk to you in the morning."

I woke up to the sound of loud knocking on my front door. In a sleepy haze I hurried to the front hall in my thin nightie and opened the door, embarrassing the very young police officer standing there.

"I brought your car," he stammered, handing me the key and nodding to the Camry in the drive. A squad car idled at the front curb.

"Thanks," I said, crossing my arms over my chest so he wouldn't see just how predictably I'd reacted to the cold gust of air he'd let in. "Hey, can you tell me anything about the guy they brought in with me last night? Victor Lloyd?"

"Sorry, ma'am. I don't know anything about that," he said, looking at his feet. "I just got the order to drive your car over here."

I thanked him, then called the vet about Pooch. She could come home today—Dr. O'Malley assured me the poison had completely worked its way out of her system. Wondering how long it would take before the poison of the last few weeks worked its way out of my system, I tried Victor's number again but got the machine. Time to go see Erin Becker—we had a lot to talk about.

Erin sat at her desk, talking on the phone, when I walked in. She waved me into a chair and finished her conversation while I looked around the room, trying not to eavesdrop. I smiled at the framed photos lined up on her side table: Erin and Matt on their Harleys at various places along the West Coast. The photos had been taken on their honeymoon. Erin hung up and looked over at me with a frown.

"How are you holding up, Ann? How's Pooch?" I filled her in on the good news, then waited for her to let me know what was happening with Liz Villardi.

"We sent someone over to interview her last night when she finally got home. She refused to talk. Said she wanted a lawyer."

"You didn't arrest her? She threatened me—paid that goon to hurt me! She poisoned my dog! What about Victor? I can't get a hold of him."

"Victor Lloyd spent the night in jail. We couldn't process him before that, but we've got him on the initial appearance calendar at two thirty this afternoon. Don't worry. He should be released on his own recognizance at the hearing."

"You're telling me that you let Liz Villardi sleep in her own bed and that you kept Victor Lloyd in the King County Jail? I might be dead if he hadn't turned up. What about Reverend Bob?"

"We're looking into the allegations that Victor Lloyd mentioned."

"Meaning Reverend Bob is running around free as well. Some legal system."

"Look Ann, there are legal channels to go through here. We need to investigate the allegations against Liz Villardi and Bob Waters. Leave the investigation to me and I'll leave the newspaper reporting to you, okay?"

I nodded and asked her about the process. She explained that the department would contact witnesses, hopefully track down Sienna

Curtis, write a report, and present it to the prosecutor's office. The prosecutor would decide on the best way to proceed: whether there would be charges against Liz Villardi and Bob Waters and how Nick Villardi factored into the scheme.

"What?" I jumped out of the chair and stood over her desk. "You mean there might not be charges?"

"Hey, hey, sit down, please. Like I said, it's early. We don't know enough yet. Leif Andersen is still at Harborview. Somebody took his statement. We'll look at it and go from there."

"Okay, I'll sit down, but only if you'll hear me out on this."

I began to lay out the whole story, everything I'd figured out about Julia's death, the details I pieced together from Julia's journals, and my conversation with Sienna Curtis, including the connection between Liz and Bob.

"At Nick Villardi's suggestion, Liz went to one of Victor Lloyd's workshops with Julia a few months before she died. Nick wanted Liz to reach out to help Julia cope with Warren's death. Instead, Liz met Reverend Bob Waters that night and recognized a kindred spirit. That started the chain of events that led to Julia's death."

"But Julia's money goes to the church—to further the work of Victor Lloyd."

"No, no, no! Victor is *not* involved."

"Settle down! I've never seen you so emotional."

"I'm fine. I'm just trying to get you to understand."

"Okay, first off, I don't see how Liz Villardi benefits from Julia's death—all Julia's money goes to the church. Or how you can connect this guy Waters to her."

I pulled out the brochure for the Satya Retreat Center, flipped to the back where Comvitek was listed as a partner in the project, and told her about my discussion with Caroline's lawyer.

"It went like this: Liz entered into this partnership with Reverend Bob Waters to develop the Satya Retreat Center, assuring herself a large share of Julia's bequest to the church in return for a loan up front. At the time, Comvitek still looked good on paper, but Liz knew from Nick that the European expansion wasn't working out as expected and that the corporation was hemorrhaging money. Waters needed money to fight a lawsuit that the state of Idaho filed against the development to collect taxes on the property, claiming Nirmala's 'retreat' did not fall under the legal category of a religious organization."

"So, the two of them enlisted this woman you found in Mexico, Sienna Curtis, to hold psychic readings with Julia, suggesting that her dead husband wanted her to join him in the great hereafter?"

"That's right."

"But how did they convince her to leave all her money to the church?"

"That was easy. Apparently Liz had asked Julia for money that same night she went to the workshop, but Julia had said she thought the church needed her money more than Comvitek. It's all in her journals," I said, as I pulled them out of my bag and placed them on her desk next to the retreat center brochure.

Erin leaned back in her chair and nodded. "I'll promise you this, Ann: if we can prove what you say is true, I'll do my best to see that Villardi and Waters get what they deserve. You can count on it."

38

Walking into the King County Courthouse always reminded me of the circus. Maybe it was the smell of the popcorn cart set up just inside the door, or the crowd of people milling about the lobby—all shapes and sizes, all manner of dress, all levels of income and personal hygiene were represented. And once you got past the security and into one of the courtrooms, there was usually quite a show, though you had to consume your food before entering. I went into the clerk's office to find out which judge was covering initial appearances this afternoon and gave the woman Victor's name, telling her he'd been in for questioning late yesterday and apparently spent the night in jail.

"Well, honey, then he'll be on Judge Beltran's two thirty calendar over at the jail, not here. Do you know where that is?"

I'd driven past the King County Jail many times, a forbidding gray concrete box visible from the freeway. There were no bars on the windows, but I'd always been struck by how small those windows were, imagining them as slits in the cells which let in a paltry amount of weak light but were placed too high in the rooms for the inmates to see out.

The jail was just a block or two over. I'd never been inside, just the thought of it made my stomach clench. And rightly so, I thought, when I arrived—the scene here was even more surreal than the courthouse. Checking the directory, I found Judge Beltran's courtroom listed as Room D1. Outside the courtroom door, a harried public defender flipped through a file while explaining the procedure for an initial appearance to his client's visibly pregnant wife. She looked barely eighteen years old and I wondered how long the father would remain in custody and what sort of future this girl would have, not to mention the child's. Suddenly my own personal problems seemed inconsequential.

The courtroom itself was small, only about six rows of wooden benches—like church pews—jammed with people, family, and friends of the accused, who would be parading through this afternoon. I found the high level of security especially unnerving—a wall of bulletproof glass divided the spectator area from the judge's bench, and armed guards stood at the door between the two spaces and in front of an interior side door.

As the judge entered from a door behind the bench, the bailiff stood and ordered us all to "Please rise." Once the judge sat down, she nodded to one of the other court personnel who opened a side door. Several men wearing prison jumpsuits filed into the courtroom and sat in a row of side benches up front. I gasped when I saw Victor was one of the bunch. He sat with his head down and I stared at him for a long time before he looked up, scanned the room, and spotted me. My stomach flipped and tears sprang to my eyes as he flashed a warm smile at me. How could he be happy to see me? I was the one who got him into this mess. I shook my head and mouthed "Sorry" at him. He just shrugged his shoulders, his smile fading as the judge's voice filled the room.

"The following prisoners are released from today's calendar. If your name is called, please leave with Mr. Stanton." The same court clerk who'd let them into the courtroom stood at the side door, nodding. "He'll see that you're processed." The fourth name on her list was Victor Lloyd. I exhaled and watched him file out of the courtroom.

As the judge called the next case, I whispered to the public defender, "Where can I find someone who's just now been released by the judge?" He directed me to an office down the hall and said, "You'll probably have a long wait. Good luck."

I left the courtroom as quietly as I could, then made my way to Room 1B to wait for Victor. After I'd established that I was in the right spot and that it would take a while, I walked back out to the lobby and called Caroline.

"Ann, I'm so glad to hear from you. What happened in Mexico? Did you have any luck? Did you find Nancy?"

Once more, I ran through the events of the past thirty-six hours in as abbreviated a fashion as possible. Stunned, Caroline suggested we get together for a longer debriefing over dinner as soon as I could manage it.

"Well, it may be a while, Caroline. I'm heading back to Mexico as soon as I make sure Victor is out of trouble. I need to see Nancy."

"Of course."

She thanked me, we said our good-byes, and I wandered back into the waiting room as Victor came in with his lawyer. He looked exhausted.

I threw my arms around him and he held me tight, then released me. "Is this all I need to do to get your attention? Shoot someone and spend the night in jail?" He pulled me close again and spoke softly into my ear. "Let's go somewhere a little less crowded. What do you say?"

"I say yes, Victor. But first I have a story to write."

The plane sat on the runway awaiting the signal for takeoff, while I looked out the window and resisted the urge to open up this morning's *Seattle Times* and read the article. I promised myself I'd wait until after takeoff—on my way to Mexico, Rancho La Puerta, and Nancy—before I read it in context, front page of the Local section, and relished the byline. I leaned over and reached into my carry-on bag, transferred the paper to the seat-back pocket in front of me, and looked out the window, my thoughts returning to the events of the last couple of days and, especially, to Victor.

I shook my head, still incredulous that the man I'd expected to reveal as a charlatan, seducer, and possible murderer had ended up in my bed. I closed my eyes and savored the memory, so fresh I could almost feel his hands on me, his body touching mine. I know Victor claimed to be a psychic medium and not clairvoyant, but I wondered how, then, he knew exactly how to please me in the first go-round. Amused by my thought that Victor's lovemaking reflected his personal qualities of intensity, athleticism, humor, mystery, and something else, something maybe even otherworldly, I smiled and hoped I'd have many more opportunities to explore all of those things.

I felt the plane suddenly speed up and roar down the runway and tucked away my carnal thoughts away along with the landing gear. I sighed, pulled out the newspaper, unfolded it, and relished the headline, "Heads of Comvitek Foundation and Nirmala Church Suspects in Comstock Suicide Investigation," by *Times* Staff Reporter Ann Dexter. I caught the guy next to me reading over my shoulder and turned to him.

"Sorry to be reading your paper—it's just that I sort of knew Julia Comstock. I was really surprised to hear that she killed herself last summer. Sad."

I agreed and listened to him talk about Julia—how they'd taken some art classes together but never really kept in touch—and thought about the chance meeting of strangers, how they might have a major impact on one another or none at all. I still didn't fully understand the path I'd taken over the past few weeks, the one that led me from Caroline Schuster to Victor Lloyd and on my way back, I hoped, to my sister. But I was glad for it.

When the bus finally pulled up to the entrance of Rancho la Puerta, I felt travel-weary and slightly nauseated from the long drive to Tecate on the winding high-desert road. After checking in, I followed a young Mexican porter along stone pathways and under arbors dripping with scented flowers to my room. The "ranchero" was one half of a small building set into the hillside and featured a cozy living area with a wood-burning fireplace, a separate bedroom, and a bathroom. It was simple and comfortable.

I checked the time and looked at the map of the ranch. I had just fifteen minutes before the end of Nancy's, or Leila's, yoga class at four. I changed into something I could work out in and filled up the complimentary water bottle with the spa's own filtered water, hoping to blend in with all the other spa inhabitants.

I felt myself slow down and soak in the serene environment as I followed the signs through the ranch to Nancy's yoga class. The Arroyo building was set up on a hill with a fabulous view of Mount Kuchumaa on one side and an old olive grove on the other. The building—one large room, really—had a wooden floor and mirrors on two walls, with the rear wall completely open to the afternoon breeze. The class was over and a few women were still collecting their mats and gear and heading out the door as I entered. I saw my sister at the front of the room crouched down, packing up her things, and was struck by how thin and frail she looked, like she might blow away if a gust of wind blew through the room. She felt my stare and turned. Nancy's eyes met mine and held them a long time before they softened and she reached out, inviting my embrace.

Epilogue

My article in the *Seattle Times* caused quite a stir when it first came out. Reverend Bob Waters threatened to sue the paper for libel, but when the court of appeals denied tax-exempt status for Satya and the probate court decided in favor of Caroline Schuster in the will contest, he didn't have the money to go forward. The Nirmala Church of Self-Actualization lost most of its congregants and last I heard the good Reverend Bob had taken off with what few funds were left in the church's account. I was sorry that I hadn't really been able to prevent the scumbag from preying on other innocent victims; I had only moved him along. I hoped that his greed caught up with him some day and that he would be punished for it, but I wasn't holding my breath.

The prosecutor declined to seek an indictment against either Reverend Bob or Liz Villardi in the death of Julia Comstock, despite the sworn declarations of Sienna Curtis, Kelly Long, and the witness, Dwight Heffron, who remembered seeing a silver Lexus SUV on the Aurora Bridge that day but couldn't positively identify the driver.

Leif Andersen was convicted of assault with a deadly weapon, reduced from attempted murder for his testimony against Liz Villardi in the attempted shooting of Victor Lloyd. Liz Villardi was charged. But her lawyers got a deal to an agreed finding of not guilty by reason of insanity.

Caroline filed a wrongful death action against Liz and Bob, which financially ruined Comvitek. It was one mess created by his wife that Nick Villardi couldn't clean up. He was, however, able to place her into the private psychiatric hospital where she remains today.

Victor continues to give psychic readings and classes, and is being courted for a position at a retreat center in California. I'm not sure how I feel about that now that our relationship has moved beyond the spiritual realm to the physical. One thing's for sure, Victor will always land on his feet.

Acknowledgements

I am so grateful to the many individuals who encouraged, mentored, pushed, taught and helped me along the road to publishing this book. I am most thankful to Waverly Fitzgerald for sharing her wisdom and experience, her keen knowledge of the writing craft and her always spot-on criticism. Waverly has been with me from the very beginning of my writing life. She convinced me early on that I could write a mystery novel and that I would have fun along the way.

I am extremely grateful for my writing group – talented writers who have spent oh-so-many Friday mornings with me reading chapters aloud and sharing their thoughts and suggestions. My writing is better thanks to Linda Anderson, Curt Colbert, Martha Crites, Corey Venema-Weiss and Janis Wildy – my sister-in-blogging.

A special thanks to Skye Moody, my first writing teacher at the University of Washington, who guided me through the first draft and read the final manuscript. I was lucky to have my friend and earliest reader, Nancy Ritter, whose editorial comments were invaluable to me in that early iteration of the manuscript. Thanks to Barbara Mugford for her sharp eyes and continued enthusiasm, to editrix, Erin Doherty, for her meticulous copy-editing and to my friend and cover artist extraordinaire, Aaron Weholt, who never complained about re-working the cover no matter how many times I changed my mind in the process.

I would especially like to thank the experts who shared their time with me: Dr. Jeb Mortimer at Green Lake Animal Hospital, who patiently explained to me how dogs react to different poisons — and helped Pooch survive; and to Linda Shaw, the real-life Seattle Times Education Reporter who gave me a tour of the newsroom and answered my questions about her day-to-day job as a newspaper journalist.

Last, and most importantly, thanks to my family, especially to my husband Dave, who has put up with the ups and downs of my writing life, listened to endless scenes along the way, and who is truly my most enthusiastic fan. To my daughter, Elizabeth, for reading the manuscript early on and declaring it "actually pretty good" and to my daughter, Julianne, who has always been encouraging and enthusiastic about her mother's writing.

A final huge thanks to Rat City Publishing for taking the *leap of faith* necessary to publish this particular novel as its debut Seattle mystery.

Author's Note

In February of 2011, after community groups successfully lobbied for the state to do something to prevent suicide, the Washington Department of Transportation installed a nearly nine foot fence along the Aurora Avenue Bridge span in Seattle. From the time the bridge opened in 1932, until the construction of the fence, more than 230 people had jumped to their deaths.

About the Author

Rachel Bukey is reading her way across the country and blogging about it at RachelBukey.com/coasttocoastbooks. When she's not writing or reading, she works part-time as a legal assistant for a criminal defense lawyer. She lives in Seattle with her husband Dave and her dog Phoebe. *Leap of Faith* is her first novel.

42319146R00175

Made in the USA
Middletown, DE
08 April 2017